ROMANTIC TIMES PRAISE FOR *NEW YORK TIMES* BESTSELLING AUTHOR BOBBI SMITH!

EDEN

"The very talented Bobbi Smith has written another winner. *Eden* is filled with adventure, danger, sentimentality and romance."

THE HALF-BREED (SECRET FIRES)

"Witty, tender, strong characters and plenty of action, as well as superb storytelling, make this a keeper."

BRIDES OF DURANGO: JENNY

"Bobbi Smith has another winner. This third installment is warm and tender as only Ms. Smith can do. . . . Ms. Smith's fans will not be disappointed."

BRIDES OF DURANGO: TESSA

"Another wonderful read by consummate storyteller Bobbi Smith. . . . Filled with adventure and romance, more than one couple winds up happily-ever-after in this gem."

BRIDES OF DURANGO: ELISE

"There's plenty of action, danger and heated romance as the pages fly by in Ms. Smith's exciting first book in this new series. This is exactly what fans expect from Bobbi Smith."

MORE *ROMANTIC TIMES* RAVES FOR STORYTELLER OF THE YEAR BOBBI SMITH!

WESTON'S LADY

"Bobbi Smith has penned another winner."

HALF-BREED'S LADY

"A fast-paced frying-pan-into-the-fire adventure that runs the gamut of emotions, from laughter to tears. A must-read for Ms. Smith's fans, and a definite keeper."

OUTLAW'S LADY

"Bobbi Smith is an author of many talents; one of them being able to weave more than one story. . . . Ms. Smith creates characters that one will remember for some time to come."

THE LADY & THE TEXAN

"An action-packed read with roller-coaster adventures that keep you turning the pages. *The Lady & the Texan* is just plain enjoyable."

RENEGADE'S LADY

"A wonderfully delicious 'Perils of Pauline' style romance. With dashes of humor, passion, adventure and romance, Ms. Smith creates another winner that only she could write!"

BOUND

"Will you bind me to you again tonight?" Marissa asked as she followed him inside.

"Yes." Wind Ryder's answer was terse.

"There is no need. I will not run away again," she said.

Wind Ryder managed to give her a cold look of distrust as he reached for the rope.

"Lie down," he directed, going to her.

Marissa lay on the blankets as he'd ordered and waited as he tied the rope securely around her leg. The night before she'd been afraid, thinking about what might happen, but tonight, the warmth of his hands upon her leg sent an unexpected thrill through her. She looked on without saying anything more as he tied the other end of the rope to his own leg and made himself comfortable.

"Did the Comanche tie you up like this when you were little to keep you from running away?" she asked quietly.

"Captives must be trained to obey," he answered without emotion.

"That must have been hard for you—as a child."

"Go to sleep," he ordered, not wanting to discuss his past with her. He was already far too aware of her. . . .

Other *Leisure* and *Love Spell* books by Bobbi Smith:
EDEN
SWEET SILKEN BONDAGE
THE HALF-BREED (SECRET FIRES)
WESTON'S LADY
HALF-BREED'S LADY
OUTLAW'S LADY
FORBIDDEN FIRES
RAPTURE'S RAGE
THE LADY & THE TEXAN
RENEGADE'S LADY
THE LADY'S HAND
LADY DECEPTION

The *Brides of Durango* series by Bobbi Smith:
ELISE
TESSA
JENNY

LONE WARRIOR

BOBBI SMITH

LEISURE BOOKS NEW YORK CITY

For Dr. Richard Murray. You're brilliant!
And for Sharon Moss Sutton and Bart Moss,
two great friends from my high school days!

A LEISURE BOOK®

July 2002

Published by

Dorchester Publishing Co., Inc.
276 Fifth Avenue
New York, NY 10001

ISBN: 0-8439-5028-5

Printed in the United States of America.

ACKNOWLEDGMENTS

Thanks to T. J. Berry and Jessica Lavy and all the other wonderful employees at Waldenbooks #1577 in Arlington, Texas. You're terrific!

Thanks, also, to my friend Sandra Welch for bringing my character Cody Jameson from *Lady Deception* to life at the *Romantic Times* Convention Costume Competition in Florida last year. You were wonderful!

And to Sharon Murphy, a true pal. Love ya!

LONE WARRIOR

Prologue

Texas, Late 1860s

Tension filled the air as the two young warriors circled each other, knives drawn. Their expressions were savage as they prepared to do battle.

Word of the fight spread quickly through the village, and a crowd of onlookers gathered. The villagers had known the day would come when the two brothers would challenge one another, for Bear Claw, Chief Ten Crow's oldest son, had long chafed under his adopted brother Wind Ryder's favored status with their father. Many years before, Chief Ten Crow had been impressed by the bravery of the captive white boy and had adopted him. The boy had taken the name Wind Ryder, and in the eight years he had lived as one of them, he had become the best rider in the village and one of the fiercest fighters. The members of the tribe looked on, wondering if Wind Ryder would prove himself to be the best again—now against his brother.

Physically, Bear Claw and Wind Ryder were both fine specimens of Comanche manhood and very evenly matched. Both were tall and strong. Their bodies were sleek and hard-muscled—and they were both determined to win. The villagers knew this would be a true test of their skills.

Bear Claw's hate-filled gaze narrowed as he prepared to make his move. Fury was driving him. Wind Ryder had taken that which should have been his! They had been out raiding when he had seen the white stallion and decided he would have it for his own. But Wind Ryder had reached the magnificent horse first and taken it for himself. The memory fueled Bear Claw's rage. He gave a bloodcurdling cry as he charged.

Wind Ryder had been waiting for Bear Claw to attack, and he was ready. He met him in that charge, and they locked together in a powerful struggle.

Tumbling to the ground, the two young warriors battled fiercely.

Each was fighting for dominance.

Each was determined not to give in.

Bear Claw managed to slash Wind Ryder's upper arm just as they broke apart. Blood flowed from the wound, and Bear Claw smiled, knowing

Wind Ryder was in pain. He was proud. He had drawn first blood. Confidence filled him.

Wind Ryder paid little heed to the wound. He ignored the pain as he had trained himself to do since coming to the Comanche. He concentrated only on Bear Claw, anticipating his every move. He saw his brother's arrogant smile and knew his overconfidence was his weakness.

"You are bleeding," Bear Claw taunted.

"It is only a scratch." He smiled back at him, wanting to push Bear Claw's anger to even greater heights.

Hatred surged through Bear Claw.

"I will kill you—" he shouted, rushing at him again.

Wind Ryder moved quickly to avoid the attack. Wielding his knife with unerring accuracy, he cut Bear Claw across his ribs.

Bear Claw was stunned that Wind Ryder had managed to slash him. The shock of the pain drove him beyond all reason. He despised Wind Ryder! No matter what his father said, this white was no brother to him! Turning, he attacked again, this time blindly.

Blood now covered both of the young men. Neither would give in. Neither would back down. It would be a fight to the death.

Bear Claw tripped Wind Ryder. Wind Ryder fell, but quickly recovered. He rolled away and jumped to his feet just in time to kick out at Bear

Claw and knock him to the ground. Bear Claw's knife flew from his grip, and in that instant Wind Ryder made his move. He threw himself upon the other warrior and, knife in hand, held him pinned to the ground.

The furious roar of Chief Ten Crow startled all those who'd gathered around to watch the battle. The villagers fell back as the mighty chief strode forward. The chief grabbed Wind Ryder and hauled him off Bear Claw.

Still caught up in the driving power of his anger, Wind Ryder struggled against the man restraining him; then he looked up into the face of his adopted father and realized what had happened. He stopped fighting and was immediately released. He stood before the chief and met his gaze without flinching.

Chief Ten Crow's expression was unreadable as he stared at Wind Ryder. After a moment, without saying a word, he nodded and then turned to Bear Claw.

"Get up," the chief ordered. "Why were you fighting Wind Ryder?"

Bear Claw flew to his feet in a rage, humiliated that he'd been overpowered. "He is the one to blame!"

The chief sneered, "Wind Ryder returned from the raid with the best horses, and he has just proven himself to be the strongest warrior. Your brother has done nothing wrong."

Bear Claw looked at Wind Ryder, his gaze filled with hatred. "This one is no brother to me!"

"He is my son—as you are."

Bear Claw said nothing more. His anger was too great. He stalked off, pausing only to pick up his knife before he disappeared into the crowd.

A great sadness filled Chief Ten Crow as he watched his son walk away. Only when Bear Claw had moved out of sight did he glance back at Wind Ryder.

"You are bleeding," the chief told his adopted son.

"It is nothing," Wind Ryder answered stoically. He would never allow himself to reveal any pain he was feeling. A proud warrior never showed a sign of weakness.

"The white stallion you brought in is a very fine animal. A mighty warrior deserves such a horse." He nodded to his son in silent approval and walked away.

The chief's praise pleased Wind Ryder. He'd wanted the horse from the first moment he had seen it. His brother and several of the other braves had wanted it, too, but he'd been lucky enough during the raid to be able to take it for himself. He would ride the stallion proudly once he'd broken it.

Wind Ryder headed to the creek to wash and clean his wound. When he'd first been brought into the camp as a young boy, Wind Ryder had befriended one of the dogs. He'd named the large brown cur Buffalo, because of his size, and it trailed after him now down to the water's edge. It was quiet there by the creek, and he appreciated the peace. He sat down on the bank to pet the dog.

Wind Ryder realized sadly that Buffalo was his one true friend in the tribe. Buffalo never worried that he was white by birth and had come into the tribe as a captive. The dog's only real concern in life was where his next meal was coming from. As long as Wind Ryder provided that, the dog was blindly faithful.

"Where were you when I needed you, Buffalo?" Wind Ryder scolded, even as he smiled down at the dog. "You could have helped me fight Bear Claw."

Buffalo just sat down beside him and leaned slightly against him as if nothing unusual had happened.

"You thought I was good enough to handle Bear Claw by myself, did you?" he said more to himself than the dog.

"And you were," came the sound of a soft feminine voice from behind him.

Wind Ryder looked back and was surprised to see the pretty young maiden Moon Cloud standing there watching him.

"Do you need help?" Moon Cloud asked as she went to him. She knew she was being bold, but she didn't care. Though she was only thirteen, she had been in love with Wind Ryder for a long time.

When she'd seen Bear Claw cut him during their fight, she'd been worried that he'd been seriously hurt.

"I am fine," Wind Ryder told her, wanting her to go away. He had come there to be alone. He didn't want to talk to anyone right then. Standing, he moved down to the water's edge and began to wash the blood from his arm.

Moon Cloud was not about to be put off. She'd brought a cloth and healing herbs with her, and she went to the creek and wet the cloth before going to his side. She pressed the cloth to his wound to stop the bleeding. She was surprised when he didn't flinch. The wound had to hurt.

"You fought bravely," she said.

"I did not want to fight Bear Claw," he answered.

"He gave you no choice."

Wind Ryder said no more as she tended his cut. When she finished, the bleeding had stopped. He flexed his arm to test it, and was pleased to find that the pain had lessened.

"It is better. Thank you."

He wanted her to leave, but she remained.

"I am glad I was able to help you." Moon Cloud looked up at him, thinking him the most handsome of all the young warriors. True, he was white, but that didn't really matter to her. He had proven himself to be the strongest and the best.

Wind Ryder felt uncomfortable under her scrutiny. He deliberately moved away.

"I must go back and see to the horses," he told her. Buffalo came quickly to his side.

Moon Cloud was disappointed that he didn't want to linger there with her a little longer. She walked back to the camp with him, but he said little to her on the way back.

Bear Claw's anger did not lessen as he sat alone some distance from the village. If anything, the hatred he felt for Wind Ryder grew as he tended his own wound. The fight between them was not over. He doubted it ever would be.

His fury burned hot within him. He longed to find some way to get back at Wind Ryder.

It was growing dark when he finally decided to return to the village.

As he made his way back, he spotted Wind Ryder's dog.

Bear Claw smiled.

Wind Ryder passed the evening sitting by the campfire with the warriors, listening to tales of their raids and telling a tale or two of his own. Bear Claw never joined them, and Wind Ryder was glad.

It was late when Wind Ryder decided to bed down for the night. As a young warrior, he had his own tipi, and he made his way there ready to seek rest. He was surprised that there was no sign of

Buffalo. The dog was usually waiting for him outside the lodge.

Then he went inside.

Wind Ryder had suffered much in his fourteen years of life. He had forced much of the horror he'd witnessed from his mind, not wanting to remember the pain of losing his white family in the Comanche raid on their ranch when he was six. But the sight of Buffalo lying dead within the tipi, his throat slashed, brought it all back in a violent rush. The pain tore at him physically and mentally, and he fought not to cry out in horror.

"Buffalo—"

Wind Ryder dropped to his knees and stared at the lifeless dog.

Only Bear Claw could have done something so vicious. Only Bear Claw would think of killing a gentle animal to take revenge on an enemy.

Wind Ryder wanted to go after the man who was supposed to be his brother and take his own revenge, but he had no real proof.

Wind Ryder reached out to stroke Buffalo's rough fur. The dog's body was cold and stiff.

The finality of death struck him again. The loss of yet another loved one tore through him.

Wind Ryder bit back the cry that threatened as long-suppressed memories tormented him. It took all the strength he could muster to repress them.

Gathering Buffalo in his arms, he carried him from the tipi and out into the dark of the night. He was glad that no one saw him as he found a secluded spot and buried his one friend.

Wind Ryder remained alone there throughout the night and did not return to the village until dawn.

Any trace of youth within him had been destroyed.

He was a solitary man—a lone warrior.

Chapter One

Ten Years Later

From a distance, Chief Ten Crow and his raiding party kept watch over the way station. He knew his braves would take many horses during this raid.

Soon the time would be right—very soon he would give the order to attack.

Marissa Williams exchanged a weary smile with her friend and traveling companion, Louise Bennett, as their stagecoach slowed to a stop before the lonely way station.

"I never thought I'd be this excited to see a way station," Marissa remarked, looking out the window at the forlorn structure in the middle of the wild Texas countryside.

"Me, either," Louise agreed, feeling battered from the rough ride in the cramped interior of the stage.

"It's been a long ride today, ladies, that's for sure," put in Thurmond Atwood, a heavyset traveling salesman. "I didn't know dawn could come as early as it did this morning. Seems to me the birds were still sleeping and we were already on the road."

"Quit all your jabberin' and open the door so we can get out of here," crotchety, white-haired Blake Randolph ordered from where he sat next to Thurmond. He had no intention of spending another minute in these close quarters, sitting on a hard seat, crammed in next to the overweight Atwood. The stage had stopped. He wanted his freedom, and he wanted it now.

Just as Blake finished speaking, Matt Hogan, the stage driver, appeared outside the door and opened it. Marissa was the first to climb out, and Matt took her hand to help her step down.

"Thank you," she told him with an appreciative smile.

"My pleasure, Miss Williams," Matt answered.

Marissa Williams was the prettiest female he'd seen in ages. She was blond and downright beautiful, not to mention friendly. Her bright smile could charm any man, and he was charmed. Her friend Louise Bennett was an attractive woman, too, though she was older than Marissa. He couldn't help wondering what two ladies of quality were doing heading for Dry Springs. He'd heard the women talking about New Orleans, and thought by the looks of them that that was where they belonged—in a sophisticated, civilized city, not in West Texas.

"We'll be spending the night here," he went on, "so you and Miss Bennett go on inside and make yourselves comfortable."

"Will we be starting at the same time tomorrow morning as today?" she asked as she waited for him to help Louise down.

"Yes, miss, we will—bright and early."

Matt ignored the mumbled complaints of the men still sitting in the stage as he aided Louise in her descent. Once Louise had gotten down, he moved off to unload the bags and take care of the horses, leaving the men on their own.

Louise went to join Marissa. They walked slowly toward the way station, taking their time, enjoying the chance to stretch and move around a bit. Louise paused to stare out across the land. She was accustomed to the sights of New Orleans, and though Marissa had warned her that West Texas was nothing like Louisiana, she hadn't expected it to be this desolate or this empty. Marissa had made the trip to Dry Springs before with her father and had always come home with wonderful tales of the beauty and excitement of her Uncle George's ranch. Right now, though, the beauty and excitement were eluding Louise. She glanced at the younger woman in amazement.

"So this is what the Wild West looks like. Do you really like this place?"

"It's beautiful, don't you think?" Marissa was gazing off in the distance.

The sun was painting the land golden with its glow as it sank lower in the western sky.

"It's certainly . . . untamed looking," Louise remarked uneasily. She was feeling a bit apprehensive as she looked around at the stark landscape dotted only by some low-growing shrubs and a few trees. It was so vast—so deserted—so isolated.

"You'll come to love it, I promise." Marissa tried to sound encouraging. "It grows on you."

Even as she spoke, sudden memories of her last visit to the Crown Ranch brought the sting of tears to her eyes. That had been a joyous, exciting trip in the company of her father. This journey, however, was anything but joyous. Her father was dead. He had died tragically and unexpectedly, and now her uncle was her only living relative; her mother had passed away several years before. Marissa had wired her uncle the news of her father's death, and he had insisted she come to Texas to live with him. She loved the ranch, and she was looking forward to seeing Mark Whittaker again. He was a handsome ranch hand who worked for her uncle. They had enjoyed each other's company during last year's visit, and she hoped he was still working there.

"If you say so," Louise replied less than enthusiastically. From the looks of things, she was not at all sure that she would find anything about this place to love. "But right now, as far as I'm concerned, we can't reach your uncle's ranch soon enough."

"You aren't enjoying our travel accommodations?" Marissa asked quietly, giving Louise a quick, knowing smile.

"Let's just say that I'm looking forward to having a clean bed again," Louise said, suppressing a shudder as she thought about the less-than-pristine bed she'd slept in the night before. Heaven only knew who had slept in it last and whether or not they had been infested with vermin. She'd found herself longing for her own bedroom in her home in New Orleans and for her maid and her freshly laundered linens.

"I'm sorry it's been so difficult." Marissa said.

"Oh, darling, there's no need to apologize. It's been an exhausting trip, but that was to be expected. I'm trying to think of this as an adventure."

"Then you're not sorry you came with me?"

"I never considered *not* coming with you," Louise insisted. She had been a close friend of Marissa's mother and had stayed in regular contact with the family even after her death. She was devoted to Marissa. She thought of her as the daughter she'd never had, and she knew how devastated the young woman was by father's passing.

"Thank you," Marissa said as she glanced at Louise.

"There is no need to thank me. Until I see you safely to your Uncle George, my place is with you," Louise reassured her, giving her a quick hug.

They started on toward the building once again, eager to go inside for the night.

The waiting was over. The time had come.

Chief Ten Crow gave the signal to the warriors waiting to raid the way station and claim the horses as their own.

They attacked.

Marissa and Louise were about to enter the station when suddenly shots rang out and chaos erupted around them. Louise grabbed Marissa's arm in panic at the sound of the war cries of the Comanche warriors.

"What's happening?" Louise asked, staring wide-eyed and fearful.

"Comanche raid!" the station master shouted.

Shocked, Marissa and Louise froze in the midst of the deadly confusion. The guards who manned the way station ran for their rifles. Several of the them were cut down by the gunfire of the attacking warriors before they could arm themselves. The two men passengers on the stagecoach were also shot where they stood, helpless before the deadly onslaught.

"Get inside!" the stage driver ordered the two women as he raced past them on his way to retrieve his own rifle from the stagecoach.

Matt's fierce command jarred Marissa and Louise from their stunned state. Terrified, they ran for the safety of the building.

A guttural scream rent the air.

At the sound, they looked back to see Matt lying in the dirt. He was writhing in agony, and blood was streaming from a gaping chest wound.

"Mr. Hogan!" Without a thought for her own safety, Marissa tore away from Louise and rushed to help the fallen man.

"Marissa—don't!" Louise gave chase, trying to stop her as the bloodcurdling war cries of the Comanche sent chills of terror through the very depths of her being. No wonder she'd felt that terrible sense of apprehension earlier. Somehow, she had sensed the danger that surrounded them. But it was too late to help Matt now—they could only try to save themselves. "Marissa! We have to get inside."

"No—I have to help him—I can't just leave him there to die! You go on!"

Marissa kept running, and she'd almost made it to Matt's side when she heard a war cry behind her. She turned to see a warrior taking aim at Louise. Marissa had no time to react as the Indian fired his weapon. She watched in horror as Louise collapsed.

"Louise!" The scream erupted from her.

"Get my gun," Matt called out to her. He had no strength to move or to help her, but he could see what was happening around them and knew she had to have some way to protect herself. It was her only hope of survival.

Marissa needed no further encouragement. She ran for the stage, suddenly filled with violent emotions she'd never experienced before. Hatred. The need for revenge. She had just seen innocent people murdered—and Louise shot down in cold blood! She was going to get that gun and shoot the savages!

But the Comanche raiding party was too close.

By the time Marissa reached the side of the stage, the bloodthirsty warriors were circling ever nearer.

Chief Ten Crow saw the woman with the golden hair climbing onto the stagecoach to grab up a gun. In that instant, a jolt of recognition shot through him. He had seen this woman before—in a vision.

The chief wheeled his horse around and rode in her direction. Snake, one of his best warriors, was ahead of him, and Chief Ten Crow watched as he closed in on the woman.

Matt could feel his life's blood draining from him; he was growing weaker by the minute. He knew he was going to die, but when he saw the Comanche charging toward Marissa, he knew he had to do something. He tried to raise himself up on an elbow as he called out another warning to her.

"Look out!"

His shout took Snake by surprise. He turned quickly and shot the white man again, this time making sure he was dead. Then he turned his attention back to the woman. She was what he wanted. She was the prize he was after.

Marissa had just grabbed up the weapon as she heard the stage driver's warning. Rifle in hand, she turned.

It was too late.

Snake was already upon her. He struck quickly, snaring her around the waist to pull her away from the stage. She fought to hang on, but Snake jerked her forcefully free.

The warrior's grip was brutal, and Marissa began to scream as she struggled in wild fury. The rifle flew from her hands as she twisted and turned, trying to break free. Marissa knew he might kill her, but she didn't care. She knew from tales her uncle had told her about the Comanche that death was preferable to being taken captive by them.

Snake fought to control both her and his horse. He was furious at the woman's fierce resistance. He shifted his powerful hold on her to try to bring her fully before him on his horse.

Marissa saw her one and only chance to escape the warrior, and took it. She viciously kicked the side of his mount and, at the same time, jerked herself sideways with all the force she could master. The horse shifted unexpectedly, and when she made her violent move, Snake momentarily loosened his hold on her.

Suddenly Marissa found herself free, tumbling to the ground. Pain jolted through her as she landed heavily, but she surged to her feet and looked around for the rifle. It had fallen too far away for her to reach it. She looked up at the warrior, and in that moment her gaze met his. Marissa knew by the fury in his war-painted face that she was looking into the face of death. She turned to run, but before she could take more than a step, another Comanche was there, snatching her up.

Marissa was silenced as the wind was knocked out of her. She fought to get away, but the Indian who held her in his grasp was far more powerful than the first. Her captor shouted something to the other warriors as he urged his horse to a run, and they galloped off.

A short distance from the way station, Chief Ten Crow reined in to wait for the rest of his warriors to join him. The building was engulfed in flames. The fierce fire cast a golden glow upon the night. The chief nodded to himself as he saw his son Bear Claw riding toward him, a silhouette with the light of the fire at his back.

It was as he'd foreseen in his vision—the flames—Bear Claw—the golden one.

The other warriors came then, too, driving the horses ahead of them, and they all raced off into the night.

Marissa managed a quick last look back at the death and devastation they were leaving behind. She could see the lifeless bodies strewn about the grounds, and pain ripped through her soul.

They were all dead—slaughtered at the hands of this deadly Comanche raiding party.

And Louise—

Memories of their last conversation tortured Marissa:

"My place is with you."

Her dear friend was dead.

It was all her fault.

If only they'd never come to Texas—

If only—

Anger and fear warred within Marissa. She offered up a tormented prayer as she tore her gaze away from the sight of the destruction. A terrible sense of hopelessness overcame her.

She wished that she had been the one to die, not Louise. She wished she were dead right then.

If she had had a weapon and had been able to use it, she would have killed herself in that moment.

Marissa was glad that the cover of night was claiming the land, for the Comanche who had taken her prisoner would not be able to see the tears she could no longer deny.

Chapter Two

The raiding party rode long into the night.

Chief Ten Crow was more than pleased with the success of the raid. His warriors had claimed many horses, and he had claimed the golden one.

The chief smiled to himself in satisfaction.

Until now, Chief Ten Crow had not understood the full meaning of the vision that had come to him some weeks ago. In it, he had seen his sons Bear Claw and Wind Ryder engaged in a life-or-death struggle, silhouetted by flames and blood. He had also seen a white woman with hair the color of the sun draw Wind Ryder away from that deadly battle. He had not been able to see her features clearly in his vision, but when he saw her for the first time during the attack, he had instinctively known she was that woman. Wind Ryder had not accompanied them on this raid, but when they returned to the village, Chief Ten Crow was certain all would be as he'd envisioned.

Chief Ten Crow realized what he had to do. He would protect the golden one and keep her safe until he could present her to Wind Ryder. The rest of his vision would then come to pass as well—the violent hatred between his sons would cease and peace would come to his people.

There was another part of the vision he deliberately didn't dwell on, but now that fate had set everything in motion, Ten Crow knew he had to face it. Soon he would be going to the spirit world. His vision had not told him how he was going to die, only that the time was coming. It was important that he see peace established between his sons before he left this world.

Marissa's fear heightened anew when the raiding party finally stopped for the night. She had managed to hold her fear at bay by keeping her mind blank, but facing the reality of being a captive terrified her.

When her captor dismounted, Marissa stiffened. She was ready to fight him, but got no chance. He pulled her down from the horse before she could react, and quickly bound her wrists tightly in front of her. He dragged her along to where the other warriors had already started building a fire, and pushed her down to sit on the ground before it.

Marissa made sure not to let her terror show. She glared defiantly up at the Comanche.

Chief Ten Crow studied the white woman for a moment as she met his gaze without flinching. Finally, without saying a word, he turned and walked away to tend to his horse.

Marissa breathed a silent sigh of relief as he left her, but then she noticed the other warriors watching her. The sight of so many of them, so close, made her want to scream. In the flickering light of the flames, the war paint on their faces made them seem even more ghoulish. With an effort, she fought down her panic. She remained unmoving, her expression impassive in spite of the looks the Comanche were giving her. They were speaking in their native tongue and laughing as they watched her.

"Snake! I thought you were a brave warrior! You let this little woman escape you?" Bear Claw chided as he looked at the white woman sitting before them. She wasn't very big and didn't look very strong either. He had little use for white women and was certain he could have controlled her with only one hand.

Snake's expression turned ugly as he responded to Bear Claw's challenge. "She did not escape me. I did not want her. I let her go."

"If you did not want her, you should have given her to me," Running Dog put in, laughing.

"Perhaps we can all have her," Hooting Owl suggested, drawing his knife and walking toward her.

Marissa sat still as the warrior approached. She fought to keep her expression from revealing what she was feeling as she stared at the wicked-looking blade he held in his hand. The way they were watching her, she could just imagine what they were saying.

Desperation filled her.

She looked around for a way to escape. She wanted to jump up and run. She wanted to save herself from the horrors she was certain they planned to inflict on her.

But there was no way out.

Forcing herself to appear calm, Marissa waited. She prayed fervently that the opportunity would come and she would be able to get away from them.

Hooting Owl came to stand over her. A sneering smile twisted his lips as he leered down at her. He was surprised when she looked up at him, seemingly unafraid. He decided she needed to learn what fear was. Ever so slowly and with great deliberation, he ran his knife down the buttons at the front of her gown, slicing them free and leaving her dress gaping open.

The other warriors called out lewd comments to him, urging him on, enjoying the scene. Each expected to have a turn with her once he was through.

Snake went to stand with Hooting Owl. He

reached out to grab the dress where the other man had cut it. In one harsh move, he ripped it open, revealing the shoulder strap of her chemise.

Marissa had managed to control her terror so far, but she cried out in shock when he tore her dress. She jumped to her feet to try to flee from the two men.

Snake grabbed her by the arm, ready to begin teaching her a few lessons.

"No!" Marissa screamed. Her flesh was crawling from his vile touch.

It was then that Chief Ten Crow returned to the campfire. He was furious to see what was going on.

"Release her!" the chief ordered angrily.

Snake and the others were surprised by their chief's fury. She was only a white captive. Snake immediately dropped his hand from her and moved off.

Marissa was startled to find herself suddenly free again. She had no idea what the man who was her captor had said to them, but they were backing away from her. She was relieved at the reprieve. She clutched the shreds of her torn bodice to her.

"You have plans for this white woman?" Snake asked.

"We thought she was only a captive," Hooting Owl explained to Ten Crow, not wanting to further anger their chief.

Ten Crow's expression was cold and commanding as he looked at them. "The golden one is mine.

I have taken her for my own. You will not touch her again."

The warriors were shocked by his declaration, but they knew better than to challenge him. They moved away. Hooting Owl slid his knife back into its sheath as he sat down across the campfire from where the chief and the woman stood.

For a time, Marissa hadn't known what to expect from the Comanche warriors. She wasn't sure if they were about to rape her or torture her and kill her. Her captor's sudden appearance had been timely, and her relief was great as he motioned for her to sit back down. She obeyed, her legs trembling.

A short time later, they all bedded down. Her captor came to Marissa's side. Absolute terror gripped her again as she imagined what was to come next.

The Comanche stared at her for a moment, then took a length of rope and bound her ankles tightly together. He said nothing, but lay down a short distance from her.

Conflicting emotions warred within Marissa—ridiculous joy that the warriors had not raped or harmed her and pure horror over the hopelessness of her situation. She was trapped with no possible chance to get away. She lay awake for a long time until exhaustion finally claimed her.

The dawn of the new day brought no relief for Marissa. For a moment when her captor gave her a horse of her own to ride, she hoped she could make a run for it, but then he took her reins to lead her mount as they got ready to move out. Sadly she realized that even if she had controlled the reins, she wouldn't have gotten very far without a saddle. She had never ridden astride before, and her skirts were a terrible hindrance as she struggled valiantly to keep her seat at the quick pace the Comanche warriors set.

The miles were endless. The sun beat down mercilessly all day long as the raiding party continued on. They stopped only to rest and water the horses, then rode off again.

A blessed numbness settled over Marissa. She focused only on staying on the horse's back and staying alive.

They made camp again, and her captor treated her in the same way as he had the previous night. This night, however, the other warriors did not come near her.

Only when the darkness surrounded her and Marissa closed her eyes, pretending to be asleep, did the pain return. She cried silently into the night for all that had been lost and the utter hopelessness of her situation.

Chapter Three

Meanwhile, at the Crown Ranch

George Williams saw the rider coming and walked out of his stable to greet him. Even at this distance, he recognized Ken Thompson, the deputy from Dry Springs, and he was suddenly concerned. It was a rare thing for a lawman to ride out to the Crown. He wondered if there was trouble.

"Morning, Ken," George called out. "What brings you out this far?"

"We need you in town," the deputy told him, his manner serious as he reined in and dismounted.

George was instantly cautious. "What's wrong?"

"Sheriff Spiller and I rode out to the way station. The stagecoach was over a day late, so we went to check on it and see if there was any kind of trouble.

It's a damned good thing we did. A Comanche raiding party has burned the way station to the ground."

George went still, fearful of what the deputy was about to tell him. His niece Marissa had sent word that she would be arriving in Dry Springs soon, depending on travel conditions, and he'd made arrangements with the stable in town to have her brought out to the Crown when she got there. "Why do you need me?"

"There was one survivor of the attack—a woman. She was shot and left for dead. I don't know how she did it, but she managed to hang on. She's been delirious and talking crazy, but she did call your name."

"Is it my niece Marissa?" George asked tightly.

"No, I met your niece the last time she came to visit you. This woman is older than Marissa. The sheriff and I transported her back to town. It wasn't easy, but we managed. Doc Harrison's taking care of her now."

"She could be my niece's companion, Louise Bennett. Did she tell you her name?"

"No, she was too weak to say much of anything. We were just shocked when she called for you."

"Is she going to make it?"

"Doc didn't know."

"What about Marissa?" He asked the question slowly. He was deathly afraid that his niece had been killed in the raid and the deputy was just trying to avoid giving him the bad news. "Was there any sign of her?"

"We found one other woman at the way station—"

George's heart sank.

"But it wasn't your niece," Ken finished quickly. "It was the station master's wife. She was dead, and so were all the men."

George felt as sick as he felt relieved. If the woman who'd survived was Louise Bennett, then where was Marissa? The thought that she might have been taken captive by the Comanche tore at him. He knew how captives were treated.

"I'll ride with you to town. Just give me a minute to take care of things here."

George left the deputy and went back into the stable to speak with Claude Collins, his foreman. Leaving him in charge, he hurriedly saddled his horse and was ready to head out. They rode for Dry Springs at top speed.

George made no attempt at conversation with the deputy, who kept pace at his side. His mood was too dark. Terrible thoughts haunted him, and his deepest fear ate at him: Had Marissa been taken captive? It seemed there could be no denying it, but first he had to talk to the injured woman and make sure. If this was Louise Bennett and Marissa had been taken, there was going to be hell to pay. He would see to it personally.

They reached Dry Springs and rode straight to

the doctor's office. George dismounted and tied his horse out front. He hurried inside to speak with Dr. Harrison, leaving Deputy Thompson to follow after him.

"Is the woman who was found at the way station still alive?" George asked. He was as ready as he would ever be to face the terrible truth.

"Yes. She's an amazing woman. She's quite a fighter," the physician told him.

"Thank God. Can I see her—talk to her?"

Dr. Harrison stood and led the way to the sick-room at the rear of his office. The doctor paused before the closed door to speak with George for a moment before they went in.

"She's in a bad way, George. She was shot in the back and lost a lot of blood. She's been drifting in and out of consciousness since they brought her in. To tell you the truth, I don't know how she managed to stay alive long enough for Sheriff Spiller and Deputy Thompson, to find her." He nodded proudly toward the lawman. "It's a miracle, that's for sure, and I'm going to do everything I can to help her pull through."

"Deputy Thompson said she called my name. Has she said anything else? Has she told you who she is? My niece Marissa was due in town, and she was traveling with a woman named Louise Bennett."

"No, except for calling your name, she hasn't

said anything else that's made sense. Would you recognize this Louise Bennett if you saw her?"

"No, I've never met the woman before."

"Well, let's see if she's awake."

The deputy waited in the outer office as the doctor quietly opened the door and went in to check on his patient. George paused, hesitating in the doorway at the sight of the woman lying deathly still on the bed. He'd always pictured Louise Bennett as a gray-haired, elderly matron, and he was surprised to see that this woman was much younger than he'd imagined. Her hair was a vibrant auburn, and though her color was ashen now, she was a delicate beauty.

"How is she?" he asked the doctor in a quiet tone as he stood there staring at her.

At the sound of a voice, the woman stirred and opened her eyes. She stared around herself blindly for a moment, frightened by her unknown surroundings. Then suddenly she tried to sit up.

"No!" she cried out.

George rushed to her side as Doc Harrison pressed her back down and spoke to her in a comforting voice.

"You're safe now, ma'am. You're in town, and you're going to be all right," the doctor reassured her gently.

She looked at the two men hovering over her. The terror that had scarred her soul screamed a warning to her to flee, that danger was everywhere.

She struggled to get away for a moment, but what little strength she had quickly gave out.

"But the Indians—they were everywhere—" she managed frantically, looking between the two men in desperation. Tears filled her eyes as she remembered the carnage she'd witnessed.

"It's all right now. No one is going to hurt you. The Comanche are gone," George reassured her as he took her hand in his.

She clung to his hand and gazed up at him. It felt good to hold on to his strength. She fought hard to focus as pain ravaged her. Something about this tall, dark-haired man standing over her seemed familiar. "Who are you?"

"I'm George—George Williams. And this is Dr. Harrison," he told her. He saw the sudden look of recognition in her eyes as she studied him.

"You're Uncle George," she said, her expression turning even more tormented when she realized she was facing Marissa's uncle. It had been her job to see Marissa safely to him. "Oh, God," she whispered. Terror once again overcame her as she thought of Marissa running to the stage driver's side. "How is Marissa? Is she here with me? Where is she?" Louise tried to sit up and look around, needing to reassure herself that Marissa was safe. "I have to see her!"

The emotions that flooded George at her words were overwhelming. His greatest fear had been realized. "So, you are Louise."

Her gaze met his, and they shared a moment of horrible comprehension.

"Yes—I'm Louise—and Marissa?" Her grip on his hand tightened even more as she started to ask, "Is she—"

"She's not dead," George told her quickly, wanting to ease her suffering.

"Thank God. Where is she? I want to see her," Louise insisted, desperate to know that Marissa was safe. "I tried to get her to go inside the way station, but she wanted to help the driver. He'd been wounded—"

George nodded in understanding. That was just like Marissa. She was always helping everyone. He could just imagine now what that act of kindness had cost her.

Grim acceptance of his niece's fate came to George. There could be no denying it any longer: The Comanche had taken her.

Louise went on quickly, wanting to explain, "I told Marissa to stay with me—I told her we had to get inside where it was safe—" She started to get hysterical again. "But she wouldn't come back! She kept going—"

"Easy," the doctor said.

Louise struggled to draw a breath as she looked up at both men, slowly shaking her head. "I'm sorry—I don't remember anything more after that. If she's not dead, then where is she? I want to see her."

George looked over at the doctor. They both knew there was no point in lying to her or trying to deny what had happened.

"Marissa was taken captive," George said quietly. "But I'm leaving right now to go after her."

"You'll find her, won't you? You'll bring her back—"

"I'm going to do everything in my power to find her, Louise. I promise you that."

Their gazes met, and Louise saw in the depths of his dark eyes the intent look of a man of his word.

"You will. If anyone can find her, it will be you," she whispered. A profound weariness overcame Louise then, and she closed her eyes against the brutal memories.

George stayed at her side for a moment longer. When her breathing became normal and her hold on his hand relaxed a little, he gently laid her hand down and quietly left the room with the doctor. They stepped out into the outer office and closed the door behind them. Deputy Thompson had taken a seat in the office, and he looked up questioningly.

"Is she your niece's companion?" he asked George.

"Yes," George answered grimly as he glanced back at the closed door.

"And your niece?"

"The Comanches must have taken her captive,"

he ground out as a fierce and terrible determination filled him.

"What are you going to do?"

"I'm going after her." George looked at the deputy, a deadly resolve showing in his eyes. He turned back to the doctor. "I'll take full responsibility for Miss Bennett's care. As soon as she can be safely moved, I want her out at the ranch. Send word if there's any change in her condition."

"I will."

George started to leave, then turned back to the doctor. "And you might want to say a few prayers for my niece."

Dr. Harrison nodded to him in silent understanding.

Without another word, George headed off with Deputy Thompson to speak with Sheriff Spiller.

The sheriff looked up as George barged into his office.

"I'm glad Ken brought you to town. Do you know the woman?" Spiller asked, concerned.

"Yes, she was my niece's traveling companion," George told him. "Her name is Louise Bennett."

"Damn. So Marissa was there at the way station, too." Sheriff Spiller's expression reflected his sudden fears. He'd met George's niece on one of her previous trips to Dry Springs. She was a lovely young lady, but he had seen no trace of her at the site of the raid.

"Yes. Marissa and Louise were making the trip

to the Crown together." He looked the lawman straight in the eye. "The Comanches must have taken Marissa, Harry. I've got to go after her—I've got to find her."

The sheriff was sickened by the news, but he understood the rancher's feelings. "I know, George, but it won't be easy."

"I didn't think it would be." His tone was cold.

"I've already notified the Rangers."

"I can't wait for them. It might be weeks before they show up, and it's already been too long. I've got to head out as fast as I can while their trail is still fresh. Who's the best tracker you know? Is there anybody here in town?"

"Hawk Morgan," Spiller answered without hesitation.

"The half-breed who works at the livery stable?" George asked sharply, not feeling the least bit kindly toward anybody with Indian blood right then.

"That's right. Hawk's as good as they come. He's helped me in the past whenever I needed him."

George nodded. "Thanks."

He turned to go, fighting down the anger he was feeling at having to deal with a half-breed, yet knowing he had a much better chance of finding Marissa with his aid. If he was going to save her, he needed the man's help.

"George."

George looked back at Sheriff Spiller.

"Be careful."

They shared a look of complete understanding. George nodded tightly, then left the office and made his way straight to the stable. He met Jim Watson, the owner of the stable, first and talked briefly with him.

"I need to speak with Hawk Morgan."

"Hawk's working out back," Jim told George. "Let me get him for you."

"I'd appreciate it." He was tense as he readied himself to speak with the half-breed.

"Hawk—someone out here needs to talk to you!" Jim Watson called out.

Hawk had been working with a horse in a corral behind the stable. At Jim's call, he went inside to see what was wanted. Hawk saw George Williams standing with Jim. He knew of the successful rancher and wondered what he wanted. "What is it?"

George eyed the tall, dark-haired half-breed coolly. He judged him to be about thirty, but he couldn't be sure and didn't care. He didn't want to take any time with niceties or trying to be polite. "Sheriff Spiller tells me you're the best tracker around. I need to hire you."

Hawk frowned. "For what?"

George quickly related all that had happened. "I've got to go after my niece while there's still time to pick up the trail. Will you do it? I'll pay you whatever you ask."

"How soon can you be ready to ride?" Hawk asked, understanding the rancher's fury and desperation.

George realized that Hawk was agreeing to go. "I want a couple of hands from my ranch to ride with us. We can be ready in a matter of hours."

Hawk asked his boss, "This all right with you, Jim? Will you be shorthanded without me?"

"I'll manage," Jim returned.

George looked at Hawk. "You didn't say how much you wanted. Name your price."

"Let's find your niece, Mr. Williams. We'll worry about the money later."

George was shocked. He would have paid whatever amount the man wanted. He would spare no cost trying to save Marissa. "Are you sure?"

Hawk nodded.

"Hawk—"

The man looked at him questioningly.

"Call me George."

Hawk nodded and shook the hand George offered him.

Jim smiled grimly, glad that things were working out. "Good luck," he told George.

"We're going to need it."

"If anyone can track them down, Hawk can," Jim said. "He's the best."

Hawk and George set up the time and place

where they would meet, and then George rode for the Crown.

They all realized time was of the essence if they were to rescue Marissa from the Comanche.

Chapter Four

Chief Ten Crow was glad when the Comanche village came into view. It had been a long, arduous trip back, but at last they were home. He shouted out to his men in triumph, and they responded with shouts of equal joy. The villagers heard the sound of their cries and ran to greet them, cheering their success. The chief and his warriors were pleased with the rousing welcome.

Marissa stared about her as they rode into the camp. It was alien to her—the tipis and open campfires, the half-naked children and the buckskin-clad women who were staring and pointing at her as she passed by. Once again she faced the fear of the unknown, and a shiver of terror trembled through her. She fought it back with fierce denial. One thing she'd come to learn in watching these Comanche who had taken her captive. They showed no fear, and they respected those who were fearless as well. Determination filled Marissa. She would face them and her future as bravely as she could.

Her captor reined in before a tipi where a woman stood. Marissa held on to her mount and waited in silent expectation to see what was going to happen next. Her gaze swept over the village again, a part of her desperately seeking help, but there was no sign of any whites—no sign of anything familiar. She was alone in a foreign and dangerous world.

Chief Ten Crow dismounted. Dropping the reins of both horses, he went to greet his wife, Laughing Woman.

"You are back, my husband," Laughing Woman said with a smile, glad to see him.

"It is good to be home."

"Your raid was successful?" she asked, looking up at the white woman. She had already seen the many horses they'd herded in.

"Very."

"You have a captive?" Laughing Woman moved closer to get a better look at the female.

"Yes."

She studied the woman intently, especially her blond hair and pale skin.

"Is she the one?" Laughing Woman asked knowingly. Ten Crow had told her of his vision of the golden woman before he'd left on the raid.

"She is." He nodded. "And she is very brave."

"It would seem so," Laughing Woman agreed, seeing how quiet the girl was. She expected her to cower, and she was surprised when the captive met her regard without showing any fear. White captives usually screamed and cried when they were brought into the village.

Chief Ten Crow came to the horse's side and pulled Marissa down from its back. Images of his vision came to him as he stared down at her for a moment.

"Have you given her a name?"

"I will call her Shining Spirit, for her hair is the color of the sun."

"It is fitting."

"Where is Wind Ryder?" Chief Ten Crow asked, surprised that his adopted son had not come to greet him.

"He left on a raid with Rearing Horse and the others. They have been gone many days, as you were."

The news troubled him. He had plans for the woman, but could do nothing until Wind Ryder returned.

"See to the woman," he directed.

"I will," Laughing Woman answered obediently.

"And keep her away from the others—except for Crazy One. I will have her come to you."

"That is good." She led Marissa into the tipi.

Chief Ten Crow was disappointed at Wind Ryder's absence. He wanted to see his vision fulfilled. He wanted to ensure the peace of his tribe.

Chief Ten Crow went to join the other warriors to celebrate the success of their raiding. He would anxiously await his other son's return.

Marissa's imagination had conjured up all kinds of terrible images of what was about to happen to her. She'd felt certain that the fate she'd been dreading during the trek to the village was about to befall her. Her surprise had been real when a woman led her away into the tipi. Any relief she'd felt quickly gave way to panic when the woman began trying to pull her clothes off her.

"No!" Marissa fought back as best she could, but it was difficult with her wrists bound.

Laughing Woman was not laughing over the captive's resistance. She was tempted to beat her into submission, but restrained herself. She knew how important Ten Crow believed this white woman to be to the future of their tribe. Pulling out her knife, she saw for the first time a glimmer of fear in the woman's eyes. That pleased Laughing Woman. She moved in on her, and with a few quick strokes cut away most of her skirt and petticoats.

Marissa was truly terrified as her garments were slashed and torn from her. She stood before the Comanche woman, half-unclothed, valiantly trying to be brave as she wondered if she was to be stripped completely naked and paraded through the camp. Horror and dread filled the very depths of her soul.

Was she to be beaten? Or given over to the warriors for their pleasure?

Laughing Woman gestured toward the rest of the clothing she still wore.

"Undress yourself," she ordered in her native tongue.

Marissa didn't know what the other woman was shouting or what she wanted her to do.

Laughing Woman repeated her command, this time gesturing toward the garments Marissa still had on.

Marissa had no intention of taking off what little was left of her clothing. She stood her ground.

Frustrated, Laughing Woman wished Crazy One would hurry. She knelt and sorted through her own clothing to find a garment for the captive to wear. When she found the one she'd been seeking, she rose and held out the fringed, buckskin dress to the white woman.

Marissa looked from the woman to the dress and back. Laughing Woman shoved it toward her again, and then Marissa understood. She grabbed it and clutched it to her breast, trying to cover herself. Once more, Laughing Woman motioned for her to undress.

Marissa finally understood what she wanted, but

knew she couldn't change clothing with her hands bound as they were. She stepped forward and held out her arms so the Comanche woman could see the problem.

Laughing Woman realized she would have to free the girl, and with one sure motion cut the rope.

Marissa rubbed her sore wrists, grateful for at least that much freedom. She kept her gaze focused on the woman as she quickly shed the remnants of her gown. Taking up the buckskin dress, she started to pull it on over her underthings, but the Comanche woman grabbed her arm to stop her, gesturing for her to strip those off too. Embarrassed, Marissa turned her back and quickly did as directed. She was glad when she finally pulled on the fringed and bead-trimmed buckskin dress. She noticed immediately that it smelled very much like a dead cow, but right then, that didn't matter to her. At least she wasn't naked. The dress modestly covered her, and the buckskin was surprisingly soft against her skin.

Laughing Woman stared at Shining Spirit's feet. The captive was still wearing shoes. Laughing Woman went through her own belongings again and took out a pair of moccasins, offering them to her.

Marissa took the moccasins, but did not really want to wear them. She glanced at the Comanche woman and found that she was watching her closely. She sat down and pulled off her own shoes and stockings, then donned the other footwear.

Laughing Woman studied Shining Spirit thoughtfully. Seeing how filthy she was, she decided to allow her to bathe. Her husband wanted the white woman to be ready for Wind Ryder when he returned. She motioned for Shining Spirit to get up so they could leave the tipi. Laughing Woman wondered why Crazy One hadn't come to them yet. She could not trust the white woman alone and could have used her help. As it was, she would have to be the one to go with her to the stream and keep watch over her.

Marissa stared at the Comanche woman, trying to understand what she wanted her to do. After a moment, she finally understood and got up to follow her from the tipi. They made their way down to the creek.

Marissa eyed the clean water, longing for a hot bath. The endless days on the trail had taken their toll. She had never been this dirty before in her entire life. She wished there was some way to scrub every inch of herself clean, but even as she wanted to bathe, Marissa wondered if she would ever feel really clean again. Still, if she was going to have the chance to wash up at all, it was now.

"Wash!" Laughing Woman ordered, pointing at the water.

Marissa watched as the Indian woman squatted down and pretended to wash herself.

"Wash!" Laughing Woman said again.

Marissa looked around, torn between her innate sense of modesty and her desperate yearning to be clean. The shrubbery on the bank of the stream provided some privacy, so she quickly stripped off the buckskin dress and moccasins and stepped into the water. It was chilling, but she didn't care. She waded out until the stream was waist deep, then dipped beneath the water and hid as she washed.

The cool, clean water washed the dirt and grit away, but even as Marissa took what small pleasure she could from feeling clean again, the reality of her situation did not change. Always in the back of her mind, torturing and haunting her, were Louise's death and the horrors of what she'd witnessed during the raid. Why had she been the only one left alive? At that moment, if the water had been deeper, she might have considered suicide. Her mother was dead, and her father, and now Louise . . .

The painful memories overwhelmed her again, and Marissa slipped under the water to hide her tears. After washing her hair and wringing the water out of the sleek, heavy length of it, she made her way back to the bank where the Indian woman awaited her.

Donning the buckskin dress again, Marissa followed the woman's lead back to the encampment, where this time she was directed to go into a different tipi. Marissa wondered whom it belonged to as she stepped inside. She waited to see what would happen next, and was relieved when the woman did not bind her hands again. The woman simply looked around and walked back outside, leaving her alone.

Marissa started to follow her back outside, but the woman turned and shouted angrily at her, gesturing for her to stay inside. She retreated into the tipi. Unsure of what she ought to do, Marissa sat down on the blankets on the far side of the lodge, across from the opening, to wait.

Bear Claw had not known the white captive would be bathing in the stream, but as he'd made his way back to his tipi he had seen the captive heading toward the stream, accompanied by his mother. He had tended to his business, and then on his return deliberately made his way past the stream. Though his mother was standing guard, he eluded her detection and watched the golden one in the water. When the captive finally emerged from the stream, her long golden hair fell around her in a natural, shimmering shield, hiding her breasts from his view. Heat had stirred within him as his hungry gaze devoured the sight of her rounded hips and long, shapely legs. Bear Claw was surprised by his own reaction to her. He usually felt no attraction to white women, but this one seemed different. He remained where he was, enjoying the view until the captive dressed again and left the stream bank.

Only when she had gone from sight did he go on to the village and seek out his father.

"Father, what will you do with the new captive?" Bear Claw asked, trying not to sound too interested.

"She will serve her purpose here," Chief Ten Crow answered mysteriously.

Bear Claw did not recognize the strangeness of his answer. He thought his father was just going to keep her in camp as he would any other white captive. "I will buy her from you," he offered.

"You do not like the whites," his father pointed out, frowning at his son's show of interest. There had been white female captives in their village before, but Bear Claw had never shown interest in any of them.

"This one is different."

"She is not for sale." Chief Ten Crow's frown darkened. The woman was meant for Wind Ryder—not Bear Claw. She was to somehow encourage peace between his sons, not cause more trouble.

"As you say, Father." Bear Claw was angered by his refusal, but struggled not to show it. He was not accustomed to being denied anything he wanted, but this was his father—the chief—so he had to accept his answer as final.

Frustrated, Bear Claw fell silent. His body was still on fire, so he bided his time, waiting for the late hours so he could find a village girl who was willing to ease the ache within him. Bear Claw knew, though, that all the while he was taking her he would be thinking of the golden one.

Marissa remained alone in the tipi. As the hours passed, her uncertainty grew. Darkness was just beginning to claim the land when she decided to take a look outside and see if there was anyone around. The thought of trying to escape taunted her as she pushed the flap farther back and looked out. She saw no one nearby, and, feeling bolder, she started outside. She didn't know how far she could get, but she had to try.

Laughing Woman had not trusted the captive. She'd sent one of the small boys in camp to keep watch over the tipi while she went to find Crazy One. She had had no success in finding Crazy One and was still looking for her when the boy rushed to alert her that the white captive had come out.

Marissa hadn't gotten very far when Laughing Woman confronted her.

"Go back!" Laughing Woman commanded in the Comanche tongue, giving her an angry look as she pointed toward Wind Ryder's tipi. Her husband had directed that Shining Spirit was to stay there until Wind Ryder returned from his raid.

Marissa's hope of slipping away undetected was ruined. She went back into the lodge, wondering if she would ever get a chance to try to save herself. As she stepped inside, she gasped in shock. There was another woman in the tipi. The woman was hunched down, visibly shaking, her face averted, a shawl covering her head.

"Who are you?" Marissa demanded, frightened. She didn't know how the woman had been able to get inside without being seen. Even as she was speaking, she realized miserably that the woman couldn't understand her.

At the sound of her voice, the woman stopped shaking and went completely still. Ever so slowly, she lifted her head to stare at the woman before her.

"Who are you?" Crazy One demanded in English, still staying huddled down.

"You speak English?" Marissa was stunned. Tears of relief burned in her eyes as she tried to get a better look at the woman.

"You speak English?" Crazy One repeated as she peered up at her.

When the woman said that, Marissa feared she was mocking her with her own words. Her spirits had momentarily soared, but now they died again. She stood there staring down at the old woman as she answered wearily, "Yes, I speak English."

Marissa did not expect an answer.

"Why are you in Wind Ryder's lodge? It is not good to be here! I must leave—quick—quick—before he returns! I must go." She stood, ready to flee, the expression on her face one of pure panic and fear.

"What?" Marissa was even more shocked as she looked into the haggard old woman's leathery face and realized she was a white woman. "You're white! Who are you?"

"They call me Crazy One."

She was taken aback by her name. "I'm Marissa—"

"No," Crazy One interrupted her. "You are Shining Spirit. Chief Ten Crow said so."

"Shining Spirit? No, my name is Marissa Williams, and I was taken captive—"

"Doesn't matter—doesn't matter," she said quickly, cutting Marissa off again as she looked nervously toward the doorway. "Wind Ryder may be coming."

"Who is Wind Ryder? Why are you so afraid of him?"

"You will see," Crazy One answered slowly, knowingly. "He is a fierce warrior—an angry warrior. I must go."

She fled the tipi.

Behind her, Marissa called out as she started to follow her, "Wait! Don't go! Can you help me? Why did you come here?"

Crazy One didn't stop to answer that she had only come because Chief Ten Crow and Laughing Woman had insisted. She wanted only to stay away from Wind Ryder's tipi.

Marissa watched Crazy One run off into the gathering darkness; then she looked around to find others in the village watching her. She went back inside.

Marissa's emotions were in turmoil as she sank down on the blankets. The relief she felt at having discovered that someone in the village spoke English was destroyed by the knowledge that the old woman had obviously been a captive for a long time and that she had a very real fear of this warrior named Wind Ryder. The very warrior whose tipi she was staying in.

Wind Ryder.

Marissa wondered who he was and what he had done to instill such terror in Crazy One. Was this Comanche warrior—this Wind Ryder—the most vicious and savage of them all? And would he really be returning soon? She had no answers. The one person who could have told her was gone.

Uneasy and greatly disturbed by Crazy One's visit, Marissa tried to rest, but sleep, again, was long in coming.

Chapter Five

At the sighting of riders approaching the village, a shout went out, and the people rushed from their lodges to see who it was.

"I hope it's Wind Ryder!" Moon Cloud told her friend Soaring Dove as they joined the others going to meet the incoming warriors.

Soaring Dove laughed at her friend's excitement. "Somehow I knew you were going to say that. It is the same thing you said three days ago when Chief Ten Crow returned."

Moon Cloud ignored her as she strained to see who was coming.

"Look!" she cried out in delight, seeing Wind Ryder riding at the front of the raiding party. "It is Wind Ryder!"

Her gaze was hungry upon the tall, handsome

brave. He was broad-shouldered, powerfully built, and darkly tanned, and he rode his horse as if they were one. From the distance, there was no evidence of his white blood. He appeared the fine warrior that he was. Her heartbeat quickened at the sight of him.

"Wind Ryder will be mine. You will see." Moon Cloud was confident.

"I am not the one you have to convince," Soaring Dove advised cautiously. "*He* is the one."

"I will do it."

Soaring Dove knew Moon Cloud was determined, but wondered if her friend really could win Wind Ryder's favor. He had shown little interest in her or any of the young maidens, and there were many who found him attractive. Still, she knew how dogged Moon Cloud could be.

They went forth to welcome the returning warriors.

Wind Ryder and the other warriors were proud of their accomplishments as they returned to the village. They had taken many horses and knew their chief would be pleased.

Wind Ryder saw his father coming to welcome them, and he reined in before him. He paid no attention to the women who crowded around, speaking only to Chief Ten Crow.

"Hello, my father."

"It is good that you are back," Chief Ten Crow told him. "I see you did well."

Wind Ryder nodded. "We took many horses. No one was injured or lost. And your raid? Were you successful?"

"All went as I had foreseen," the chief answered cryptically.

Wind Ryder nodded, assuming he meant everything had gone well. "I will tend to my horse and then come to tell you of our raids."

Chief Ten Crow watched him go and smiled to himself. He did not doubt that his son would return to him quickly.

Crazy One had hidden behind a tipi to watch the raiding party's return. She looked on nervously as Wind Ryder spoke briefly with the chief and then left him, striding toward his own lodge. Conflicting emotions filled her. She was torn between the desire to flee from the fury she was sure would come and the need to stay and try to help Shining Spirit. During the past three days, she had tended to the captive as Laughing Woman had ordered her to do, taking meals to her and guarding her when she went to the stream to bathe. She hadn't wanted to. She didn't want to have anything to do with Wind Ryder, but now, seeing that he was returning to his lodge, she wondered what was going to happen to the woman. She knew how he'd felt about having her around—as a boy he'd chased her away any time she'd come near him and she had learned through the years that he avoided her because she was white. She could only imagine how he was going to react to finding Shining Spirit in his tipi.

Crazy One crept away.

She did not want to witness his fury.

Marissa was surprised by all the excitement she heard outside the tipi. In the time that she'd lived with the Comanche, the village had been very quiet. She wondered what had happened to cause such a celebration.

The temptation to take a look outside was strong, but Marissa knew there was always someone nearby, keeping watch over her. The moment she showed herself, her guard would descend and force her back inside. She was only allowed to leave the lodge to bathe and to take care of her private needs. Otherwise, she was as much a prisoner in the tipi as she would have been in any jail, visited only by Crazy One several times a day when she brought her food.

Once she had discovered that Crazy One was white, Marissa had hoped she would help her, but the old woman had offered no help at all. She did not say much, but when she did, she only babbled about how she had to stay away from Wind Ryder.

Marissa was constantly praying for someone to rescue her, but she was losing heart. Surely her uncle had received word of her disappearance by now. That knowledge gave her one last hope she could hold on to—that Uncle George had put together a search party and he and Mark were trying to find her even now. But the raiding party had traveled so many miles so quickly after attacking the way station, she wondered if anyone would ever be able to track them down.

Being helpless this way didn't suit Marissa. She hated being afraid. She hated being at the mercy of the Comanche. She hated this idleness that left her sitting alone, worrying about the fate that awaited her.

Anger stirred within her breast and emboldened Marissa. In a moment of brazenness, she decided to tempt fate and go outside. She moved forward ready to throw open the flap.

Marissa had taken only one step when suddenly the door covering was drawn aside and a tall, powerful Comanche warrior stepped into the lodge. She stopped, startled by the intrusion. The sun was at his back, so it was difficult for her to make out his features. Uneasiness gripped her. Since she'd been kept captive in the tipi, no men had been permitted to come near her—and now this warrior had walked in.

Wind Ryder entered his tipi completely unaware of what he was about to discover. He straightened, letting the flap close behind him, and found himself face to face with a woman—a white woman with hair the color of golden sunshine.

"Who are you?" Wind Ryder demanded curtly in the Comanche tongue. It was shocking enough to find a female there, but the fact that she was white and beautiful disturbed him even more.

At the harshness in his deep voice, Marissa gasped and stepped back. She got her first good look at him then as he stood before her clad in the traditional Comanche loincloth and moccasins, and she realized she had never seen this warrior before. If she had, she certainly would have remembered.

The warrior's presence was overwhelming. He was tall, his shoulders broad, his body lean and hard-muscled. On his upper arm Marissa could see a wicked scar, pale against his darkly tanned flesh, a silent testimony to the violent life he led. The warrior's black hair was long and held back by only a headband. Slashes of war paint colored his features, and his expression was fiercely arrogant as he glared down at her. He seemed to fill the entire tipi as he loomed over her.

A shiver of fear trembled through Marissa as she realized this might be the warrior Crazy One had warned her about. This man might be Wind Ryder. She could understand the old woman's fear of him. He exuded an aura of danger. Marissa took another step back, wanting to get as far away from him as she could.

"What are you doing here?" Wind Ryder demanded, again in the Comanche tongue. He knew everyone in the village, but he had never seen this woman before. He was irritated by her presence in his lodge.

He sounded so angry that Marissa wanted to turn and flee, but she knew there was nowhere to go, nowhere to run. Drawing upon what little bravery she had left, she lifted her chin and glared back up at him.

Wind Ryder grew even more angered by her show of defiance. He closed on her and grabbed her by the upper arm to drag her to him.

Fear—sudden and real—tore through Marissa.

Was this the moment she'd been dreading all this time?

Was this the moment when she was to be sacrificed to a Comanche warrior's lust?

Had she been offered up to this man as some prize to be claimed—to be taken and used as he desired?

"No! Let me go!" she cried as she fought wildly against his hold. She was desperate to break free, to try to save herself. The fear she'd held at bay for so long erupted into pure terror. She would not surrender easily.

Wind Ryder was surprised by the fierceness of her resistance, but he was just as determined not to let her get away. He pulled her tightly to him, and a shock of instinctive physical awareness jolted through Wind Ryder at the feel of her soft body molded to him.

Crushed against the hard-muscled width of his

chest, Marissa gasped. She looked up at him and found herself staring into a pair of green eyes. Her eyes widened in shock at the discovery.

This Comanche warrior was a white man!

How could that be?

"You're white!" Marissa's gaze locked with his. She remained frozen in his arms as she tried to understand.

Her words stunned Wind Ryder. Hearing English after all this time had a powerful effect on him. He released her immediately and moved away, denying any knowledge of the language of his childhood.

"Please!" she began desperately, a faint glimmer of hope sparking within her for the first time. This man could help her! This man could save her!

Wind Ryder didn't show any reaction. He just stared at her, seeing her frantic desperation and wondering how she had come to be in his tipi.

Marissa came toward him, pleading, "You're white, so you understand. You've got to help me!"

He still did not respond.

She went on, her desperation growing, "They murdered everyone at the way station! They killed Louise. Please—can you do something to help me? Can you help me get away?"

For an instant, a distant, fragmented, painful memory threatened to surface, but Wind Ryder savagely denied it. Without a word, he turned his back on the woman and left.

Wind Ryder strode back toward the tipi where his father was waiting for him. He remembered his father's earlier statement—*"All went as I had foreseen."* He wondered now if there had been a secret meaning behind his father's words.

Chief Ten Crow had been sitting before his own tipi, awaiting Wind Ryder's return. When he saw his son striding across the camp in his direction, he smiled inwardly, but revealed nothing in his expression. He looked up as Wind Ryder came to stand over him. Seeing his son's stony expression, he got slowly to his feet.

"You have found the present I have given you?" Chief Ten Crow asked.

"I have no need for a white woman," Wind Ryder answered tersely.

"You would refuse my gift?" The chief pinned him with a penetrating gaze.

"Why have you given this woman to me?" he challenged.

"It came to me in a vision. This golden woman was meant for you."

"Your vision was wrong," Wind Ryder said angrily, refusing to believe him.

"My visions are never wrong," the chief responded with confidence. "There is much you do not know, my son."

"Then help me. Tell me what it is I do not know, but do not put this white woman in my care."

"You will guard Shining Spirit well." He stated it as fact, ignoring Wind Ryder's protests.

"Shining Spirit?"

"It is the name I have given her."

"But I have no need of a slave."

"I have spoken. Come, let us join the others and hear the tales of your raids."

Wind Ryder knew there was nothing more he could say or do. He accompanied his father to the fire, where the other warriors had gathered to speak of their feats of daring.

Even as he passed the long hours with the other men, Wind Ryder found images of the golden woman drifting into his thoughts. He decided he would stay away from his tipi for as long as he could.

Marissa's thoughts were racing as she sat alone in the lodge. Darkness had come, but still the warrior had not returned. When the flap was thrown open, she looked up, startled, unsure of what to expect.

"I must hurry," Crazy One said as she came in carrying the evening meal. She was glancing behind herself as if fearful that someone was following her.

"Is something wrong?"

"I told you he would be back." She was nervous as she put the food down. "Wind Ryder has returned to the village."

"Is Wind Ryder the white warrior?" she asked.

"Yes, and he is a fierce one." The old woman started to back away, wanting only to be gone from his tipi. "And now you are his."

"What?" Crazy One's words shocked Marissa.

"I must go."

"Will you tell me—?"

Marissa got no further. Crazy One slipped outside and was gone. She was alone again.

Wind Ryder was back—

And she was his—

Marissa's confusion was real. Her nerves were on edge as she tried to understand what Crazy One had meant.

Wind Ryder was back—

The knowledge that he was a white man still shocked her. Over and over, she found herself wondering how he had come to be there with the Comanche, living as one of them. Had he been taken captive and raised in the village, or had he joined the tribe of his own free will? She couldn't imagine any white man going there of his own free will, yet he seemed so natural in this setting, so attuned to the Comanche ways, that he must have lived among them for a long time.

And she was his—

Marissa's imagination conjured up images of what might happen in the long hours of the night ahead that left her trembling. She knew she had to find a way to communicate with Wind Ryder, yet having witnessed Crazy One's fear of him, she was unsure of what to do. When he returned to the lodge, she would try to talk to him again in hopes that some part of him remembered his life in the white world and would be able to understand her desperation.

Even as she allowed herself that small hope, Marissa realized that little had really changed. The man who had stood before her in the tipi had been as much a Comanche warrior as any of the other men in the village. He had been fearsome, and the look in his eyes—no matter that they were green in color, a testimony to his white heritage—had been cold and unfeeling. A shiver trembled through her as she remembered the way it had felt when he'd held her prisoner in his arms.

Emotionally exhausted, Marissa lay down and pulled the blanket up over her. It was a meager defense against the dangers that threatened, but somehow she felt safer that way.

The hours dragged on, and a great weariness settled over her. When at last she could fight no more, she closed her eyes and fell into a troubled slumber.

Wind Ryder sat with his father and the other braves before the campfire. Many stories had been told and many feats of courage recounted, including the tale of the raid on the way station and taking the white woman captive.

"She was almost Snake's captive, but she was

too quick for him," Running Dog taunted Snake. "We will find out soon if Wind Ryder is a better warrior than Snake. We will find out if she can get away from him, too."

The warriors laughed.

"Your father has given you a fine prize," Snake said, looking coldly at Wind Ryder across the fire. He had been wondering ever since they'd returned why Chief Ten Crow was giving the woman to his adopted son. Wind Ryder was no real Comanche. Though some of the others had come to accept him as one of them, Snake never would. To him, Wind Ryder would always be white—and he hated him for his white blood.

"Yes, he has," Wind Ryder agreed, but did not say more. He was in no mood to discuss the woman.

Bear Claw grew angry as he listened to the talk of Wind Ryder and the captive white woman.

He had wanted her.

He had offered to buy her from his father, and his father had refused to sell her to him.

Finding out now that she had been a gift to Wind Ryder left him furious. He had wondered why his father had kept her in Wind Ryder's tipi since they'd returned to the village, and now he knew. Hatred seethed within him.

His father had never given him such an important gift. He stared at the man his father claimed as a son. Nothing had changed between them since that day when they had fought all those years ago. Bear Claw had no brother.

The talk among the warriors continued until the hour grew late.

Wind Ryder stayed away from his lodge for as long as he could without drawing attention to himself. When at last the hour came to retire for the night, he made his way slowly back to his tipi. His mood was as dark as the moonless night that surrounded him.

Chapter Six

Wind Ryder walked silently to his lodge. He drew back the flap and went in. It was dark and very quiet inside. The weather was warm, and no fire had been lit, so he stood there with the flap held up to give him just enough light to see the woman asleep on the far side of the lodge. She was a vision as she slept, her long, golden hair unbound and spread out around her in a shimmering halo.

The golden one—

Shining Spirit—

Wind Ryder understood why his father had called her these things. In sleep, she looked soft and delicate, but he caught himself in that self-deception. He knew what a fierce fighter this woman was. She had been a she-cat when he'd held her earlier, and he'd heard how she'd escaped from Snake during the raid.

He could imagine how she'd respond if he tried to touch her now. As quickly as the thought had come to him, he dismissed it.

He would not touch her—not now—not ever.

Wind Ryder was glad that she was asleep. He needed peace in his soul. He didn't want to hear her speak English. He didn't want to be reminded of things he'd long ago put from him—memories that were powerful enough to destroy the life he'd created for himself. He was Wind Ryder, Comanche warrior, son of Chief Ten Crow and Laughing Woman.

Dropping the flap, Wind Ryder settled in on his own blankets to get some much needed rest. He would deal with the woman in the morning. For now, he just wanted to sleep. He stretched out and closed his eyes, trying to put all thoughts of Shining Spirit and his father's troubling vision from him.

Marissa's dreams were tormented. During the past few nights she'd managed to get some rest, but the warrior's unexpected appearance today left her frightened and desperate again. Bloody visions of the raid at the way station returned. In her mind, she heard the screams of the dying, along with the sounds of the gunfire and the smell of the fire.

And then Marissa saw Louise—

Louise calling out; Louise warning her and trying to protect her—

Then finally, the gunshot that had taken her life.

Marissa awoke with a start and sat up quickly. Terror surrounded her in the darkness. She didn't know where she was or why she was there.

"No!" she cried out, and tears fell freely as she relived the horror of Louise's death. Her heart was pounding and her breathing was ragged. She stared around her, trying to understand what was real and what was not.

At the sound of her cry, Wind Ryder was instantly awake. Expecting trouble, he was on his feet, knife in hand, ready for whatever danger was near.

Still caught in the grip of her nightmare, Marissa screamed at the sight of the warrior standing over her.

Wind Ryder moved instinctively, pulling her to her feet and clamping a hand over her mouth to silence her.

Mindlessly, Marissa fought his hold on her. She kept screaming even though the sound was muffled by his hand.

"Be still!" Wind Ryder commanded harshly in a low voice, using English with her for the first time.

She continued to struggle for a moment until the realization that he'd actually spoken English penetrated her terror. She stopped.

The moment she gave up the fight, Wind Ryder

released her. He stood there staring down at her, his expression revealing the anger he felt at being so awakened.

Marissa thoughts were still chaotic. Memories of the raid and Louise's death tormented her. She was shaking as she looked up at him.

Marissa saw the fury in his face and backed as far away from him as she could. What little bravery she'd felt earlier vanished as she wondered whether he would attack her now. The night had become a living nightmare.

Horrified, Marissa waited for him to make his move—to begin beating her or to rape her. He hadn't responded to her earlier pleas for help in any way, and she could only imagine that he had no sympathy for her plight.

"Don't kill me," she whispered in a frightened voice, unable to deny her fear any longer.

Her words struck savagely at Wind Ryder, and the memory they awoke in him angered him even more. He pushed the painful vision away, turning his anger on Shining Spirit.

"Lie down," he ordered.

Marissa was stunned.

So this was to be her fate. He was going to rape her. She didn't know what to do—Should she try to flee or should she obey him?

Panic filled her. Mindlessly, she tried to dodge past him, to escape from the tipi and the fate she was certain was about to be hers.

Wind Ryder was shocked by her daring move, but he reacted quickly. He snared her around the waist when she would have darted by and brought her against him, her back to his chest.

Marissa went instantly still when his arms closed around her. She waited for what she believed was to come next. Understanding Crazy One's fear of this man, she began to tremble as he walked toward the side of the tipi where she'd made her bed.

Wind Ryder released her.

"Lie down!" He pointed at her blankets.

The look on his face was as frightening as the tone of his voice. Marissa knew there was no way out. She did as he commanded and sat down on her blankets, but she never took her gaze off him. Instinctively, she clutched one of the blankets to her breast as she stared up at him, waiting—expecting him to attack her, for though his skin was white, his heart was Comanche.

Wind Ryder appreciated that she was a beautiful woman, but the look of pure terror in her expression left him cold. He knew what she was thinking and silently cursed the fact that his father had put her in his care. He wanted nothing to do with her. The farther away from him she stayed, the better. If he could have taken her to another tipi in the village, he would have.

"Sleep." The word was harsh.

Marissa blinked in confusion, shocked by his order.

"What?" she choked out.

"Sleep." He didn't want to say anything more to her. He just wanted her to be quiet.

Relief swept through Marissa. She couldn't believe what was happening, but quickly did as he'd ordered. She wrapped the blanket tightly around her, for it was her only defense. She did not say another word and remained quiet, fearful that any move she might make would stir his wrath again.

Wind Ryder looked on and gave a grunt of some satisfaction when she obeyed him. He went back to his own bedding and lay down. He shut his eyes and sought sleep. He wanted to rest. But the pain of hearing her words ate at him.

Don't kill me—

How old had he been when his mother had cried those same words? How old had he been when he'd seen her murdered before his very eyes?

Don't kill me—

As much as he wanted to, Wind Ryder wondered how he could deny the reality behind Shining Spirit's fears. She had seen the other warriors raiding and knew the terror of being helpless before them—just as he had been all those years ago.

The unexpected thought jarred him.

Everything Shining Spirit had said to him earlier returned to haunt him. Long-denied, unwanted memories of his own past crept back into his consciousness—of how he'd felt when he'd been brought into the Comanche camp for the first time.

He tried to remember how old he'd been. He had a vague recollection of being about eight years old, but he wasn't sure.

It had been many years ago.

Wind Ryder realized, too, that it had been almost that long since he'd spoken English. The language did not come easily to him now, but that did not surprise him. It pained him to draw upon his knowledge of his past. That was why he had refused to speak English to her earlier.

More memories assaulted him now even as he tried to deny them. In order to survive his ordeal, he had pretended that none of his life before the Comanche raid had really happened. He'd told himself that he hadn't really lost his white father, mother, and brothers to the savage raiding party—that the boy he had been had never existed. Zach Ryder, the oldest son of Michael and Catherine Ryder and the brother of Jeff and Will, was dead.

Zach Ryder had died the day he'd watched his family slaughtered by the Comanche who had taken him with them as they rode away.

In his place, Wind Ryder, the fearless warrior, had been born. He had focused all his energies on becoming the best warrior in the village. It had been hard for him, for the Comanche boys had hated and resented him, but that had only spurred him to work harder. He had been fortunate that Chief Ten Crow had taken such a liking to him or he probably would have been dead by now or traded off to another tribe.

Zach Ryder—

Just thinking of his white name tore at Wind Ryder, and it took all his considerable willpower to force the thoughts of that time away. As he gave in to the weariness that gripped him, he did allow himself to remember how he had quietly celebrated every time one of the warriors who'd murdered his white family had been killed on a raid.

Wind Ryder slept, but not before he had taken one last look at the golden captive asleep across the lodge from him.

Marissa lay unmoving, barely breathing, making no sound. She was acutely aware of the warrior's powerful presence so close to her within the confines of the lodge. As the hours dragged on, Marissa found herself wondering if dawn would ever come. Yet even as she longed for the start of the new day, she feared it.

Wind Ryder had returned to take command of the tipi—and of her. What did he want with her? What was to become of her?

Marissa had no idea what her future held, and it was that uncertainty that left her unable to sleep. Anxiety was her only companion there in the darkness. She prayed that her uncle would find her.

Wind Ryder awoke with the dawn. He glanced over at Shining Spirit and was glad to see she was still asleep. Rising soundlessly, he left the tipi.

The village was just stirring to life as he made his way down to the stream to bathe. He stripped off his clothing and waded out into the water.

The cold water was refreshing, and Wind Ryder took his time. His thoughts were troubled as he scrubbed the war paint away. He did not know what he was to do with Shining Spirit. Beauty though she was, he did not want her. She meant nothing but trouble for him. She was a complication he did not need. The restless night he'd just passed was proof of that.

But his father had decreed that she was to be his as had been foreseen in his vision. In irritation, Wind Ryder wondered what else his father had seen in the vision.

Annoyed, Wind Ryder left the water and dressed. He strode through the village, deliberately not returning to his tipi. He sought out the other warriors, wanting to stay as far away from Shining Spirit as he could. The less time he spent in the company of the white woman, the better.

Marissa awoke to find the warrior gone. Relief swept through her, and amazement filled her at what had transpired during the night just past. The man Crazy One tried so hard to avoid had returned and spent the night in the tipi with her, but he had not harmed her in any way. She had remained untouched. After witnessing the old woman's fear of being near him, Marissa had expected the worst from him, and yet nothing had happened.

Marissa rose, but she was unsure of what she should do. Crazy One always came for her early in the morning, but she wasn't sure if she'd appear now that Wind Ryder had returned. Marissa wondered if she was free to move around the village on her own. She decided to wait awhile to see if anyone came.

Laughing Woman was eager to reach Wind Ryder's tipi to find out what had happened overnight. She had told Crazy One that she would tend to the captive today, and, as she'd suspected, the old woman had been relieved. Laughing Woman knew Crazy One wouldn't want to chance seeing Wind Ryder.

Ten Crow had said Shining Spirit was the woman from his vision, so Laughing Woman wanted to make sure all was going as it should. If it did, her worries would soon be over. There would be peace in the village.

Peace. Laughing Woman smiled at the thought. She knew how much Bear Claw hated Wind Ryder, and she understood. The white captive had disturbed the tribe and her family. She had tried to convince her husband not to adopt the boy, but he had been too impressed with the white youth's fearlessness and his abilities. Once he had become their son, Wind Ryder had stolen that which should have been Bear Claw's—he had stolen Ten Crow's favor.

Laughing Woman had tried all these years to accept Wind Ryder as her son, but she had never fully succeeded. Though the white boy had grown into a strong and powerful warrior, she could never forget that he was not Comanche. Others in the tribe had been able to, but she could not.

Reaching the tipi, Laughing Woman saw that the door flap was thrown back. She called to Wind Ryder, but when he did not come out, she looked inside and saw that Shining Spirit was alone. She wondered where Wind Ryder had gone so early in the day. She gestured for the white woman to come out and was pleased when the captive obeyed her.

Marissa found she was almost glad to see the Comanche woman instead of Crazy One this morning. After the night just past, she wasn't sure she was ready to listen to the old woman. Marissa was puzzled, though, by the strange look this woman gave her when she stepped outside. She felt almost as if the Comanche were inspecting her for some reason.

Laughing Woman eyed Shining Spirit closely, trying to guess what had transpired during the night. It puzzled her that the white woman seemed no different after spending time alone with Wind Ryder. She had expected the warrior to use the captive the way her son or Snake would have if she had been theirs. Laughing Woman motioned for

Shining Spirit to follow her, and they started off.

Marissa trailed after her. As they walked through the village, she found herself looking around for some sign of Wind Ryder. She was nervous about seeing him again.

Wind Ryder was sitting with the warriors when he caught a glimpse of Shining Spirit following his mother through the camp. Satisfied that there was no need for him to concern himself with the troubling female, he turned his attention back to the other warriors. As they were talking, Chief Ten Crow and Bear Claw came to join them.

"Good morning, Father, Bear Claw," Wind Ryder greeted them.

Chief Ten Crow asked, "Where is your woman?"

Wind Ryder didn't like hearing the woman called 'his,' but did not argue. "She is with my mother."

The chief nodded.

"How was your night?" Bear Claw asked. His thoughts were lewd as he imagined what must have gone on between captor and captive. He certainly would have enjoyed having the white woman for his own. "Is the talk true that screams were heard coming from your lodge? She must have fought you as hard as she fought Snake."

Wind Ryder looked at him steadily. His expression was closed as he answered, "But Shining Spirit did not get away from me."

Bear Claw smiled thinly at him as he thought, *Yet.*

Wind Ryder saw his sneer and knew what Bear Claw would have done with Shining Spirit had she been his. The terror that had possessed her last night would have been merited. Shining Spirit had been worried he might kill her—but Wind Ryder knew there were many fates worse than death, and she would have suffered them all at Bear Claw's hands.

Wind Ryder pushed thoughts of Shining Spirit from his mind.

It did not matter what she suffered. She was a captive. Her destiny was to submit to his will.

"They are coming," Chief Ten Crow told him some time later when he saw the two women returning.

Wind Ryder turned to look their way. Across the distance his gaze met Shining Spirit's.

Chapter Seven

Wind Ryder noticed a change in Shining Spirit's expression as their gazes locked, but he did not understand it. What he did understand was the sudden physical reaction he had to the sight of her. There was no doubt she was a beautiful woman. The golden mane of her hair tumbled down her back in a mass of soft curls, and she moved with an easy grace that drew all eyes to her. As Shining Spirit and Laughing Woman came toward them, Wind Ryder felt his desire grow. He frowned and fiercely denied the feelings she was stirring within him.

A shock ran through Marissa at the sight of Wind Ryder standing with the other warriors. She was stunned by the change in his appearance. She would never have imagined that he could look like this without the harsh camouflage of his war paint. Though his dark hair was long and he was wearing a loincloth and moccasins, there was no mistaking his heritage. Her warrior was truly a—

Marissa stopped, startled by the way she'd thought of him—

Her warrior.

He wasn't *her* anything!

Wind Ryder might look like a white man, but that was where it ended. His appearance didn't change his actions.

She knew what he was.

He was a Comanche.

The memory of how he'd treated her the night before, however, slipped into her thoughts and tempered them, for he had not harmed her in any way.

Marissa dropped her gaze away from Wind Ryder as Laughing Woman led her to where the men had gathered.

Bear Claw and Snake were both staring at the captive hungrily. Snake, in particular, wanted to get his hands on her so he could teach her a lesson. The screams everyone had spoken of last night would be nothing compared to what he would rouse from her if he got the chance. He looked on in silence as Wind Ryder went to speak with his mother and the woman.

"I have been keeping her safe in your lodge, but there is no need now that you have returned."

"You are right, Mother," Wind Ryder agreed. "Can you teach her the ways of our women?"

"It is what you want?"

"Teach her well." Wind Ryder nodded, though he really didn't care if Shining Spirit learned the Comanche ways or not. He just wanted to keep her away from him.

"I will do this," Laughing Woman agreed, glad to have extra help with her work.

Marissa wished she knew what they were saying, but the Comanche tongue was still foreign to her even after being in their midst for all these days. The older woman took her arm to draw her away. Marissa glanced up at Wind Ryder to find that he was already walking back to rejoin the men. Unsure whether to be relieved at being taken away from him or concerned about where the woman was leading her, Marissa went along without resistance.

"She does not have any bruises," Bear Claw taunted Wind Ryder as he joined them again. "Why was she screaming in your lodge last night if you were not beating her?"

Wind Ryder cast a quick glance at him, then smiled slightly. "It is you who said she was screaming because I was beating her."

The rest of the men laughed loudly at Bear Claw's expense.

Bear Claw grew angry.

Chief Ten Crow sensed the growing tension and stood. "Let us see to the horses. There is much to be done."

Snake looked at Bear Claw as Wind Ryder and the others went off after the chief to break the new horses.

"She is a beautiful one, this captive," Snake remarked, staring after Shining Spirit. His expression turned to a leer as he watched the sway of her hips and imagined her lying naked beneath him as he . . . "I am sorry she got away from me."

"My father should never have given her to Wind Ryder," Bear Claw snarled. Then an idea occurred to him. He glanced at Snake, his eyes narrowing. "You still want this woman. Together, we could find a way to take her from him."

Snake did not like Wind Ryder. He never had. Like Bear Claw, he had always resented the white man's presence among them, but he knew what a fierce warrior Wind Ryder was. He knew better than to challenge him. Wind Ryder would make a deadly enemy.

"No, I will not go against Wind Ryder."

"You are a coward?"

"I do not want to die. Wind Ryder protects what is his. If you go after the woman, you will do it on your own."

Bear Claw was disgusted by Snake's refusal and stalked away.

* * *

Marissa wasn't sure which was worse, sitting alone in the tipi for days on end or doing the women's work in the camp. Under Laughing Woman's tutelage, she learned how to sew buffalo hides together and had been working at it since they'd left the men that morning. Activities went on around her, and she kept watch, hoping to come up with a plan to escape now that she was being given a little more freedom.

Marissa's hope of returning to the white world was the only thing that kept her from complete despair. She could tell that the other women were watching her and talking about her, and for once she was glad she could not understand what they were saying. Mostly, they seemed to be laughing and sneering at her. She tried to ignore them, but occasionally one of them would get up and come over to poke her or yank on her hair. She fought to stay calm and concentrated on doing the task set before her.

"She is ugly," Moon Cloud sneered to Soaring Dove, jealousy filling her as she watched the golden-haired captive working with Laughing Woman.

"She is very ugly," Soaring Dove agreed. "I am sure Wind Ryder only took her because she was a gift from his father and he could not refuse."

"But I want Wind Ryder for my own. She is the one sharing his tipi."

"As his captive," Soaring Dove insisted. "Shining

Spirit is not his wife. *You* will be his wife."

"That is what I have wanted for as long as I can remember, but he has never asked me."

"Then perhaps it is time for you to go to him," Soaring Dove suggested.

Moon Cloud smiled at the prospect of humiliating the white woman that way. "Soon. Yes, very soon."

"And perhaps it is time for this captive to learn her place in the village."

The thought intrigued Moon Cloud and her smile broadened. "That would be good."

Word came to them that the men were about to start breaking the horses. The women knew it would be a challenge. They quit what they were doing and hurried off to watch.

Marissa had been hard at work, and she was surprised when the other women got up and left. She had no idea what was going on, so she decided to follow them. She trailed after them to what she discovered was a corral made of posts and surrounded by brush and branches that were stacked high against the posts to discourage the horses from jumping out. The other villagers were already there, shouting and yelling, and as she drew closer she saw what all the excitement was about. A brave was in the corral trying to break one of the wild stallions. The stallion was bucking and twisting wildly, trying to dislodge the warrior Black Eagle from his back. Then with one particularly violent move, it threw the man off.

A roar of laughter went up from the other warriors as Black Eagle landed heavily in the dirt. He scrambled to his feet and ran to get away from the angry, rearing stallion.

"Where is Wind Ryder?" someone shouted. "Only Wind Ryder can break this one!"

Wind Ryder heard them calling him and went forward, eyeing the powerful stallion knowingly. It was a fine-looking horse, and Wind Ryder knew it would prove a challenge. He approached the animal slowly and took up the rope that was serving as its bridle. The stallion was watching him, rolling its eyes nervously as it waited for him to make his move. Wind Ryder knew what it expected, though, and he wasn't going to comply. Drawing on the rope, he led the resisting horse from the corral and down to the stream nearby. He waded out into the middle of the water, bringing the stallion with him. It wasn't too deep there, but deep enough to slow the horse's movements, and that was just what Wind Ryder wanted. In one fluid movement, he vaulted onto its bare back and prepared himself for the violent ride he knew was to come.

Marissa found herself caught up in the drama unfolding before her. Wind Ryder seemed so calm and deliberate as he took charge. She had to admit he looked magnificent as he sat on the stallion's back. His expression was serious, and his body was tense and ready. The black stallion and the proud warrior looked evenly matched, and she wondered which would prevail. Marissa could feel the excitement growing in the crowd around her, and a thrill went through her.

The stallion stood unmoving for a moment, tension etched in every quivering, taut muscle of its sleek body. Then the horse erupted in fury, rearing and bucking with all its might, trying to rid itself of the man who dared ride him. Arching, twisting, turning, the horse was determined not to surrender.

Wind Ryder was equally determined to win the confrontation. He held on tightly as the stallion fought both him and the water. He had broken many horses in the past, but this one was proving particularly stubborn. Even with the help of the water, the stallion was testing his abilities.

Marissa watched in awe as Wind Ryder kept his seat, staying with the bucking, surging stallion.

The whole scene suddenly seemed unreal to her. Here she was in the midst of the West Texas wilderness watching a Comanche warrior break a horse.

She felt almost dazed as she wondered how she had come to this. Just weeks ago she had been living the life of a lady in New Orleans, and now here she was living in an Indian village, dressed in buckskin, watching Wind Ryder attempt to tame a stallion.

The horse reared suddenly, pawing at the air as it tried with all its might to throw Wind Ryder from its back.

Marissa gasped in awe as he kept his seat.

She didn't want to admire anything about this man. She hated the Comanche for what they had done. They were killers, cold-blooded murderers.

But as she watched, Wind Ryder continued to amaze her with his ability to stay with the horse. He held on, the powerful corded muscles of his arms straining as he fought for control over the animal.

The horse continued to battle his domination. The hindrance of the water drained its strength, though, and made it harder and harder for the stallion to move.

Wind Ryder felt the weakening of its resistance, and he smiled confidently to himself. Soon it would be over. The stallion was an excellent, spirited animal. Whoever ended up with it was going to be well served.

After fighting a few minutes more, the horse realized the battle had been lost. Its sides were heaving as it stopped bucking and stood in the stream, trembling and sweaty from the exertion of its lost fight for freedom.

Wind Ryder reached down and patted the proud horse's lathered neck.

Cheers arose from those who'd gathered round to watch the challenge.

Marissa looked on as Wind Ryder rode the exhausted horse from the stream up into the corral. He dismounted and handed the reins to another warrior.

Around Marissa, the villagers hurried forward to congratulate him on his hard-fought victory. She did not join them. She stayed back to watch. It was then she noticed that two of the warriors had walked away without saying a word. Their backs were to her, so she could not see who they were. She found it strange that they alone did not want to share in Wind Ryder's victory celebration.

After a time, another wild horse was brought forward, and another brave prepared to mount. The crowd backed away once more to give them room.

Wind Ryder went to stand with his father.

"As always, you have made me proud, my son," Chief Ten Crow told him, smiling at his accomplishment.

"The stallion will make some warrior a fine raiding pony," Wind Ryder said.

"He was a stubborn one," the chief agreed. "You have once again proven your ability. You are the best horseman in the village."

Wind Ryder was pleased by his praise, but before he could say anything, Black Eagle joined them.

"Wind Ryder—it was good that I wore the stallion down for you, wasn't it?" Black Eagle laughed.

"It was very good," Wind Ryder answered, laughing good-naturedly with him.

They turned their attention back to the corral where the brave was trying to mount the new horse.

Marissa quietly moved to the back of the crowd. Glancing around, she noticed that no one was keeping watch over her, and it looked like the villagers would be busy watching the warriors with the horses for some time to come.

The lure of freedom called to her.

She wondered if she dared try to get away now while everyone was so distracted. She quickly made her decision. Without drawing undue attention to herself, she edged her way through the gathering. As the villagers concentrated on the drama in the corral, Marissa slipped off.

Determination filled her as she walked calmly away. She wanted to break into a run, she wanted to flee as quickly as she could, but she forced herself to walk slowly. She headed back toward where she had been working with the women earlier, hoping that by going in that direction, she would fool anyone who might see her into thinking she was returning to her work.

Marissa tried not to appear nervous, but a part of her wanted to keep looking around to make certain that the way was clear. Somehow, she controlled the desire. She walked at an even pace, appearing outwardly calm, while in truth her heart was beating a frantic rhythm. She was imagining herself away from the Comanche—

Free at last—

Going home.

Bear Claw and Snake had seen enough of Wind Ryder breaking the stallion. The cheers of the villagers had driven them away in disgust. They went to sit on the far side of the encampment. They did not want to listen to everyone singing his praise.

"Snake! Look!" Bear Claw spotted the white captive walking alone through the village. "Shining Spirit is by herself."

"No one's watching her," Snake agreed, surprised.

"I wonder where she is going. If she wanders away from the camp, she might not be found again."

"What of Wind Ryder? Should we tell him?"

Bear Claw gave him an angry look. "Why? He is the one who let her out of his sight. If she disappeared, no one would know what happened to her."

"There isn't much time." Nervousness took Snake as he thought about what Bear Claw wanted to do. Snake knew the fierceness of the revenge Wind Ryder would exact if he ever found out what had happened to her.

"I will do this alone." Bear Claw was disgusted

that Snake was still worried about angering Wind Ryder. He didn't have the time to argue with him. He knew what he wanted to do, and he was going to do it.

Bear Claw trailed after the white woman, watching her as she wandered farther from the gathering by the corral, heading ever away from the village.

Wind Ryder looked up from where he'd been standing with his father and Black Eagle to discover that Shining Spirit was nowhere to be seen. She had disappeared. His gaze swept over the villagers gathered there, and he found no trace of her. Knowing how badly she wanted to escape, he went to look for her without a word to the other men.

Chapter Eight

Marissa knew her plan might be dangerous. She didn't care. This might be the only chance she ever got to make her escape. She wished she could find a way to take a horse without being noticed, but that was impossible. The horses were the Comanche's most prized possessions. She resigned herself to the fact that whatever she was going to do, she would have to do on foot. Offering up a silent prayer, she forged ahead and never looked back.

Bear Claw followed Shining Spirit easily. He stayed behind her, silently stalking her, letting her get farther and farther away from the village. He would take her, but in his own good time. He did not want to risk anyone finding them.

The warrior smiled to himself as he imagined what he was going to do to Shining Spirit. He could not let her make any sound, though. No one could ever know what had happened, and when he was finished with her, he would make sure her body was never found.

Marissa tried not to get too excited as she stayed along the bank of the stream where the foliage was the heaviest and would shelter her passing. Her pace quickened as she drew away from the village.

Time was of the essence.

She had to get away while she could.

The terrain grew rockier, and Marissa was glad. It gave her more places where she could hide if necessary and made her trail harder to follow. She rushed on and kept her thoughts focused on being reunited with her uncle. She did not allow herself even to consider that Wind Ryder might discover she was missing and come after her. She permitted herself to have hope that she could do this.

And then the fierce-looking warrior stepped out in front of her.

Marissa stopped, horrified. She recognized the man as one of the savages from the raiding party, and she would have screamed, but he moved too quickly for her. Grabbing her, he covered her mouth with his hand before she had time to utter a sound. His hands on her body were brutal as he dragged her behind some bushes and wrestled her to the ground.

Bear Claw couldn't believe that he had taken Shining Spirit so easily. He had worried that she would fight him as she'd fought Snake, but she had offered little resistance. He grew even more confident. Things had gone better than he'd hoped. He smiled coldly down at her as he kept her mouth covered.

"My father should never have given you to Wind Ryder," he taunted in his native tongue as he roughly groped her breasts with his free hand.

Marissa had never been touched so intimately before. The shock of his hated hands upon her jarred her and started her fighting him in earnest. She struggled against his overpowering strength.

She had to get away from him!

She had to save herself, for there was no one else to do it.

Marissa swung out at him with her fists, trying to knock his hands away.

Bear Claw was more amused by her struggles than threatened by them. He was already hard with wanting her, and her resistance just heightened his lust. He was eager to take her, to abuse her.

"You will be a fine one to mount," he said, leering at her as he reached down to pull up the skirt of her buckskin dress. He was more than ready to bury himself between her thighs.

Marissa didn't know what he was saying, but she had a good idea. She kicked with all her might, trying to dislodge him, trying to keep him from touching her. She screamed against his hand and moved as violently as she could to escape his assault. His touch was painful and deliberately cruel, and she could only imagine what he was going to do to her next.

From the moment she'd been taken prisoner, she had lived in terror of just this moment—of being completely helpless before a Comanche attacker. The vicious warrior was far more powerful than she was, and he was intent upon his deed. It was her worst nightmare realized.

Thoughts of Wind Ryder came to Marissa. Her warrior hadn't exactly been kind to her, but he had not abused her in any way. Not like this. Her attacker pawed at her thighs and roughly shoved her legs apart in spite of her best efforts to keep them together. Marissa continued to try to resist him, but he was too strong for her.

She was helpless.

Still, Marissa fought on. No one would be coming to save her. She was alone. Her arms were free, and she desperately groped about on the ground beside her, hoping to find some weapon to use against him.

And then her hand closed on a rock.

Without any pause or thought, Marissa grabbed the rock and swung at him. Her blow caught him alongside the head and stunned him for an instant. Shocked as he was, he drew his hands away, giving Marissa time to utter only one sharp cry for help before he viciously backhanded her.

"You will pay for that!" Bear Claw snarled, grabbing her wrists and pinning her arms above her head. Blood trickled from a cut high on his cheek, infuriating him even more.

Marissa was terror-driven. She continued to resist him, but there was little she could do except try to twist free.

Bear Claw laughed at her feeble efforts now. He could tell her strength was failing, and he was glad. He wanted her completely submissive beneath him.

Wind Ryder might have mounted and tamed the stallion, but he was going to mount and claim this woman.

Bear Claw knelt between her legs and leaned forward, pinning her body to the ground as he shoved her skirt up even higher and groped at her with cruel hands.

At first, Wind Ryder had not been too concerned that Shining Spirit was gone. He thought she might have returned to work with one of the other women. As he crossed the village looking for her, though, he saw no sign of her anywhere. The village was nearly deserted, for most of the people had gone to watch the men with the horses. He checked in his tipi, but found it empty. Finally he began to suspect that she might have tried to get away. He decided to circle the encampment and search for signs of her passing. It didn't take him long to discover her tracks. He immediately set out to bring her back.

Wind Ryder hadn't gone far when he noticed that another set of tracks covered hers, tracks belonging to a man. Tension grew within him. He stood silently for a moment looking ahead, frowning as he tried to imagine where she was going and who might be following her. Wind Ryder took care to be as quiet as possible as he hurried on. He hoped Shining Spirit hadn't gotten too far ahead.

The realization that he was worried about her startled Wind Ryder. He told himself he didn't care, that he was only going after Shining Spirit to bring her back because his father had given her to him. In truth, though, just the thought that someone might harm her infuriated him. A vision of the golden captive played in his mind as he tracked the path she'd taken.

The sound of a distant cry came to Wind Ryder, and he charged forward. The scene he came upon put him in a mindless rage. There before him was Bear Claw with blood on his cheek, attempting to rape Shining Spirit. Wind Ryder threw himself bodily at the other warrior and knocked him away from the helpless woman. The two men grappled in the brush in their fight for supremacy. Wind Ryder won easily, having taken Bear Claw by surprise. He pinned him to the ground and glared down at him with pure hatred in his eyes.

"She is mine!" Wind Ryder growled. "You do not take what is mine!"

"She wanted me. She lured me out here." Bear Claw lied, the lust he'd felt for the captive vanishing in the face of Wind Ryder's attack.

Wind Ryder knew different. He looked at Shining Spirit, who was trying to cover herself. She was dirty, her clothing was in disarray, and there was a mark on her face where she'd been struck. He knew she had not been trying to lure Bear Claw anywhere.

"The blood on your face and your trail tell me otherwise," he said with deadly intent.

Bear Claw realized his mistake too late. Wind Ryder was an expert tracker and would have known just by checking the trail that he had been following her, not walking by her side. He went still, trapped by his own lie and by the blood on his cheek where Shining Spirit had hit him.

Wind Ryder was furious. He wanted to draw his knife, but managed to control his rage as he stood up. He remained standing over Bear Claw, looking down at him, his expression savage.

"Go. Now." It was all Wind Ryder could say. He had been angry in the past with this man who was supposed to have been his brother, but never as angry as he was at this moment.

Bear Claw slowly got to his feet and, without looking back at the white woman, walked away.

Fury filled him, too, but his need for revenge would have to wait.

Marissa had been visibly trembling as she'd watched Wind Ryder face down the other warrior. She had never thought she would be relieved to see him, but he appeared a savior to her right now as he stood there so tall and magnificent before her. He had driven the evil warrior away.

When Bear Claw had disappeared from sight and Wind Ryder looked her way, she suddenly felt naked and vulnerable before him. She struggled to cover herself again, but still felt exposed. Worse, Wind Ryder had seen the other man's hands upon her.

Wind Ryder stared down at Shining Spirit and saw the uncertainty in her eyes. He went to her.

Marissa was unsure of what to expect next. She wondered if he was going to finish what the other warrior had started. She waited, huddled and frightened, as he came toward her. When he bent down, she cowered away from him even more.

He understood her terror. In one move, he scooped her up into his arms and stood, carrying her much as he would a small child.

"I can walk," Marissa gasped in protest and looked up at him.

"I will carry you."

Their gazes locked.

For a long moment, they stared at each other. She searched his expression for some sign of danger, but found none. She sensed he was no threat to her—she was safe. She drew a strangled breath as a shudder wracked her.

"Thank you," Marissa managed in a choked voice.

Wind Ryder did not respond, but turned back toward the village.

As he began to walk, Marissa looped her arms around his neck to steady herself. She allowed herself to lean against him, her emotions in turmoil. Anger over her failed escape attempt ate at her. She had believed she was going to get away, but she'd been terribly wrong. If Wind Ryder hadn't appeared, there was no telling what might have happened to her.

Thank God Wind Ryder had shown up when he did.

Marissa was shocked by the revelation that she truly was grateful to this warrior.

The power of her turbulent emotions was nearly overwhelming as she tried to accept her failure. She had to accept, too, that her fate was now sealed.

She was Wind Ryder's.

Wind Ryder's own thoughts were deeply troubled as he made his way back to his lodge with the golden one in his arms. He had not wanted to care about Shining Spirit. He had not wanted to get close to her. In truth, he'd wanted as little to do with her as possible; he had wanted to keep a physical distance between them. The less time he spent with this white woman, the better. But then he'd heard her cry out and had found Bear Claw about to rape her. In that moment, any semblance of indifference within him had been destroyed. It had jarred him to discover that he did care what happened to her, that he would protect her with his life.

Now, carrying her close to his heart, Wind Ryder felt a stirring of some strange emotion within him. The awakening disturbed him. He had guarded his heart and his soul for so long now, he feared allowing himself to feel any tender emotion toward anyone—and especially toward a white woman.

It had been difficult enough for him through the years just seeing Crazy One around the camp. He had deliberately been harsh to her so she would stay away from him. He hadn't wanted to be reminded of his past life. He hadn't wanted to remember his white family and all that had been lost to him.

But that was over now.

This woman had changed everything.

Shining Spirit had proven herself to be a fierce fighter, yet as he held her in his arms right now, he was amazed at how delicate and fragile she was. Though he was angry with her for trying to escape, he had to admit that he was impressed by her courage. There were not many captive women who would have been brave enough to try.

They drew near the tipi, and Wind Ryder was glad it was late in the day. Once they returned to the lodge, he would make sure Shining Spirit did not leave it again that night. Though she was quiet now, he did not trust her to give up her attempts to reclaim her freedom. He had been the same way—at first. He did not trust Bear Claw, either, to accept the fact that Shining Spirit would never be his. He was going to stay with her and keep watch over her to make sure she was safe from all harm.

As Wind Ryder entered his lodge, he did not notice Snake watching him from across the campsite.

Snake saw Wind Ryder return, carrying the white captive, and he was instantly curious about what had happened to Bear Claw. Obviously, his friend's plan to take Shining Spirit had failed.

Snake went looking for Bear Claw to find out what had gone wrong. He found him a good distance from the camp, sitting alone, staring off into the gathering darkness.

"Bear Claw?" he called as he drew near. "What happened with Shining Spirit? I saw Wind Ryder take her back into his lodge."

The warrior turned to look at him. His expression was ugly, filled with hatred.

"Wind Ryder was tracking the white woman,

too." He would not tell the other warrior any of what had happened. He would not admit his humiliation.

Snake could see the injury to Bear Claw's face, but did not remark on it. He knew just how ugly his friend's temper could be. "There will be another time," he reassured him.

"And I will be ready," Bear Claw snarled, the promise of violence in his voice.

Wind Ryder set Shining Spirit on her feet once they were inside the tipi.

Marissa looked up at him, uncertain of what was to come. "What do you want of me?"

"Lie down." His order was terse.

Marissa's reaction was immediate. She did as she was told, but she was surprised when he turned around and walked out of the lodge. He was gone for only moments, then returned with a rope in hand. Marissa swallowed nervously, knowing he was probably going to tie her up to keep her from trying to run away again. She had sealed her own fate with her failed attempt to escape.

Wind Ryder picked up his bedding and moved it next to hers, then sat down beside her. He saw her eyes widen as he reached for her leg, taking her by the calf just above the ankle.

Marissa stiffened, expecting him to be as rough with her as the other warrior had been. She was surprised when his hands were gentle upon her.

Wind Ryder pushed her skirt up a little. She tensed even more, and then he started to tie the rope around her ankle.

Wind Ryder stopped when he saw the bruises already forming on her legs. He knew they were from Bear Claw's rough handling of her, and his anger renewed itself, along with his determination never to let any harm come to her again.

"There is much danger here in the village," he told her, staring first at the bruises, then lifting his gaze to hers. "Do not try to run again."

He finished tying the rope to her ankle, then knotted the other end around his own. He lay back on his blankets and tried to relax, closing his eyes. It was still early in the evening, but he had no desire to leave her again that night.

Marissa stared at Wind Ryder, startled by this development. He seemed oblivious to her presence as he lay there beside her. She sat on her bedding for a moment, not certain what to do. Finally she stretched out next to him.

Marissa scooted away until the rope that bound them together brought her up short. She glanced nervously at the warrior to find his green-eyed gaze steady upon her. He made no move toward her, though, so she stopped where she was and lay still, closing her eyes. She knew that sleep would be long in coming, though.

Chapter Nine

Wind Ryder had known he wouldn't sleep much that night, but he had never imagined he would still be lying wide awake in the predawn darkness. The night had been long and troubling for him. Shining Spirit's presence disturbed him deeply. Several times he'd wanted to get up and leave the lodge, but bound to her as he was, he could not.

Glancing over at her now, Wind Ryder could make out the beauty of her features as she slept. She was relaxed, not wary or frightened, and looked even more lovely than before. He studied her, visually caressing her features. He thought of all the hardships she'd endured and survived. He understood her misery far better than she would ever know.

Wind Ryder stared off into the darkness, refusing

to allow himself to think about his life before that fateful day when he'd been taken captive. He had long ago put the memories from him, for they caused too much pain.

Much had happened in the years since. He had managed to make a life for himself as one of the tribe. It had not been easy, but he had done it. His youth had helped him to adapt.

Shining Spirit, though, was older than he had been when he was captured. He wondered how she would deal with what had happened to her. How long would she mourn the life she'd left behind? How long would it take her to accept that she would not be going back?

As if sensing that he was thinking of her, Shining Spirit stirred in her sleep. There was a chill in the night air. Unconsciously, she shifted closer to the warmth beside her, instinctively drawn there.

Wind Ryder all but groaned at the jolt of sensual awareness that went through him as she nestled against him. He would have moved away, but the rope bound them together. He was caught in a trap of his own making.

The powerful feelings Shining Spirit aroused in him were confusing. He found the innocent press of her body against him almost unbearable. Wind Ryder swallowed tightly, trying not to think about the softness of her breasts against his side.

His jaw locked as he fought for control, and sweat beaded his brow. He did not want to desire her. He did not want to care about her.

He looked down at the sleeping golden one and realized she was completely, blissfully unaware of his inner turmoil.

Wind Ryder wondered what the future would bring. He knew he would have to keep as much distance—physically and emotionally—between them as he could.

It would be better that way.

Marissa awoke slowly. She had found forgetfulness in sleep. She had been at peace.

She smiled, still keeping her eyes closed to enjoy the sensation. She was warm. She was safe. And she was—

Marissa almost gasped out loud as she finally opened her eyes to find herself staring at the broad expanse of Wind Ryder's tanned, hard-muscled chest. Suddenly she realized why she was so warm—she was curled up next to him! She thought about bolting, but the feel of the rope around her ankle held her immobile.

Wind Ryder hadn't moved, so she lifted her gaze to his face and discovered that he was still sleeping. Relief swept through her, and her tension eased. He had slept beside her all night, and no harm had come to her. If anything, she had been safer because of his nearness. After the attack by the other warrior, she was tempted to stay tied to Wind Ryder forever.

Marissa hadn't meant to smile, but the thought of being physically bound to this man, and riding double with him as he broke a stallion like he'd done the day before, almost made her laugh.

Wind Ryder awoke to find Shining Spirit watching him, a soft, gentle smile curving her lips. He had never seen her smile before, and he was amazed by the way it transformed her. He realized then that he wanted to see her smile more often.

"Oh! You're awake," Marissa gasped as she found his gaze upon her. Her smile instantly disappeared.

"I have not seen you smile before," he said in a quiet voice.

"There has been nothing to smile about."

"Perhaps that will change."

"You'll take me back?" she asked hopefully, quickly sitting up to face him.

"No. This is where you are to stay."

"But I don't belong here."

"You are mine."

"But you don't belong here either," she countered.

"This is my home."

"But it hasn't always been your home, has it? Where is your family?"

"Chief Ten Crow is my father, and Laughing Woman is my mother."

"But you're white. Where's your real family?

Your white family? Were you taken captive, too, like I was?"

Wind Ryder's expression turned stony at her questions.

But Marissa wasn't about to be deterred.

"My name is Marissa Williams. What's yours?"

He did not answer, but sat up and worked at untying the rope that bound them together. He had to get away from her.

"One of the women will come for you." The tone of his voice had gone cold.

"But, Wind Ryder—why won't you—"

With that he was gone, leaving her alone in the lodge and her questions unanswered.

Marissa did not smile as she stared after him. She wondered if she would ever smile again.

Louise lay in the bed in her room at the boardinghouse, staring listlessly out the window. Dr. Harrison had moved her there when she had begun to recover from her wound. He wanted her to stay in town for another week until she was physically strong enough to make the trip out to George Williams's ranch. So she was biding her time, waiting, worrying, and agonizing about Marissa.

A knock sounded at the door.

"Come in," Louise called out. It wasn't often she got visitors, and she was hoping it was someone with good news for her.

"Mrs. Bennett?" Sarah Collins let herself in.

Her husband, Claude, worked for George and had ridden with him to find Marissa.

"Sarah, it's so good to see you," Louise said, her spirits lifting at the sight of her. Sarah had been coming to see her regularly, and Louise appreciated her visits very much. "Have you heard anything new? Has there been any word about Marissa at all?"

"No, none," Sarah answered honestly, knowing there was no point in lying. "It's too soon. They've barely been gone a week."

"How long could this take?" Louise asked, fearful of the answer.

"It could take months." Sarah saw Louise's devastated expression and empathized. "I'm sorry."

"There's nothing for you to be sorry for. It was foolish of me to hope we'd hear something already, but I've been so frantic, worrying about Marissa."

"We all have been, Mrs. Bennett," Sarah said kindly.

"Please, call me Louise."

"All right, Louise." They shared a warm smile, a silent acknowledgment of friendship formed in trying circumstances. "I just wanted to come to town to see how you were feeling. I spoke with the doctor, and he thought you might be recovered enough by the end of next week to make the trip out to the Crown. Are you about ready to come stay with us at the ranch?"

"I am more than ready."

Louise was relieved by the doctor's report. There were days when she wondered if she really was getting any better. The pain was great, and she was very weak, barely able to get up and move around by herself. It was good to know the doctor saw some improvement in her condition. He checked on her daily, and Tildy, the woman who ran the boardinghouse, kept a close eye on her, too.

"Sarah, have you ever been through anything like this before with the Comanche?" she asked. "I've heard terrible stories of how captives are treated. Do you honestly believe they'll be able to find Marissa and bring her home?"

Sarah was quiet for a long moment, then answered, "If anyone can find them, it will be George. He loves Marissa very much, and he's going to do everything in his power to track her down."

"But he's only a rancher going up against an entire tribe of Comanche."

"No, he's George Williams, and that's saying a lot in this country. Everyone knows what a determined man George can be when he wants something. He took my husband, Claude, and Mark, one of the hands from the ranch, with him. Mark is quite fond of Marissa and was looking forward to seeing her again. George also hired a man named Hawk from the livery in town to help with the tracking. I've heard he's very good at it."

"I wish I had been more help to them." Louise sighed. Her memory of meeting George was vague, for she'd been very weak and feverish that day. She just remembered he was a determined, angry man.

"There was nothing more you could do. George was just thankful you were alive," Sarah said kindly as she smiled at Louise. She wanted to offer her what comfort she could.

"When will we know for sure that I can make the trip out to the ranch?"

"Dr. Harrison said he'd make the decision the first of the week."

"Good. At least that gives me something to look forward to."

"I'll see about finding you some clothes, too."

Louise suddenly realized her desperate and destitute situation. "But I don't have any money. Everything I brought with me was lost in the raid."

"Don't worry about a thing. It'll be fine. George is taking care of everything."

"I'll have to find a way to pay him back."

"I wouldn't worry about it. He told me to take care of you while he was gone, and I intend to do just that."

Louise was touched by his kindness, and tears shone in her eyes. "Thank you."

Sarah stayed on to visit with her for a time, then left when Louise showed signs of tiring. She promised to return later in the week or sooner if she received any word from the men.

* * *

George Williams's mood was grim as the search party continued on across the vast, untamed expanses of West Texas. The days they'd spent tracking Marissa had been hell for him. He longed to find her quickly, to bring her safely home, but with each passing day and each passing mile, he knew his chances of finding her safe and unharmed were lessening.

"I don't like the look of those storm clouds up ahead," Hawk told George as he dismounted to check the trail. "We've been lucky so far, but if we get rain . . ."

The two men shared a knowing look.

If the trail washed out, they would be lost. There would be no way to track the raiding party that had taken Marissa.

"We'd better keep moving, then," George said, his determination never fading.

Hawk nodded and mounted up. He led the way, following the trail they hoped would lead them to the missing girl.

Hawk had realized George had had trouble dealing with him at first, but he was used to that kind of reaction from folks. There weren't many white people who could ignore his Indian blood. Over the course of the last week, though, as they'd worked together to find the stolen woman, the two men had come to regard each other with mutual respect.

"Let's ride," George urged.

George knew the other men were tired, but he

was not about to give up on his niece. He would not rest. He wanted to stay on the trail of the raiding party while they could. He wouldn't quit until he had Marissa back.

As they continued on, George's thoughts turned to Louise Bennett, and he wondered how she was doing. He hoped her recovery was going well. Doc Harrison was a good man, and George was sure the physician would do all he could to help her.

George felt sorry for the woman—for all that she'd been through. She was a lady, and life was hard in West Texas. She'd found that out firsthand. He hoped he could show her it wasn't all bad when he returned with Marissa.

George was trying to convince himself that that day would come when the storm hit.

Hawk had feared the threatening weather, and with good reason. The power the storm unleashed was brutal. Violent lightning strikes exploded an around them, but Hawk refused to stop until they absolutely had to. When the torrent hit full-force, there could be no continuing. The four riders sought what shelter they could find in overhangs among the rocks. They hoped that it would hit quickly and move on.

But the storm was a vicious one, lasting nearly an hour. It was a gully-washer. The downpour scoured the land with its torrential rains and high winds.

With every passing minute, George's rage

against the heavens grew. His scowl darkened, and his mood turned as black as the sky overhead.

Mark and Claude could see the change in their boss's expression, and they understood. After a storm like this, there would be nothing left for them to follow. Hawk was one of the best trackers they'd ever seen, but he wasn't a miracle worker.

Hawk studied the clouds, looking for a sign that the storm would be letting up soon, but it continued. He stared out across the rain-soaked land, his expression stony. There was nothing they could do but wait it out.

And finally the storm started to let up.

The parched land had been thirsting for a good rain. Streams flowed now, where earlier there had only been rock beds. The sky overhead lightened as the cloud cover lifted.

"Wait here," Hawk told George and the others.

They understood. They stayed with the horses as Hawk moved out alone in an effort to find any trace left of the trail they'd been following.

The time passed slowly for George. He knew that the longer it took Hawk to come back for them, the worse the news was going to be. It was nearly an hour later when Hawk returned.

"What did you find?" George asked hopefully, but deep inside he already knew the answer.

"Nothing. Everything's been washed away," Hawk told him. "We can ride on a mile or so in the direction we were heading and check there. It might not have rained so hard farther out, and we might get lucky and be able to pick up the trail again."

"Let's go." George was ready.

Hawk didn't have much hope as he led the way. It had been difficult enough tracking the Comanche over the rocky terrain before the heavy rainfall, but now it was proving impossible.

Several hours passed before they stopped their search.

"George—there's nothing more we can do," Hawk told him, his own frustration as great as the rancher's.

"No!" George argued. "I'm not giving up."

"We have to keep going!" Mark insisted.

Claude knew, as Hawk did, that they had reached a dead end. There was no way of knowing which direction the raiding party had gone.

"They could be anywhere out there," Claude said, looking across the vast, empty land.

"I'll go on alone," George declared. Miserably, he knew Hawk was right. The storm had been too severe, but his desperate need to save Marissa was driving him. He couldn't abandon her to the torturous life he knew would be hers in a Comanche village. "You go on back. I'll be fine."

He kneed his horse onward, not looking at the other men.

"You're not going without me," Mark said, riding to his side.

Hawk glanced at Claude, then nodded toward George and Mark.

They fell in behind them.

Chapter Ten

Marissa had been nervous and uneasy for most of the morning as she'd worked with the women. She'd been fearful that Bear Claw might come after her again. Wind Ryder seemed to have left camp, and she felt vulnerable.

As the morning aged, thoughts of Wind Ryder drove Marissa to seek out Crazy One. She'd hoped the old woman would join her in working with the others, but it seemed she liked to keep to herself. Marissa supposed that was part of the reason why they'd given her the name Crazy One. The old woman was sitting alone by the stream, working with some hides when Marissa found her.

"You are working hard," Marissa noted as she went to stand beside her.

"Always—always." Crazy One suddenly looked

a little worried. "Wind Ryder isn't coming after you, is he?"

"No," Marissa said.

"Good. He's starting to trust you."

Marissa wondered how he could trust her after her escape attempt the day before, but no one had tried to stop her when she'd left the tipi. "I haven't seen him since early this morning."

Marissa wanted to understand him, but was finding it difficult. That was why she wanted to talk to Crazy One. She hoped she could learn something about Wind Ryder's past that would help her deal with him.

"May I sit with you for a while?" Marissa asked.

Crazy One nodded as she continued her work.

Marissa sat down on the bank beside her. It was a peaceful place, shady and quiet. She understood why the other woman liked to work there.

"I wanted to ask you about Wind Ryder," Marissa began hesitantly.

Crazy One gave her a cautious look. "What about him?"

"How long has he been with the tribe? Was he very young when he was taken?"

"I have watched him grow."

"So he was young," she said thoughtfully.

"He was only this tall," Crazy One went on, holding her hand at the height of about a six- or seven-year-old child. "And he was so afraid." Her expression turned sad.

"Why are you sad?"

"I went to him. I knew what he was going through, and I wanted to comfort him."

Marissa could imagine how terrifying his capture must have been to a small boy. She was a grown woman, and she was still frightened. "That was kind of you."

"He was a warm child—a gentle child. He reminded me of my own son—"

"You had a son?" Marissa was shocked by the news. She stared at Crazy One, trying to envision her as she'd been all those years ago.

Crazy One nodded. "I had a husband and two children—a boy and a girl. My husband was killed by the raiding party that attacked our ranch. They took me and the children, but they separated us. They traded me to Chief Ten Crow, and I never saw my son or daughter again."

Marissa's heart was breaking for her. She reached out to touch her hand in sympathy.

Crazy One jerked her hand away as if she'd been burned. She turned back to her work, holding herself rigid.

"If Wind Ryder reminded you of your son, why are you so frightened of him now?"

"It was Chief Ten Crow," she said as she looked up again. "He beat me when he found me with the boy. He told me to stay away from him."

"Why would he do that?"

"The chief wanted him to forget his white past.

He wanted him to become a Comanche—and Wind Ryder did. Later, as he grew older, whenever Wind Ryder saw me, he would chase me away."

Marissa's heart ached for her and the horror that her life had been. Her heart ached for Wind Ryder, too, who as a small boy had been torn from his family and forced to survive in a world foreign to him in all ways—a world without any warmth or love. She could only guess that Wind Ryder chased Crazy One away because her presence reminded him of what it had been like when he'd first come to the village and of all that had been lost to him.

"Do you ever think about running away?" Marissa asked.

"Oh no," Crazy One answered seriously. "I couldn't go back. Not now. Oh, no. But Wind Ryder—he tried to escape when he was little. But they found him each time and brought him back. He was a brave one—Chief Ten Crow saw that in him. That's why he took him as his son."

It surprised Marissa to learn that Wind Ryder had tried to escape, and it also gave her a glimmer of hope that that same little boy still existed somewhere inside the fierce warrior Wind Ryder had become. All she had to do was find a way to reach that part of him and make him understand how badly she wanted to return to her family in the white world.

Marissa remained there with Crazy One for a

little longer, then left to make her way back to the camp.

"Look, Moon Cloud! There she comes now," Soaring Dove told her friend as she saw Shining Spirit returning.

"I was hoping she had run away or maybe drowned in the creek," Moon Cloud snarled.

"The water is not deep enough." Her friend laughed.

"That is a shame."

"So, have you made your plan."

"Oh yes. Tonight I will go to him. Tonight I will tell Wind Ryder of my love."

Soaring Dove smiled. "It is good. You have waited long enough."

"I want him and I will make him mine," Moon Cloud declared.

She grew excited as she thought of the night to come. Among her people, if a maiden was interested in a particular warrior, she could sneak into his lodge at night and let him know of her feelings. That was her plan for tonight. By morning, she was certain she would have Wind Ryder's heart.

Moon Cloud glanced toward the white captive who shared Wind Ryder's lodge, and her lip curled in disgust. She hated the white woman.

Tonight she would teach Shining Spirit her place in the village.

Tonight she would make Wind Ryder hers.

* * *

Wind Ryder deliberately stayed away from the village for most of the day. He had ridden out early to hunt with several other warriors. While on the hunt, he'd found himself thinking about Shining Spirit and worrying about her, and that had irritated him. He wasn't used to caring about others or fearing for anyone's safety. Wind Ryder wanted to believe that Bear Claw would not try to harm her again, but a sense of distrust and uneasiness stayed with him, distracting him.

Returning to camp late in the afternoon, Wind Ryder was anxious to seek out Shining Spirit and reassure himself that she had come to no harm during his absence. He saw no sign of Bear Claw in the village and was glad. He didn't know where his adopted brother was, and he didn't care. He just wanted to make sure the other man stayed away from Shining Spirit.

Wind Ryder walked toward the group of working women.

Marissa had been scraping hides ever since she'd returned from her visit with Crazy One. She had not seen Wind Ryder anywhere in camp, and so she stayed there, passing the time and honing skills she had never, even in her wildest dreams, thought she would master.

As Wind Ryder strode across the camp, he saw her safely working with the women. The feeling of relief that filled him annoyed him even more than his earlier anxiety. When she looked up and saw him, he again felt a strange emotion tug at him. He scowled.

Marissa had somehow instinctively known that Wind Ryder was near. At the sight of him striding toward her, her heart actually skipped a beat, surprising her. Her gaze went over him. He was tall and powerful, and there was an air of arrogance about him that set him apart. He was a man to be reckoned with. She could understand why Chief Ten Crow had wanted to adopt him. Marissa tried to imagine him walking toward her dressed as a gentleman would dress in New Orleans. She pictured him with his hair cut, wearing a suit and tie. The image was striking, and she looked away.

"Come, Shining Spirit," he dictated as he came to stand before her.

Delighted to be away from the women, Marissa quickly rose to obey him. He nodded and led her to the chief's tent. There, they shared the evening meal with Ten Crow and Laughing Woman. Wind Ryder only spoke Comanche with them, so again Marissa was at a loss. She merely sat in silence, eating and waiting for the visit to end.

"Bear Claw is not here?" Wind Ryder asked his father.

"He left with a raiding party this afternoon," Ten Crow told him.

"This is good. I do not want him near Shining Spirit," he told his father. He went on to explain what his brother had done to Shining Spirit the day before.

Chief Ten Crow's expression darkened at the news. Again he found himself worrying about what was going to happen in the future between his sons. Shining Spirit was supposed to make things better—not worse.

Night came far too quickly for Wind Ryder's peace of mind, and he realized he could linger there no longer. He stood to go, and Marissa did the same. She followed him outside.

Wind Ryder led the way to his own tipi. He knew there could be no avoiding it—it was time for them to bed down for the night.

While he'd had his father's conversation to distract him, he'd been able to ignore Shining Spirit's presence. Alone with her in the darkness now, her hair silvered by the moon's pale glow, he was acutely aware of her. Soon he would be lying with her in the privacy of his lodge. Wind Ryder was concentrating so hard on convincing himself that he could make it through the night without touching her, he did not notice Moon Cloud watching him as they passed through the village.

Marissa walked quietly by Wind Ryder's side, unaware of his inner turmoil. She was nervous in her own right. It was time again to bed down for the night. She wondered if he would insist on sleeping beside her again. She glanced up at him as they reached the tipi, and he brushed aside the door flap to enter.

"Will you bind me to you again tonight?" Marissa asked as she followed him inside.

"Yes." Wind Ryder's answer was terse.

"There is no need. I will not run away again," she said.

Wind Ryder managed to give her a cold look of distrust as he reached for the rope.

"Lie down," he directed, going to her.

Marissa lay down on the blankets as he'd ordered and waited as he tied the rope securely around her leg. The night before, she'd been afraid, thinking about what might happen, but tonight the warmth of his hands upon her leg sent an unexpected thrill through her. She looked on without saying anything more as he tied the other end of the rope to his own leg and then made himself comfortable.

"Did the Comanche tie you up like this when you were little to keep you from running away?" she asked quietly.

"Captives must be trained to obey," he answered without emotion.

"That must have been hard for you—as a child."

"Go to sleep," he ordered, not wanting to discuss his past with her. He was already far too aware of her. . . .

"Good night," she said softly as she closed her eyes, pulling the blanket up over herself.

Her gentle words touched a chord within him, but he did not let on. He kept his eyes closed and only grunted in response.

He made sure to lie so he was not touching her in any way.

He wanted to sleep.

He hoped he could.

Moon Cloud waited breathlessly for the village to quiet. She had watched Wind Ryder return to his lodge and couldn't wait for the moment to go to him. She knew the white woman would be there, but she didn't care. If anything, she would humiliate Shining Spirit tonight when she made the handsome warrior hers and hers alone.

Smiling at the thought, Moon Cloud gazed up at the night sky. The moon and stars shone brightly above her. Everything was perfect. All she had to do was go to Wind Ryder and declare her love for him. She had wanted him for what seemed like forever, and now she was going to have him.

Moon Cloud admitted to herself that her experience with other warriors should help her. She had met a few of the other men under the cover of night to taunt and tease them, but she had never wanted any of them the way she wanted Wind Ryder.

An ache grew deep within her in anticipation of the long, hot, exciting hours to come.

Soon she would be lying with him.

Soon she would feel the heat of his flesh next to hers.

Moon Cloud wandered away into the darkness to calm herself.

It was not quite time yet—

But it would be soon.

Wind Ryder stirred at the press of the lush feminine body against him. He did not open his eyes, but gritted his teeth against the unbidden desire that pounded through him. Shining Spirit must have rolled over in her sleep to end up pressed so tightly to him. He told himself that if he didn't move and just stayed quiet, he would be able to keep himself under control until she moved away again. He thought it odd that the close contact with him hadn't awakened her, but then realized she was probably too exhausted to awaken easily tonight.

And then the woman's hands were upon him—aggressively.

The caress was very intimate and very knowing as a woman's voice—not Shining Spirit's—breathed in his ear, "Wind Ryder—I want you."

He tensed at the sound of her voice, and his eyes flew open to find it was Moon Cloud who had slipped beneath his blanket—Moon Cloud who'd been caressing him. She was raising herself up over him now as she gave him a knowing, hungry smile.

"You want me, too—I can tell," she purred with

confidence as she hiked her skirt up and ground her naked hips against the hardness of his need.

Moon Cloud gazed down at him, a look of pure hunger on her face. She knew the white woman was in the tipi, but she didn't care.

All she cared about was Wind Ryder.

All she wanted was Wind Ryder.

She was offering herself to him completely—freely. She wanted him to lose control and make love to her. It surprised her more than a little when he did not instantly grab her and bring her beneath him to make her his.

"Wind Ryder—" Moon Cloud said his name breathlessly, wanting him—needing him—urging him on. She leaned down and kissed him fully and hungrily.

Wind Ryder took her by the upper arms and pushed her away from him. "Moon Cloud? No."

Marissa had been sleeping, but awoke when she felt the rustling beside her.

Sitting up in confusion, Marissa found the Comanche woman with her dress hiked up to her waist, sitting astride Wind Ryder. He was holding her by the arms and seemed to be enjoying that very intimate contact.

Moon Cloud was startled when Marissa sat up right next to them. She had been so intent on making love to Wind Ryder that she hadn't noticed the other woman sleeping so close beside him. She had expected her to be bedded down across the lodge.

"Moon Cloud—you must go. Leave now!" Wind Ryder told her, lifting her off him. He quickly got to his feet and stood, glaring down at her.

"You want me! I could feel your desire," she said defiantly. "It does not matter that the white one is here. She could watch us and learn how to please a man—for I would please you well." She murmured the last in a suggestive tone and ran the tip of her tongue across her lips.

"The desire you felt was not for you," he said, showing her the rope that bound him to Marissa. "Go now."

Moon Cloud stood up, her humiliation complete. She jerked her skirt back down and started to storm from the lodge. She paused to look back once in the hope that Wind Ryder might have changed his mind, but he was staring after her, his expression cold and inscrutable. Moon Cloud glanced down at the white woman and found her watching, smiling triumphantly. Shining Spirit's smile only made Moon Cloud's rejection more complete. She stomped away into the night, filled with fury.

Chapter Eleven

Marissa was glad Moon Cloud had gone. The other woman had obviously wanted Wind Ryder, but for some reason he'd turned her down. When he sat back down on the blanket beside her, Marissa looked over at him.

"You are smiling," Wind Ryder pointed out, remembering how the night before she'd said there was little to smile about.

"She is gone," Marissa replied.

"You are glad?" he asked. The heat that had risen in his body was still with him.

"Yes."

Their gazes met. A silence stretched between them there in the intimate confines of the lodge.

The recognition of the power of his desire shocked Wind Ryder even as he realized he'd wanted Shining Spirit all along. He could deny it no longer after his reaction to Moon Cloud.

Moon Cloud was an attractive woman. She could have been his for the taking. But he had not wanted her. He wanted Shining Spirit.

Marissa was entranced by the wonder of Wind Ryder's gaze. The jealousy she'd felt when she'd seen the other woman trying to seduce Wind Ryder had shocked her. She'd thought this man meant nothing to her, but now Marissa wondered what she truly did feel for him. What she had learned about Wind Ryder from Crazy One had touched her deeply. There was much more to him than just the fierce and fearless warrior.

"Do women throw themselves at you that way often?" Marissa asked.

He gave a slight shrug.

"You could give me my own tipi. Then you would be alone so you could—"

"You will stay here with me," he stated firmly, his gaze still upon her. His voice lowered as he added, "This is where I want you to be."

Wind Ryder was drawn to Shining Spirit. He shifted closer to her, wanting to kiss her, wanting to taste the sweetness of her. The need he felt for her was overpowering, undeniable. He lifted one hand to gently cup her cheek, and then his lips sought hers in a tender-soft caress.

A thrill shot through Marissa at the touch of his lips. She held her breath as Wind Ryder took her in his arms. She was so caught up in the moment that she almost succumbed to the temptation, but then the memory of Moon Cloud's brazen attempt to seduce him returned. She drew back, pulling away from him, ending the embrace.

"No," she whispered, unsure that the desire he was feeling was really for her and not left over from the other woman's passionate ploys.

Wind Ryder stared down at Shining Spirit, surprised by her withdrawal from him. He said nothing as she lay down with her back to him and drew the blanket up over herself.

The fire of his need burned within him. He had felt her response to him. He was tempted to go to her and take her in his arms, to kiss her again and force her to admit that she desired him as much as he desired her, but he held himself back.

Marissa lay quietly beside him, waiting to see what he would do. She knew she was taking a chance. If Wind Ryder wanted to take her, he was certainly strong enough to force her to his will. She would not be able to fight him off for long. She was tense as she anticipated what was to come.

Wind Ryder fought down the heat in his body and lay back on his blankets. There were still many hours until sunrise, and he hoped to somehow find a way to sleep. Shining Spirit's presence beside him was both arousing and comforting. He wanted her, and he also wanted to be sure she was safe. In frustration, he closed his eyes to await the dawn.

Several hours passed, and still Wind Ryder could find no rest. His body was on fire with the hunger he felt for the golden one, and he reached out idly to caress one soft golden curl. Even that simple touch proved a mistake. Her hair was silky and begged a man's caress, and yet he was forbidden that pleasure.

He wanted to kiss her.

He wanted to caress her.

He wanted to slip between her silken thighs and possess her fully—to lose himself within her and seek the perfection that only their union could bring.

But she had said no.

Fighting for control, Wind Ryder carefully sat up and untied the rope from his own leg. There was no way he could spend the rest of the night so close to her without making love to her. She stirred slightly as he got up and she murmured something in a soft voice, but she did not awake.

Wind Ryder was glad.

He left the tipi and went straight to the stream. Stripping, he walked out into the flowing water. Its iciness cut through him like a knife, but the pain was worth it to him. The cold water did what he'd hoped it would do—it successfully killed the fiery, passionate need within him.

The relief he felt was great.

When he finally left the stream, Wind Ryder dressed and remained sitting there on the bank for the rest of the night. He did not trust himself to return to the lodge—not after having kissed her.

Marissa was surprised when she awoke and found it was morning. As upset as she'd been, she hadn't expected to get much rest that night. But eventually she had fallen asleep, and the hours had flown. Girding herself for a confrontation with Wind Ryder after all that had happened, she rolled over.

Marissa was shocked to discover her warrior had already left the lodge. She must have been sleeping deeply not to have awakened when he'd left her side. She wondered when he'd gone and where.

For an instant, she wondered if he'd gone after Moon Cloud, but then she remembered the kiss he had given her. If he had wanted Moon Cloud, he could have taken her last night. Certainly, the other woman had been ready and willing. But he had sent Moon Cloud away.

Wind Ryder had kissed *her*.

Even as she thought about Wind Ryder's kiss, she smiled. She had told him no, and he had stopped. He could have taken her against her will—certainly he was strong enough to force her, but he had not. Warmth filled her as she found, to her amazement, that she was beginning to trust him, and with that trust also came respect.

Marissa arose to start the new day.

* * *

Soaring Dove had been anxiously watching for Moon Cloud to appear that morning. She could hardly wait to hear all about the night just past. She had no doubt that Wind Ryder would soon be taking Moon Cloud as his wife. When she saw her friend come out of her tipi, she hurried over to speak with her. She saw that Moon Cloud looked tired and believed that was a good sign.

"You had a good night, Moon Cloud?" Soaring Dove asked, giving her a knowing smile.

Moon Cloud scowled at her.

"Is something wrong? What happened? I thought you had it all planned."

"I will tell you later," Moon Cloud answered curtly.

"It was not good?"

When Moon Cloud gave her a discouraging look, Soaring Dove fell silent, shocked by her unspoken message.

Moon Cloud was glad that she'd managed to silence Soaring Dove's questions. The last thing Moon Cloud wanted to do was stand there in the middle of the village talking about what had happened between her and Wind Ryder. Her fury was still raging, and she had yet to give vent to her tears.

The pain she felt over Wind Ryder's rejection was real. She had loved him for a long time and had always believed that one day he would be hers. Now, it seemed that dream would never come true.

She felt humiliated and angry, and she hated the white captive with a passion. The woman had dared to smile at her humiliation! Somehow, Moon Cloud vowed to herself, she would find a way to exact revenge upon her.

Moon Cloud and Soaring Dove went to join the other women, only to find that Shining Spirit was already there, working beside Laughing Woman. Moon Cloud was angered by her presence, but knew she could do nothing about it.

They settled in to work. The hours passed slowly.

Marissa was well aware that Moon Cloud had come to join them and that the other woman was watching her closely. She pretended to ignore her, concentrating on the task Laughing Woman had given her. She had to admit to herself, though, that she was glad everything had gone as it had the night before. She could just imagine her own embarrassment if Wind Ryder had taken Moon Cloud up on her offer and she'd had to witness their love-making.

Moon Cloud stared at Shining Spirit.

"She is truly the ugliest white woman I have ever seen," she said to Soaring Dove.

"And she is stupid, too," her friend agreed, laughing at the way Shining Spirit was doing her work.

A few of the other women chuckled at her remark, for they knew the captive was still learning their ways and was not very proficient at her tasks.

Marissa sensed they were laughing at her and again cursed the barrier of language that kept her from understanding all that was going on around her. She'd been trying to pick up words and phrases, but was having little success. When Laughing Woman gestured for her to come along, she was glad of the reprieve. Rising, she started to follow Laughing Woman.

Moon Cloud saw her opportunity for revenge, and she took it. As the captive walked past her, she deliberately stuck her foot out. She laughed uproariously as Shining Spirit tripped and fell face down in the dirt. Soaring Dove was laughing, too.

"Not only is she ugly and stupid, she is clumsy, too!" Moon Cloud said loud enough for everyone to hear.

Marissa had been born a lady.

She had been raised a lady.

But there came a time when enough was enough.

Any semblance of the Marissa Williams who'd charmed New Orleans society vanished in that instant. She was mad—fighting mad. She surged to her feet in righteous fury and without pausing, launched herself at the laughing Moon Cloud.

Marissa knew very little about physical fighting, but she didn't care. With all her might, she began to pummel the other woman. She landed several punishing blows to her face before Moon Cloud got over her shock at being attacked and began to fight back.

Soaring Dove and the other village women scrambled to get out of their way as the two grappled in the dirt.

Marissa and Moon Cloud rolled on the ground, kicking and punching, each shrieking in anger.

"Should we stop them?" one of the women asked.

"Why?" Soaring Dove returned smugly. "Shining Spirit will get what she deserves."

Laughing Woman, however, thought differently. She was too old to pull them apart herself, so she ran to find Wind Ryder.

Marissa had never been in any kind of physical confrontation before. Moon Cloud's blows were painful, but they were not enough to stop her.

They continued to battle, scratching and clawing, yanking and punching. They were both bleeding and filthy, but neither thought of quitting.

Moon Cloud had been shocked by Shining Spirit's attack. She had thought the woman would be easily intimidated and tormented, but she realized now, as she snared a handful of her blonde hair, that she'd been wrong.

Marissa responded with a cry of pain and hit out at her rival, bloodying her lip. Moon Cloud grabbed a handful of dirt then and tried to throw it in her face, but Marissa was able to block her arm just in time to stop her.

"Wind Ryder was to be mine!" Moon Cloud shrieked as she tried to throw off her opponent.

Moon Cloud had just spoken those words when suddenly the white captive's weight was lifted from her. She looked up to see Wind Ryder standing over her, holding Shining Spirit with her back against his chest. The white woman was trying to break free of him, but his grip on her was as ungiving as iron.

"No, Moon Cloud. I was never yours. If I had wanted you, I would have taken you," Wind Ryder told her. His tone was angry, but the words were only loud enough for her to hear. He did not want to debase her any further than he already had the night before, but he did want to discourage her from thinking that he cared anything for her. He also wanted to warn her away from Shining Spirit. "Shining Spirit is my woman." He said the Comanche words to her first, and then looked up at those who were gathered around. "Know this—Shining Spirit is my woman. I have taken her as my wife."

He was making the announcement to let everyone know that Shining Spirit was not to be abused in any way. As his captive, she had been his property, but by proclaiming her his wife, he was giving her his complete protection. He didn't want a wife, but then he hadn't wanted a captive either. Now, no one would dare try to harm her. She would be safer this way.

"Shining Spirit is Wind Ryder's woman—" A murmur of interest spread through the onlookers.

Marissa was totally unaware of what Wind Ryder had just said. She didn't want to listen to all this Comanche talk. She just wanted to get loose and go after Moon Cloud again.

"Let me go!" Marissa was shouting, swinging her fists and violently trying to twist free.

Wind Ryder ignored her command and walked away with her, carrying her easily in spite of her protests.

The villagers watched them go, smiling to themselves at the sight.

Moon Cloud struggled to her feet and stared after him.

"You would have beaten her," Soaring Dove told her, trying to be supportive. "Too bad Wind Ryder showed up when he did."

"It does not matter," Moon Cloud said, and in that moment she meant it. She was thoroughly disgusted with Wind Ryder, and angry with herself for having thought he was worthy of her love. She had been foolish. He was not worth it. Wind Ryder was welcome to his ugly, stupid white wife. "It does not matter any more about Wind Ryder."

"It doesn't? You don't care?" Soaring Dove was surprised.

Moon Cloud smiled at her friend. "If he wants a white wife, he can have her. I will waste no more time on him." She lifted her gaze to look around the camp.

"You won't?" Soaring Dove's tone was disbelieving.

"No. I want to see Running Dog. Do you know where he is?"

"Running Dog?" Soaring Dove's eyes widened in surprise at her friend's complete change of heart. "When I last saw him, he was working with the horses."

"Good. As soon as I have cleaned myself up, I think I will have to run an errand by the corral." She moved toward her own tipi.

Soaring Dove was surprised that Moon Cloud had set her sights on another warrior so quickly, but then she realized she shouldn't have been. Moon Cloud wanted a man, and since she wasn't going to get Wind Ryder, she was ready to go after her second choice. Soaring Dove smiled to herself and returned to her work with the women.

Chapter Twelve

Marissa was still wriggling against Wind Ryder's hold as he crossed the village, but he tightened his grip around her waist and she stopped. She felt almost like a recalcitrant child as he stormed back toward the lodge. She didn't know what was about to happen, but she knew he was angry.

And this time he was angry with her.

Once they were inside the tipi, Wind Ryder released Shining Spirit. He stood there glaring down at her. She was filthy from head to toe, and her hair was in disarray. A bruise was forming on her cheek, and one of her knees was cut and bleeding.

Wind Ryder had to admit he was proud that she'd held her own with Moon Cloud. Judging from the way the other woman had acted, he could imagine how the fight had come about. It surprised him and pleased him that Shining Spirit had been so fierce.

And he had claimed her as his wife—

He did not regret his words, for they would keep her safe, but he had no intention of telling her what he'd done. She had no interest in being his wife, and he had no interest in having a wife. Things would continue as they had between them, but the rest of the tribe didn't need to know that. In the eyes of the village, they were married.

Wind Ryder found that Shining Spirit was looking up at him now, defiantly meeting his gaze straight on. It seemed as if she were ready to fight him, too.

"You are bleeding," Wind Ryder said, unthinkingly speaking to her in Comanche.

Marissa was angry already.

She had just been forced to fight another woman, and now he was speaking to her in the foreign tongue and that made her even more furious.

"Speak English!" Marissa all but shouted at him.

"You are bleeding," Wind Ryder repeated in English, realizing his mistake.

"Well, Moon Cloud is bleeding more," she shot back at him, lifting her chin.

"And you are dirty," he pointed out.

"Moon Cloud's dirtier!" she countered again.

"Well, I am not sleeping with Moon Cloud," Wind Ryder pointed out. "Let's go."

"Go where?" She eyed him cautiously.

"We're going to the stream so you can get cleaned up," he dictated, starting toward the door of the lodge.

"I'm not going to take a bath in front of you!"

"Yes, Shining Spirit, you are," he stated easily, confident of what he was about to do.

"My name's Marissa—not Shining Spirit!" she ground out. "Say it! Marissa!"

Wind Ryder ignored her as he crossed to where she was standing. In one easy move, he lifted her up and threw her over his shoulder.

Marissa grunted at being so manhandled.

"What do you think you're doing?" She shouted, the wind knocked out of her by his unexpected ploy. "Stop!" She started pounding on his back as he left the tipi and headed for the stream. "Put me down! How dare you?"

Wind Ryder didn't pause or bother to argue with her. Her protests meant nothing to him. He barely felt her blows. She needed a bath, and she was going to get one. He hoped the shock of the cold water would cool down her temper. She was certainly a wild one when she got angry. He suppressed an unbidden smile.

Word of the fight between Moon Cloud and Shining Spirit had spread through the village, along with the news that Wind Ryder had taken the white captive as his wife.

When Crazy One heard this, she grew worried

about Shining Spirit. She went to hover near Wind Ryder's tipi, fearful that something bad might have happened to Shining Spirit. She was still afraid of Wind Ryder, but she was concerned for the other captive woman.

Crazy One knew that Shining Spirit would be more respected and protected in the village as Wind Ryder's wife, but she also knew that Shining Spirit wanted to go home to her family. There would be no chance of that happening now.

When Wind Ryder came out of the lodge carrying Shining Spirit over his shoulder, Crazy One gasped and darted away to hide. She admired the white captive even more as she watched them. For although Shining Spirit was dirty and bruised, she was fighting him as best she could—considering her position.

Trailing after them, the old woman was ready to go to the younger's aid if he tried to harm her in any way. It was the bravest thing she'd done in years, but she'd come to like Shining Spirit and didn't want to see her hurt.

Others in the village heard Shining Spirit shouting at Wind Ryder, and they came rushing out to see what was going on. They found the sight of the warrior carrying his female captive amusing and decided to follow the pair. They all stayed back a distance, fearful of angering Wind Ryder by appearing too eager to know his business. He was a

mighty warrior, a man to be reckoned with, and nobody wanted to make him mad.

Wind Ryder was so preoccupied with keeping Shining Spirit under control that he didn't pay any attention to those around him. He stalked straight down to the water's edge.

"Put me down! What do you think you're doing?" Marissa yelled. "Put me down now!"

Without ceremony or warning, Wind Ryder did just what she had demanded. He lifted her off his shoulder and tossed her straight into the deepest pool in the stream.

Marissa let out a scream as she landed with a big splash in the ice-cold water. Furious and indignant, she struggled to her feet. Her knee was stinging where it had been injured, and her buckskin dress was a heavy, sodden weight upon her. Her expression was one of pure outrage as she pushed her wet hair out of her eyes and glared up at him, arms akimbo.

Wind Ryder stood on the bank, gloating.

"Wash," he ordered smugly.

"Why you—"

This was Marissa's day to lose any and all semblance of civilized behavior. Without another thought, she attacked the arrogant, overconfident man standing over her. She started splashing him with all the force she could muster. She didn't just do it once. She kept on splashing water at him, wanting him to be just as wet as she was. She was delighted when he was drenched.

Wind Ryder was shocked by the iciness of the water, and it took him a moment to react to her unexpected and continued assault. When he finally did react, he moved quickly, charging forward into the stream to stop her.

Marissa saw him coming after her and turned to run.

As with the stallion Wind Ryder had broken the day before, the water slowed her efforts to escape. He was there before she could reach the far bank.

"I'm sorry!" Marissa said quickly, trying to hide her smile. She'd seen the determination in his expression and wanted to discourage him from doing whatever it was he had in mind for revenge.

"Sorry? You're going to be sorry all right! You're going to pay for that!"

Wind Ryder grabbed her up and deliberately tumbled backward into the deeper water, taking her with him.

They both surfaced sputtering and choking.

Amazingly, Marissa found herself laughing at his antics. She'd feared he was going to beat her, and instead he had only dunked her again.

"You think this is funny?" Wind Ryder asked in a threatening voice, even as he was smiling back at her. He didn't give her a chance to escape. He snared her around the waist before she could run and brought her tightly against him.

The moment was startling—and revealing for them both.

They went still as the shock of sensual recognition hit them. Sleek and wet, they clung together.

They were suddenly and completely oblivious to the real world around them. It was just the two of them, standing hip to hip, breast to bare chest in the waist-deep water of the stream.

Marissa was stunned by the power of her physical reaction to Wind Ryder's nearness. She was breathless as she looked up at him, her eyes wide, her lips parted in anticipation of . . . She didn't know what, but she did know that being this close to him left her breathing labored and her pulse pounding.

Wind Ryder remained unmoving, completely caught up in the unexpected arousal of the moment. The feel of her breasts crushed against him sent heat pounding through his body. It settled in his loins and left him aching.

He had never felt this way about a woman before.

Even when Moon Cloud was sitting so brazenly atop him the night before, offering herself freely to him, he hadn't felt this kind of desire.

What was there about Shining Spirit that affected him so profoundly? He wanted to lay her down and make her his own. He was ready. He needed her. He had taken her as his wife—

And then Wind Ryder heard the muffled laughter.

The sound of chuckling jarred him back to the reality of where he was and what he was doing. He looked up toward the bank of the stream to find nearly half the villagers standing there, watching them and laughing at their antics.

Marissa had been in the grip of a sensual daze. It took her a moment to realize that they had become the center of attention in the village. When she saw the people gathered around laughing at them, she blushed and looked nervously away from the onlookers. It embarrassed her that she had completely forgotten herself in his arms.

And then Wind Ryder released her and stepped away.

Marissa felt suddenly lost without his powerful arms around her, supporting her, warming her. She looked up at him to find his gaze riveted upon her for a moment before he looked away.

Wind Ryder faced those who were watching them from the banks of the stream.

"Have you never seen anyone take a bath with clothes on before?" he asked in the Comanche tongue as he smiled wryly up at them.

Everyone roared at his humor. People began to wander away, now that the excitement was over.

Even Crazy One found herself actually smiling a little bit. She was relieved that Shining Spirit was unharmed.

* * *

Wind Ryder was glad when the villagers began to move away from the stream. Fighting to bring his desire for Shining Spirit under control, he turned back, ready to help her out of the water. He stared down at her, seeing the way the wet dress clung to her every curve and seeing how her golden hair was a sleek cascade down her back. Neither observation helped quell his need. He lifted his gaze to hers and saw confusion mirrored there. He wondered if she was as troubled as he was by what had happened between them.

Then he noticed the small smudge of dirt that remained on her cheek.

"You need to wash your cheek," he told her, unable to resist gently lifting one hand to touch the spot.

"Oh—" she said nervously.

Marissa didn't understand why Wind Ryder had such an effect on her, but his simple touch sent a thrill through her unlike anything she'd known before. Desperate to distract herself, she scrubbed at her cheek until she'd washed away the last trace of the dirt.

Marissa looked up to find his gaze still upon her. What she saw mirrored in the depths of his gaze unsettled her so much, she quickly started from the stream on her own. Marissa had only made it a few steps when she slipped.

Her loss of footing gave Wind Ryder just the excuse he needed to sweep her up into his arms. He carried her from the water and on toward their tipi.

Their return to the lodge was far different from their earlier exit. Though they were both dripping wet, Wind Ryder was carrying her with the utmost tenderness, and he was thoroughly enjoying the feel of her body against him. She was not pounding on his back or shouting at him to put her down. She was quiet in his arms, although she was shivering a little. He thought that was probably from the dampness of her dress. He ducked to enter the lodge and set her on her feet once they were inside.

"Take off your dress," Wind Ryder ordered.

Chapter Thirteen

Marissa looked up at Wind Ryder quickly, eyes widening at his command. "No—I can't—"

"You're wet, and you're shivering," he pointed out.

"Well, you're the one who threw me in the water," she returned, not wanting to admit the real reason she was trembling. True, the dress was damp and cold, but it was his overpowering nearness and the excitement he'd created within her that were taking their toll on her peace of mind.

"Give me your dress."

"But I . . ." The thought of being naked before him unnerved her completely. She started to tremble even more. "I don't have any other clothes."

"Here." Wind Ryder scooped up one of his own blankets and held it out to her. "Use this."

She took it and clutched it to her breast, eying him warily.

"Turn around," she insisted.

Marissa was surprised when he responded to her request without argument. Wind Ryder acted in a most civilized manner, turning his back on her. She realized that if he'd been dressed in a white man's clothing and had had his hair cut, he would have seemed the perfect gentleman.

With great relief, she started to peel off the clinging, sodden garment.

Wind Ryder stood facing away from Shining Spirit, his shoulders set, his posture rigid. He did not peek as she struggled out of the wet clothing, but he wanted to.

Marissa was glad to be rid of the dress, but she longed for something more to cover herself than just a simple blanket. She wrapped it around her as best she could, then tucked the end in over her breasts to secure it. As decent as she could be, she picked up the wet clothing and went to Wind Ryder.

"Here." She held the dress and shoes out to him.

Wind Ryder turned back to her and felt another powerful jolt of desire at the sight of her wrapped in the blanket. The blanket did cover most of her, but it left her shoulders bare to his gaze. He reached out to take the garments from her, and as he did, his hand touched hers.

Wind Ryder stopped and stood staring down at

her. He saw a beautiful woman—a brave woman—a woman who had survived many terrible trials and still was able to laugh. The memory of the sound of her laughter echoed in his mind. He wanted to hear her laugh again. He wanted to see her smile more. His gaze roved over her face, stopping at the bruise on her cheek. He tenderly reached out to touch it.

"Moon Cloud hurt you," he said quietly.

Wind Ryder was surprised by the sudden anger that flared within him at the thought of the Comanche woman hitting her. Ever so slowly, he bent toward Shining Spirit and pressed a soft kiss to the injury.

Marissa went still at the touch of his lips on her cheek. When he moved to really kiss her, she did not resist or pull away. She met him in that exchange, tentatively at first, then turning toward him and welcoming him warmly.

It was a wondrous moment of pure discovery and pleasure for both of them as they gave themselves over to the desire they'd each tried so hard to deny.

Marissa reached up to link her arms around Wind Ryder's neck and draw him closer to her. Her encouragement emboldened him. He crushed her to him, reveling in the softness of her lush body against his.

Wind Ryder deepened the kiss. He sought the sweetness of her, parting her lips to taste of her.

Marissa was enraptured. A part of her told her

to end the embrace now, while she still had the willpower to do it. But her heart overruled her. She relaxed in his arms and gave herself over to the power of his kiss.

Wind Ryder felt her surrender. He broke off the kiss to seek the softness of her throat and neck, pressing heated kisses there.

Marissa shivered at the sensations coursing through her. She had never been so intimate with a man before. She had kissed a few men while courting, but their kisses had never evoked any feelings in her like she was experiencing now. The excitement building within her thrilled her even as the power of it frightened her a bit. When Wind Ryder picked her up and laid her upon the bedding, she could only gaze up at him in wonder.

Wind Ryder followed her down, joining her there, stretching out fully beside her.

A small logical voice within Marissa cried out that Wind Ryder was a Comanche—

She should run from him while she still could—

She should try to save herself—

But another part of her looked up at him and saw the white man he could have been. She saw the passion in his eyes and knew her passion matched his.

Wind Ryder sought her lips in a wild exchange, and Marissa responded fully. She drew him down even closer to her, and he went eagerly. Their kiss was long and hungry, and as he was kissing her, his hands began a gentle foray over her sweet curves. One hand skimmed the top of the blanket over her breasts, drawing a gasp of excitement from her.

Wind Ryder freed the blanket from where she'd secured it and brushed it aside to bare her breasts to his caress. Marissa was shocked by his move and by the intimacy of his touch. She tried to cover herself.

Wind Ryder only smiled down at her, amused by her innocent efforts.

"Don't," he told her in a husky voice. "You're beautiful. I want to look at you."

He took her in his arms. Marissa reveled in being held against the hot, hard-muscled strength of his chest. His warmth and nearness ignited fires of desire within her. She sought his lips again as he began to caress her more intimately. With each touch, he created new and thrilling feelings within her.

Marissa reached out to him, wanting to touch him as he was touching her. Her hands skimmed over the hard planes of his chest and back, sculpting the rock-hard muscles. As she let her hands move lower down his back to his waist, she felt him shudder in excitement. It gave her a sense of power to know that she could arouse him, too.

Wind Ryder was on fire for her. With every touch and kiss, his desire grew. He moved away only long enough to take off his loincloth, and then he returned to her, ready to know the fullness of her love. He moved over her.

Marissa was caught up in a haze of delight. She opened to him like a flower to the sun.

Wind Ryder felt her unspoken invitation. He fit himself to her in love's perfect union.

She tensed as he moved to make her his own. She was surprised by the intimacy of their joining and by his power. She cried out softly as he breached her innocence.

Wind Ryder shuddered at the power of the emotions that surged through him at the proof of her virginity.

She was his wife.

He had made her his own.

Unable to deny himself what he wanted most, Wind Ryder pressed his entry home, making her his in all ways. He began to move within her. He was careful to be gentle, caressing her and kissing her until she, too, was caught up in the perfection of what was happening between them.

They moved together in love's ageless dance. The rapturous rhythm swept them away from reality. They were two lovers seeking only the pure pleasure that complete surrender could give.

With Wind Ryder's every touch, Marissa's excitement grew. Her body was on fire. She was being consumed by the heat of her need. Mindlessly she clutched at him, holding him close, thrilled at being one with him. It seemed she couldn't get close enough to him.

And then ecstasy burst upon her.

She was lost to the myriad of sensations that throbbed through her as she clasped Wind Ryder to her heart.

Wind Ryder felt the tension in her as she attained the heights of passion. Knowing he'd pleased her heightened his own already driving desire. He quickened his pace, wanting to join her in that sweet release.

"Marissa—" He groaned her name as his own rapture claimed him.

Wrapped in each other's arms, they gave themselves over to bliss.

Later, in the aftermath, they lay quietly together, their bodies still joined. Neither spoke. There was no need for words between them.

Later, they would talk.

Wind Ryder rested with Shining Spirit in his arms, savoring the contentment of the moment. He had not been surprised that she was a virgin; he had sensed an innocence and a purity about her. What he was surprised about was the power of his need for her. Even now, as he lay quietly holding her, he could feel the fire stirring within him again. The touch of her bared breasts, her long, slender legs entwined with his, just thinking about taking her another time aroused him.

Marissa gazed up at him, her eyes widening as

she felt the proof of his renewed arousal deep within her. He bent ever so slowly down to her and captured her lips in a devastating kiss that erased any thought of stopping from her mind. She became a creature of the flesh, wanting only to be one with Wind Ryder again.

Darkness claimed the land, but they did not notice. They were too entranced by the beauty of what they were sharing. It was well into the night before they slept, exhaustion claiming them in the aftermath of their spent passion.

Marissa awoke slowly to find herself curled against Wind Ryder's side, her head resting on his shoulder, her hand splayed upon his chest. It was dark in the tipi, and he was sleeping soundly. She was glad he was still asleep, for her sanity had returned with a vengeance and she was trying to come to terms with what she'd done.

She had made love to Wind Ryder.

Her emotions were in turmoil as she relived in her mind their passion-filled night. How could she have given herself to him so wantonly?

She had never desired any man the way she desired Wind Ryder. He had had only to kiss her and caress her, and she'd been lost in the wildfire of passion that had flamed to life between them.

Marissa studied her warrior as he slept. He looked even more handsome in the dark shadows of the lodge—the dark curve of his brows, his straight nose and high cheekbones. Her gaze dropped to his lips, and her heart stirred as she remembered his kiss and the feel of his hands tracing paths of ecstasy over her.

Was this love? Did she love him? Marissa didn't know.

He was a Comanche warrior. She was his captive.

It seemed impossible that she could love him. They had only known each other a short time.

She was filled with conflicting feelings. A part of her couldn't believe she'd surrendered her innocence to him, and yet she found, deep inside, that she still wanted him—

She wanted to touch him and hold him.

Her turbulent emotions tormented her. Their lovemaking had changed everything.

Marissa was agonizing over her need for Wind Ryder when he rose on one elbow to gaze down at her.

"You're awake—" She was startled by his unexpected move.

"And I want you," he told her. "Again."

Before Marissa could say anything, Wind Ryder kissed her. It was a deep, soul-searching exchange that stirred to life her hunger for him. He was ready for her, and she welcomed him passionately. He took her quickly, their union exquisite. They reached the heights together and crested there, clinging to one another as they drifted slowly back to reality.

They quieted.

Marissa lay in his arms, her head pressed to his chest, listening to the powerful beat of his heart. As she rested there, she could see a scar on his arm. It must have been a bloody gash and caused him much pain. She wondered how it had happened. She wondered, too, if his heart and soul had been scarred as deeply as his body. She lifted her gaze to his face to find him watching her.

"How did you get that scar?" Marissa asked, reaching out to gently trace the mark with one finger.

"In a fight with Bear Claw when we were young," he answered without emotion.

"Did you win?"

"Bear Claw was far bloodier than I was," he said, echoing her words about Moon Cloud.

"Good." And she meant it. Her mood turned somber as she thought of the other warrior. "That must have been hard for you—coming to the village when you were so young. How old were you?" She wasn't sure he would answer her, but she wanted to know. She wanted to learn everything she could about him.

"Six."

"Only six," she said sadly, his answer confirming her fears. Her heart ached for him. "What was your name?"

"My name is Wind Ryder," he answered, balking at revealing any more about his past.

"But who were you then?" she asked, watching his expression, trying to read his thoughts.

Her questions, though softly asked, tore at him. He finally managed, "My name was Zach. Zach Ryder."

"Zach." She repeated his name gently.

Wind Ryder liked the way it sounded on her lips, but quickly denied the feeling.

"And your family, Zach? What were they like? I'm sure they still miss you."

At her words, she could feel him tense.

"They're all dead," he said tightly as he moved her away from him and sat up. "Everyone in my family was killed that day."

She was stunned by his revelation. Tears burned in her eyes as she wrapped her arms around him and held him. "I'm sorry, Zach."

"My name is Wind Ryder," he repeated, holding himself rigid.

"You can still go back—"

"No. That life is over."

"Your life isn't over. It doesn't have to be this way. We can go back together."

"You don't understand," he said, tearing himself from her arms. "Zach Ryder died that day. He died with his parents and his brothers."

Wind Ryder donned his breechcloth, then stood up and left the lodge.

Chapter Fourteen

Wind Ryder stalked through the dark village. He was used to being by himself, but he had never felt more alone.

Zach Ryder—

Feelings he had long refused to acknowledge stirred within him.

He had convinced himself that Zach Ryder was dead. He had created a new life for himself with the tribe, and he had come to be accepted as one of them. Chief Ten Crow had adopted him. It had been hard, but he'd survived.

But now Shining Spirit was threatening to destroy the world he'd created for himself and what little inner peace he had.

Wind Ryder made his way out of the village and stood alone, staring up at the heavens. The moonless night was clear, the sky a star-spangled canopy above him. He thought of the hours just passed in Shining Spirit's arms. He had never known that loving could be so beautiful. He remained lost in thought, trying to understand all he was feeling.

Laughing Woman was in a bad mood when she arose just before dawn. She had not slept well. It seemed to her that the captive who was supposed to bring peace to the tribe was causing more trouble than ever. The fight with Moon Cloud had been bad enough, but the news that Wind Ryder had taken Shining Spirit as his wife troubled her even more deeply.

Ten Crow awoke to find his wife moving about the tipi, her expression troubled. "Is something wrong?"

"I was thinking of all that's happened since Shining Spirit came into the village. I thought she would bring peace to our people, but it seems there is to be no peace for Bear Claw."

"Our son tried to take what was not his," Ten Crow said flatly.

"He wanted her. He even offered to buy her from you. Why could you not give her to him?"

"In the vision, it was not so."

"I hope your vision proves true."

"As do I."

"Sometimes I think bringing Wind Ryder into

the tribe was wrong. Look at the trouble he has caused!"

"Wind Ryder is our son," Ten Crow said.

"Wind Ryder is not *my* son," Laughing Woman denied angrily.

"You raised him as your own."

"Only because you took him in. Bear Claw is our one true son. Wind Ryder doesn't belong here—he never has."

Ten Crow had always known his wife resented Wind Ryder, but she had never stated it so bluntly before. He defended his adopted son. "He is a fine brave."

"So is Bear Claw, and yet you have always favored Wind Ryder over him! Wind Ryder should have remained a captive. If he had, there would be no worry right now about peace in our tribe."

Ten Crow stood up. His expression was angry as he towered over her, but she did not back down or cower before him.

"We will speak of this no more," he ordered. "All is as it should be."

With that, the chief started from the lodge. He did not want to listen to his wife speak of Bear Claw's bravery anymore. Time and again through the years, the son of his flesh had proven himself to be less than a man.

As he emerged from the tipi, Ten Crow did not see Wind Ryder disappear into the shadows.

He did not know that Wind Ryder had heard their every word.

When the eastern sky had begun to brighten, Wind Ryder had made his way toward his father's lodge. He knew the chief always got up early, and he'd wanted to talk with him. As he'd drawn near the tipi, he'd heard his father and mother talking inside. He'd been glad that they both were awake, but as he'd started to make his presence known to them, he'd overheard what Laughing Woman was saying.

"Wind Ryder is not my son."

"You raised him as your own."

"Only because you took him in. Bear Claw is our one true son. Wind Ryder doesn't belong here—he never has."

Her words had been like a lash upon him. He'd considered this woman to be his mother, and yet now he'd learned the truth of her feelings for him. He had remained there, listening to the rest of their conversation, until he had realized that Ten Crow was about to leave the tipi.

Tormented by all that he'd learned, Wind Ryder had moved away before his father could see him. He wandered a distance from the camp, not wanting to see or speak to anyone. He couldn't go back to his own lodge, for Shining Spirit was there. He sought solitude and returned to the secluded spot where he'd been earlier. As he sat there, the memory of his parents' talk replayed in his mind.

"Wind Ryder is not my son."

"You raised him as your own."

"Only because you took him in. Bear Claw is our one true son. Wind Ryder doesn't belong here—he never has."

The words tortured him.

Wind Ryder realized now that all along he'd had doubts about the way Laughing Woman had treated him. She had never been outwardly cruel to him, but she had always taken Bear Claw's side against him.

Laughing Woman had said he didn't belong there.

Slowly, painfully, Wind Ryder was coming to believe that the woman he'd thought of as his mother might be right—he truly didn't belong with the tribe.

He thought about Shining Spirit's words and realized he did have an alternative now.

He was a man full-grown.

He could walk away—if he wanted to.

The confusion he'd felt earlier deepened. And with the confusion came the memories he'd so long suppressed.

In his mind's eye, Wind Ryder saw his true parents—his white mother and father. Their names came to him in a painful rush—Michael and Catherine Ryder. Images of his brothers played before him, too—his big brother, Will, and his younger brother, Jeff. He remembered playing with them and working with his father and saying grace together before eating dinner.

It came to him bitterly that he'd continued to pray after he'd been taken by the Comanche. He had prayed for his family—that somehow, in spite of the murderous attack, they'd survived. He had prayed to be rescued. But no one had ever come to rescue him. After endless months, he'd given up praying. After endless months, he'd realized Zach Ryder was dead.

Until now.

Until this moment.

"Zach." He said his own name out loud.

Again memories overwhelmed him.

He heard his mother screaming his name, and he saw far too clearly his mother running toward him, her arms out, trying to save him from the warrior who'd grabbed him. He saw, too, how she'd been struck down by an arrow in her back—how she'd fallen, yet had tried to get back up to keep coming after him, until finally her strength had failed and she'd collapsed and lain unmoving.

Silent rage filled him.

The burning house—

The screams of his brothers trapped inside—

The sight of his father, lying dead by the stable.

He had witnessed it all as the Comanche had ridden off, taking him with them as their captive. The scenes were seared into his consciousness.

Wind Ryder had denied the memories because he'd been just a boy and had needed to adapt to survive. But they could never be forgotten. They were still a part of him—of the man he'd become.

He thought about his first days as a captive, of the terror and abuse he'd suffered. His rage intensified as he remembered his own hopelessness and fear. Crazy One had been the only white person in the village. She had sought him out to try to help him, but Ten Crow had been furious when he'd caught her tending to him. Ten Crow had beaten Crazy One severely and had forbidden her to go near him. He had seen the chief beating her, and he had been horrified by the violence done to her. From that day on, he had done everything in his power to make sure Crazy One didn't come near him, for he hadn't wanted her to be hurt in any way because of him.

His thoughts turned to Shining Spirit. He could only imagine how difficult it was to be taken captive as an adult. He had been a mere boy when he'd been brought into the village. He had been young enough and strong enough to fit in. But Shining Spirit was a grown woman. She had had a life of her own, and they had taken it from her.

Wind Ryder wondered about her life. He knew she wasn't married, for he had been the one to take her innocence, but he wondered if she had left behind someone she'd loved. And if she had—what right did he have to take her life from her? And what right did he have to make her stay?

Shining Spirit had begged him to take her back to her world. She had told him he could return to the white world.

Wind Ryder didn't know if that would be possible. He had no life there, no family.

But then, he had no family here either.

There was only Ten Crow—the man who'd taken him as his son, the man who had raised him in the tribe and taught him what he needed to know to become a warrior. Wind Ryder cared about Ten Crow; he admitted to himself that he loved him. It was because of the chief that he was still alive today.

But was there anything holding him in the village now that he knew the truth of Laughing Woman's feelings?

Was there any hope of his returning to the white world after he had lived as a Comanche for so long?

Instead of being able to clear his thoughts as he'd hoped, Wind Ryder found they grew even more troubled.

Daylight had come, and he knew what he had to do. He needed time alone, time away from everyone.

If he returned to his lodge and Shining Spirit, he did not know if he would be able to keep himself from her, not after the pleasure he'd found in her arms during the night, not after knowing the beauty of her love.

Wind Ryder returned to the village and went straight to get his mount. One of the other warriors was there working with the horses as he prepared to ride out.

"Are you going on a raid?" Black Eagle asked. "Wait, and I will ride with you."

"No. I am riding alone."

"You will be back soon?"

Wind Ryder swung up on his horse's back and looked down at the other man. "I do not know when I will return. Tell my father."

Before Black Eagle could say more, he wheeled his mount around and rode off.

Unnoticed, Crazy One had been watching and listening a short distance away.

Black Eagle finished what he was doing, then went to find the chief. He gave him Wind Ryder's message.

Ten Crow was troubled by the news that Wind Ryder had left the village. He thought of all Laughing Woman had said earlier, and he wondered for the first time if his vision could have been wrong. His visions had always been proven right in the past, but the sense of foreboding he felt could not be easily ignored.

He thought of his vision again—of Bear Claw and Wind Ryder fighting, of the blood and flames, of the golden one drawing Wind Ryder away, and of peace for his people. Was the golden one going to bring that peace? He was no longer certain.

* * *

It was already daylight when Marissa stirred. She awoke slowly, clinging to the serenity she'd found in sleep. But as she opened her eyes, she was forced to face reality—to remember what had transpired the night before.

"That life is over. Zach Ryder died that day."

Even now, pain filled her as she remembered how tortured Wind Ryder had sounded. She had hoped, after all they'd shared, that she would be able to reach him, but he had refused to listen to her pleas. He had walked out after the passionate night of loving they'd shared, and he hadn't come back.

Marissa got up, determined to find him. After dressing, she left the lodge and went looking for him. She was surprised when she could find no sign of him anywhere in the village. She returned to the tipi and was about to go back inside when Crazy One approached her.

"He's gone," Crazy One told her solemnly.

"Yes, he is. You're safe."

"No. No." She shook her head as she drew closer. "He's gone. He left the village. He rode away by himself. I saw him. Don't know when he'll be back."

"You saw Wind Ryder leave?"

"Yes."

"When?"

"At dawn. I heard him tell Black Eagle he didn't know when he'd be back."

Marissa was stunned—and heartbroken.

How could Wind Ryder have left her without saying a word?

Had last night meant so little to him that he could just ride away and not look back?

"Is that all he said?" she asked Crazy One.

"That is all I heard. He's gone. Now I have to go, too. I have work to do."

She walked away without saying anything more.

Marissa went back inside the lodge and stood alone, staring down at the blankets where she and Wind Ryder had made love just hours before—where she had given him her innocence. She wanted to get a horse and go after him, but she couldn't. She would be forced to wait there for his return—whenever that would be.

As she considered remaining alone in the village, Marissa thought of Bear Claw and fought down a shiver of fear. She would have to be watchful every minute, for she did not trust the other warrior to stay away from her. Without Wind Ryder's protection, she was vulnerable.

A thought came to her, and Marissa knelt down to quickly go through the few personal belongings Wind Ryder kept in a buckskin bag in the tipi. She was hoping to find a weapon of some kind so she could defend herself against Bear Claw if the need arose. Digging through his belongings, she was glad to find a small knife. She secured it in her waistband and had just started to put everything back when she saw something shining in the bottom of the bag. Marissa reached down and drew out a gold chain and cross.

A shiver went through Marissa as she stared down at the cross. The cross belonged to Zach. This was the only connection to his family he had left. Despite his words, he had not severed all ties with Zach Ryder.

There was hope.

Marissa carefully put the cross and chain back in the bag.

Tears threatened, and she paused, waiting to regain control of her emotions before she went back outside to join the women at work. She did not know if the tears were tears of joy at the knowledge that she might be able to convince Wind Ryder to leave the village or tears of sorrow at knowing he still kept that one connection to the past he so vehemently denied.

He was Zach Ryder.

She had to find a way to convince him of that truth when he returned.

Chapter Fifteen

Bear Claw's mood had not improved with the passing of the days, and he was glad to be heading out of the village with his father and the raiding party. He needed time to plan what to do next. He wanted to take the golden one, but he now knew that he would have to kill Wind Ryder to claim her.

He smiled to himself. He found the thought quite pleasant.

He hoped Wind Ryder would be back in the village when they returned. He was looking forward to their next encounter.

It was useless.

Everyone riding with the search party knew it, but no one wanted to be the first to admit it.

They continued on day after day, doggedly

searching, always hoping, scouring the land looking for a trail, for some clue as to where the Comanche had taken Marissa, but there was nothing. There was only the vast, deserted Texas wilderness.

They made camp and settled in for the night—hot, dirty, exhausted, frustrated, and angry.

"What do we do now, Hawk?" George asked as they sat around the campfire. His mood was black, for he realized how desperate their situation was.

"There is nothing more we can do, unless you just want to keep searching in ever widening circles. But even if we keep on another week or another month, there's no guarantee we'll ever turn up any trace of them."

"That's what I was afraid of."

Hawk looked up at George, his expression troubled and sympathetic. "I wish there was some way to give you hope. Hell, I wish there was some way to give myself hope that we'd find her if we kept on, but there isn't."

"I know."

George had come to respect and trust Hawk's opinions. Though it was painful to admit it, he knew Hawk was right. The storm had destroyed their only hope of locating Marissa quickly. Now it would be a matter of pure luck if they ever found her. He'd offered up silent prayers every night for help, but all his praying seemed to have come to nothing.

"So, what do you want to do? Do you want to

keep heading west in the morning?" Hawk asked.

George was silent as he searched his soul for an answer. He would have ridden on forever if he believed there was even the slightest chance of finding the Comanche's trail. The long days in the saddle and the endless hours of tracking would be worth it if they could found a clue to Marissa's whereabouts, but since the storm, they hadn't found a thing. It was as if she and the raiding party had disappeared off the face of the earth.

George could hide from the truth no longer. They were defeated. It was time to give it up.

George looked up at the man who'd become his friend. They shared a look of painful understanding as he answered, "No, we'll head back at first light."

"We can't just quit!" Mark argued. The thought of Marissa as a helpless Comanche captive angered him.

George looked up at his young ranch hand and understood his anger. Marissa was George's blood relation; no one wanted her safe return more than he did.

"Mark—we've done everything we can. Hawk's right. There's no point in going on."

"There's got to be something more we can do! We can't just give up," Mark argued.

"Nobody's giving up on her," George told him.

"But you want to go back!"

"There's nowhere else to go right now. Hawk's the best tracker around, but we could search every inch of West Texas for the next six months and not find a thing. You know that."

Mark fell silent. Though logic told him George was right, a part of him didn't want to quit. He considered going on by himself, but if even Hawk couldn't find their trail, Mark knew he didn't stand a chance.

"You all right?" George asked when Mark remained silent.

"Yeah." His answer was terse. He turned and stalked away from the campsite.

George and Hawk watched him go, knowing what he was feeling, knowing he needed time alone.

Claude had kept his silence as he'd listened to their exchange. He realized how difficult making that decision had been. But their course had now been decided.

In the morning, they would turn back.

Mark walked a distance away, needing time to sort out his feelings. When he'd first learned that Marissa was coming to live at the ranch after her father's death, he'd been glad. She was an attractive girl, and they had spent some time together during her last visit. He'd been seriously considering courting her when she arrived. Marrying George's only heir would be a smart move, for the Crown Ranch was very successful.

Now, though, Mark wondered about his plan. If

they had managed to find Marissa, he would have won George's favor by marrying her. Certainly, no one else was going to want her after she'd been held by the Comanche. He smiled at the thought. There would be no competition for her hand in marriage. But their failure to find her had ruined everything. He didn't know what he would do next, but he was sorry they weren't going to keep looking for her.

Louise was moving slowly and painfully, but at least she was moving, and for that she was grateful. She made her way down the hall of the boarding-house, leaning heavily on Dr. Harrison's arm.

"Are you certain you're up to this?" the doctor asked, concerned.

"Oh, yes," she said with determination.

The endless days of lying in bed had taken their toll on Louise. Her worries about Marissa were consuming her. She wasn't the type of person to sit idly by when others were in trouble. She had to get up and try to do something to help.

It took a great effort, but she made it down the stairs and into the physician's buggy.

"Sarah has things all ready for you out at the Crown. I'll have you at the ranch in no time," the doctor promised as he climbed in beside her and took up the reins.

"Thank you for everything you've done for me,"

Louise told him, truly grateful for his compassionate care.

"I'm just glad you're doing so well. There was a time early on when I wasn't sure you were going to make it." He smiled over at her, glad that she was looking so much better. "You're a strong woman, Louise Bennett."

"I've been told that before," she said quietly, sitting back and trying to make herself comfortable.

She noticed that the doctor had a rifle in the buggy, and she was glad. She had made up her mind to learn how to ride astride and how to fire a gun when she got to the ranch. There would never be another time in her life when she would be left defenseless the way she had been in the raid on the way station. If she'd had a gun that day and had known how to use it, she might have been able to save Marissa from the Comanche. Louise had vowed to herself never to be helpless again.

The trek to the ranch passed far too slowly for Louise. Lingering terror from the Comanche attack left her nervous and unsure as they traveled the long miles across the open country.

"You're on Crown property now," Dr. Harrison told her after they'd been on the road for over an hour.

Louise was tremendously relieved some time later when the Crown ranch house and outbuildings finally came into view. She'd had no idea the ranch was so successful. She was impressed by the empire that George had carved out of the wild Texas land.

As they drove up the main road toward the house, Louise saw Sarah come out on the front porch and wave to them in welcome. Once they'd drawn to a stop, Sarah approached the buggy.

"It is so wonderful that you're finally here," Sarah told Louise, smiling brightly.

"Have you heard anything from George and the others?" Louise asked quickly, desperate for news about Marissa.

"Not a word in all this time," Sarah answered honestly. "I wish I could tell you different, but there's been nothing."

Dr. Harrison climbed down from the buggy and then assisted Louise in her descent.

Louise realized all too painfully how weak she still was. She was forced to cling to the doctor's arm just to make it inside the house. With the doctor's and Sarah's help, she settled on the sofa in the parlor.

"Will you be all right now?" the physician asked Louise once he'd made sure she was comfortable.

"Yes, thank you."

"Don't worry about her, Doc. We'll take good care of her," Sarah promised.

"I'll be holding you to that," he said.

"Can you stay for a while?" Sarah invited.

"No, I've got to get back. But if there's any change at all in Miss Louise's condition, you send word to me right away. We don't want to take any chances."

"I'll do that."

"You take care of yourself," Dr. Harrison said to Louise. "I'll check back in on you in about a week."

Sarah went out to see him off, then returned to join Louise.

"I turned the dining room into a bedroom for you so you wouldn't have to climb the stairs," Sarah explained.

"Thank you. And, Sarah?" When the other woman turned to her, "Thank you for providing all the personal things for me." The doctor had told her that Sarah had left money with him to buy the personal things she needed.

"No need to thank me. George was the one. He told me to make sure you were taken care of, and I knew you would be needing clothes and such. I'm just glad that you're finally well enough to be here. Now all we have to do is pray that they return soon with Marissa. It's been far too long already."

Their gazes locked.

"I've been praying for that since the day they left," Louise admitted.

"So have I."

It was almost dusk when Marissa returned to the tipi for the night. She was just about to go inside when she saw a warrior in the distance.

She stopped, her heartbeat quickening at the sight of the brave riding in.

Was it Wind Ryder?

Had he finally returned to her?

She waited, unsure what to do. Her first impulse was to run forward and greet him, but she stayed back, uncertain of his response.

Marissa grew nervous. She hated to admit it, but she had missed Wind Ryder desperately. She'd been worried about him, too. As excited as she was about the chance to see him again now, doubt held her in place. He'd been angry when he left, so she did not know what to expect. She walked slowly in the warrior's direction, trying to ignore the quickening of her heartbeat.

Marissa was almost holding her breath as she watched the warrior draw nearer, but finally she realized it was not Wind Ryder. She was surprised by the surge of disappointment that filled her.

Turning away, she quickly returned to the lodge and settled in for the night. She had heard that Bear Claw had ridden out with a raiding party, but even so, she fell asleep with Wind Ryder's knife close at hand.

Chapter Sixteen

It was more than a week before Wind Ryder made the return trip to the village. Time held little meaning in the wilderness. He'd deliberately lost himself, seeking solitude and peace.

He had found the solitude, but the peace had been harder to achieve. It seemed that Shining Spirit haunted his thoughts every moment. He'd tried to put the memories of the last night they'd spent together from his mind, but whenever he attempted to fall asleep, images of her were there before him—images of her naked in his arms, taunting him with her beautiful body and tempting him with her innocent love.

He had realized quickly there would be no forgetting Shining Spirit.

The understanding had come to him in the dark

of night when he had stirred in his sleep and reached out for her, only to discover she was not there.

It had been a revelation for Wind Ryder to discover that he no longer wanted to be by himself—to be a lone warrior.

He wanted Shining Spirit.

As he accepted that truth, another realization struck him. Feeling as he did, he did not know if he still belonged with the tribe. Laughing Woman's words had been like a knife in his heart, severing the ties he'd believed he'd had with her and the people.

During his time alone, Wind Ryder considered all that Shining Spirit had told him about the white world. He was not a man who admitted to fear. He faced any and all challenges straight on. He had learned to do that under Ten Crow's tutelage, but the thought of trying to make a life for himself among the whites troubled him.

He was a Comanche warrior. How would he ever fit into the white world? Did he want to?

Wind Ryder looked up as he neared the village. All was calm. He knew the village was the same as when he'd left, but somehow it appeared almost alien to him.

The village might be the same, but he had changed.

He quietly greeted the brave keeping watch,

then tended to his horse before making his way to his tipi.

Silently Wind Ryder lifted the door flap and let himself into the lodge. Shining Spirit was asleep, and he stopped just inside the entry to stare down at her. In his thoughts and dreams, she had been beautiful, but as he gazed down at her now in the semidarkness, she was even more lovely.

Wind Ryder let the door flap fall down as he moved closer to her. He had been a driven man on the ride back to the village. He had thought of nothing except losing himself in the heat of her passion. He wanted to take her in his arms, to feel her against him. He stretched out beside her and drew her to him.

Marissa had been deeply asleep, but when she felt a man's hands upon her, she jerked awake in a panic. Fearing it was Bear Claw, she reached for the knife and scrambled away to crouch across the lodge. She was trembling, but she was ready to fight if she had to.

And then Wind Ryder whispered her name.

"Marissa—"

He moved nearer, wanting to calm her, wanting to reassure her.

At the sound of his voice, a shiver of a different kind trembled through Marissa.

"You're back," she breathed, and lowered the knife.

"You were afraid?" He saw the weapon, and he

was glad she had it to defend herself, but a sudden fear raged through him. "Has Bear Claw tried to harm you?"

"No, but I did not know when you would return. You've been gone for so long." The days had seemed endless.

"I missed you," he said simply.

Then, unable to resist her any longer, he lifted one hand to caress her cheek as he bent to capture her lips in a sweet, soft kiss.

The knife fell unheeded from her hand as Marissa surrendered willingly to his embrace.

Wind Ryder had returned to her. And he wanted her.

She welcomed him to her now without question.

Their time apart had only heightened the desire they felt for each other. They came together in a rush of passion. Clothes were quickly stripped away in their need to be close to one another. They lay together upon the softness of their blankets, completely caught up in the glory of their nearness.

Wind Ryder moved over her, claiming her as his own. The excitement of their union swept them both away. They were alone in the world they'd created, lost in the splendor of their loving.

Marissa responded wildly to his every touch, and she returned his every caress, wanting to please him as he was pleasing her. They crested together, ecstasy sweeping over them, taking them to the heights of pleasure.

Afterward, Marissa lay quietly in Wind Ryder's arms, her head resting on his chest.

He had come back to her. She hadn't been sure that he would.

"I'm sorry I upset you," Marissa said in a soft voice as she trailed one hand across the width of his chest. It felt good to touch him, to have him near. "I only wanted to learn more about you—about who you really are and what your life was like before—"

His long days alone had changed the way he felt. The anger was no longer there.

"I know," Wind Ryder finally answered after a long pause. "I remember a little about my family—my parents and my two brothers. We had a ranch near San Antonio. Life was good then—until the raid."

"I understand," she said, thinking of Louise and all that she'd witnessed at the way station. "I lived in New Orleans with my father until he died. That was when I decided to make the trip to Dry Springs to live with my Uncle George on his ranch. Louise Bennett, a friend of my parents, was making the trip with me. I was the only one who survived the attack on the way station." Her voice was choked. "I don't know why I had to be the one. I saw everything. I saw Louise die."

"I understand," Wind Ryder said quietly. "I saw everything, too."

"Then why do you stay?" She remembered what

Crazy One had told her, but she didn't want to let him know she'd spoken to the old woman about him.

"I did try to get away in the beginning, but Ten Crow found me every time. After a while, I gave up and did what I had to do to survive."

"You became one of them."

"There was no other way. Then Ten Crow took me as his son, and I was accepted." He did not tell her what he'd heard Laughing Woman say.

"But you're a man full-grown now. You could leave the tribe if you wanted to."

"There's nothing for me in the white world. My family is all dead."

"If you took me back, I would be with you. You wouldn't be alone. We could go to my uncle's ranch."

Wind Ryder could just imagine the reception he'd get in the white world. He would be an outcast.

"I don't belong there."

Marissa fell silent. She wanted to press Wind Ryder, but this wasn't the time. He had opened up to her a little, and for now she would be thankful for that much. He had returned to her. She would wait and hold on to the hope that maybe, in time, she could find a way to convince him to take her to her uncle.

Wind Ryder said nothing more, for he was lost deep in thought. The days alone in the wilderness had proven to him that he wanted her with him. He wondered if he could bear to be parted from her.

Rising up on an elbow over her, he kissed her.

He didn't belong in the white world. Nor did he belong in the village. The only place he felt he did belong was in her arms.

"The boss is back! They're riding in!"

"They're back?" Louise asked Sarah, her hopes soaring at last.

With each day that had passed during the weeks since she'd come to stay at the ranch, her fears had increased that she would never see Marissa again.

"Thank God!" Sarah said as she got up to look out the window. She'd been worrying about them, too, fearing for her husband's safety.

Louise had regained most of her strength, and she rushed from the house, desperate to see Marissa. Sarah followed her outside on the porch. The ranch hands were coming up to the house to greet the newcomers, too.

Louise shielded her eyes against the sun as she stared down the road. She could see a group of riders in the distance, and her heart leapt in excitement.

Marissa was back!

Joy filled her, and she offered up a prayer of thanks for Marissa's safe return. George had told her he was going to find her, and he had.

And then she heard one of the ranch hands mutter, "Damn. There's just the four of them."

"What?" Louise went still at his words, every fiber of her being denying the truth of he'd just blurted out.

Sarah reached over to take her hand in a supportive gesture, but said nothing as the riders drew closer. Sarah knew there was nothing more to be said. The fact that it was just the four men returning after all this time said it all.

Louise began to tremble. Sarah clutched her hand even more tightly, but still said nothing. She understood what Louise was feeling.

Tears welled up in Louise's eyes. "George was going to find her. He promised me he would."

The men reined in before them, tired, dirty, and defeated.

"Boss, you're back," the hands greeted him.

George only nodded to his men, then turned to meet Louise's gaze. He was thrilled that she was looking so well. She appeared fully recovered, but he hated giving her the bad news.

"How did it go?" one of the hands asked. "Did you find anything?"

"No." The word was dragged from him. "A storm came through and wiped out the trail. We kept searching as long as we could, but there was no use. The trail was gone."

Louise had been watching him, trying to read his expression. At his answer, all the pain he was feeling was revealed in the depths of his eyes. She had lain awake night after night, agonizing over what she would do if the worst came to pass.

And now it had.

She wanted to scream and cry and rant and rave, but she drew upon her deepest inner strength and left the porch to go to George. Her heart ached for him and for all that he had suffered and lost.

"George—" She said his name softly, reaching his side just as he dismounted.

"We did everything we could, Louise." George was not a man who admitted defeat easily, and the words were choked from him.

She saw the torture in his eyes, the pain in his soul. Her own sorrow and misery matched his. Her worst fears had been realized.

Louise's voice was tight as she asked, "Is Marissa dead?"

"No—I don't think so," he answered quickly, but in his heart he wondered if she might not have been better off dead than living as a captive. He would never say that aloud, though.

"Then there's still hope." Louise was relieved that she still had something to cling to—and that George did, too. She put her hand reassuringly on his arm. "If it's possible, I know Marissa will come back to us."

George knew the odds were against that eventuality. He was trying to accept what he believed was the inevitable truth—that he would never see his niece alive again—but he did not have the heart to deny Louise her one last, slender thread of hope.

"Marissa's a strong girl," he said.

"Yes, she is," Louise agreed.

"Let's go inside," George said, then turned to the men who'd ridden with him. "Hawk, you're more than welcome to spend the night."

"Thanks, but I'd better be getting back to town," he said. "If you hear anything more, let me know."

"I will," George promised. "And, Hawk—"

Hawk had started to mount up again, but paused to glance his way.

"Thanks."

George left Louise's side for a moment and went to offer Hawk his hand in friendship. Hawk nodded solemnly. The bond they'd formed was a strong one. Then he swung up in the saddle and rode out, lifting one hand in a farewell gesture.

"I'm glad you're back," Sarah said as she went to her husband and hugged him in welcome. She was devastated over the news that they hadn't found Marissa, but relieved that Claude had returned safely.

"I just wish things had turned out different," Claude remarked.

"We all do," Sarah agreed.

"I'll take care of the horses," Mark offered, knowing Claude wanted time to be with Sarah, and George would want to talk more with Marissa's aunt.

"We got 'em," the other hands spoke up, helping him with the horses.

Mark appreciated their help. It wasn't in his nature to give up, but there had been no choice. His mood was dark as he walked with them to the stable.

Chapter Seventeen

Word spread that the raiding party was riding in, and the villagers went to meet them. There was always a great celebration when Chief Ten Crow returned, for he always led the most successful raids. The welcoming mood changed quickly when they saw the chief being brought in on a travois.

Laughing Woman rushed to kneel at her husband's side. She was shocked to find him unconscious.

"Was he wounded during the raid?" she asked, looking up at Bear Claw when he dismounted and came to her.

"No, a rattlesnake struck at his horse two days ago, and he was thrown."

"Take him inside. I will send for the medicine man," Laughing Woman ordered.

With the help of another warrior, Bear Claw moved his father into the lodge. When he came back outside to see if the medicine man was coming, Snake approached him.

"What do you want to do with the captive?" Snake asked.

Bear Claw didn't care if the young white boy he'd taken captive lived or died.

"Tie him to the pole at the center of the village. I will see to him after we have cared for my father."

Snake went off to do as Bear Claw had directed. He dragged the bound and beaten captive through the village to the center pole. He tied him there, his arms extended above his head, and left him alone to be subjected to the ridicule and taunting of the villagers.

Wind Ryder had been working with the horses when word came to him that the raiding party was back, and that his father had been seriously injured. He rushed to the tipi to find Laughing Woman and Bear Claw waiting outside.

"What happened?"

"A rattlesnake struck at his horse, and he was thrown. The medicine man is with him," Laughing Woman told him.

Wind Ryder was shocked by the news, for Ten Crow was one of the best horsemen in the tribe. He looked at Bear Claw and Laughing Woman worriedly, "Will he be all right?"

"We do not know. The medicine man will call us in when he is ready."

Conflicting emotions tore at Wind Ryder as he awaited word of his father's condition. He did not want to be with Bear Claw and Laughing Woman, but his concern for Ten Crow held him there. The chief had cared about him and loved him as if he were his own. He could do no less.

Except for the ecstasy and forgetfulness Marissa found during the long, dark hours of the night in Wind Ryder's arms, the days and weeks of her captivity were passing with agonizing slowness. There were times when she wondered if she would ever be reunited with her uncle. She made the best she could of things, and this day sought out Crazy One to visit with her near the stream. They were there talking when they heard shouting coming from the village.

"I wonder what's happening," she said, looking in that direction.

Crazy One listened for a moment, and then her expression changed. Her eyes widened as a tremor of terror shook her.

"What is it?" Marissa asked, puzzled by her reaction.

"We cannot go there," she said, her fear obvious.

"Why? Is something wrong? Should we go see if we can help?"

The older woman's expression grew more fearful. She grabbed Shining Spirit forcefully by the arm, her fingers digging into her flesh. "Do not go there."

Her insistence left Marissa even more worried. She tore herself loose and started off toward the village.

Crazy One stood uncertainly where she was. She knew what was happening, and she feared for Shining Spirit's safety. A part of her wanted to run, to find a place to hide, but her heart was moved by Shining Spirit's daring. She thought her aptly named. She was brave and courageous, and her goodness shone for all to see.

But ever since the early days when Wind Ryder had come into the tribe, Crazy One had made it a point never to care for anyone. Somehow, though, this strong, determined young woman had found a place in her heart. Though her mind screamed at her to go hide, her heart led her.

Crazy One went after Shining Spirit; she knew her friend was going to need help.

The closer Marissa came to the center of the village, the faster she ran. Something was telling her that there was trouble.

The sight that greeted her shocked her to the depths of her already tortured soul.

There, tied helplessly to a pole, was a young white boy. He was bloodied and nearly unconscious. The Comanche children were throwing rocks and sticks at him, and they cheered when they hurt him.

Outrage filled her, and she reacted without thought. She ran screaming at the children. She was shocked when she heard someone behind her shouting and looked back to see Crazy One following her. At that moment, she loved the old woman.

Crazy One grabbed up the biggest stick she could find and waved it at the children, who stayed just out of range. She deliberately acted wild and insane, wanting to keep them away as Shining Spirit worked at freeing the injured youth from his bonds.

"Do you need help to get him down?" Crazy One asked.

"No, I can do it," Marissa told her with determination.

The boy was barely conscious, but at the feel of gentle hands upon him, he opened his eyes. His expression was both pained and dazed as he tried to focus on her. His terror eased a little at the sight of her blond hair.

"Who are you?" he asked, his voice barely above a whisper.

"A friend," she told him. She knew there would be serious consequences for her actions, but she didn't care. All that mattered was saving the boy from further abuse.

One of the boys ran to find Bear Claw to let him know what was happening. He found the warrior at his father's lodge.

"Bear Claw! Hurry!" the boy shouted.

"What is it?" he asked, jumping to his feet when he heard the urgency in the boy's tone. He had been waiting outside the tipi for word of his father's condition.

"Your captive! Shining Spirit is trying to free him from the pole!"

Wind Ryder had been standing nearby. He had not known that Bear Claw had taken a prisoner, and he could only imagine Shining Spirit's reaction to witnessing the torture of a captive. He knew he had to get to her before Bear Claw did.

Wind Ryder reached the women just as Shining Spirit finished untying the boy's hands.

Crazy One saw him coming. For a moment, she started to run, then stood her ground, stick in hand.

"Stay back! You will not harm them!" she shouted at him.

He looked from the two women to the boy. A jolt of recognition seared him to the depths of his being. The pain was unlike anything he'd experienced. Wind Ryder could tell the boy was young, not even ten. His face was battered, and he was cut and bloodied. His wrists were raw from being bound. Shining Spirit had her arm around his shoulders, trying to help him stand, but he was sagging weakly from the abuse he'd suffered.

Wind Ryder remembered when he had felt the same way—when he had been beaten and abused—when he had been alone and desperate.

Crazy One had been the only person to help him—in the beginning.

Wind Ryder knew what he had to do. He started to walk past Crazy One, unafraid that she might hit him. He knew only that he had to help this boy.

Crazy One stood her ground for a moment, then backed off and let him pass without attacking him.

"What are you going to do?" Shining Spirit asked, not wanting the boy to come to any more harm.

The boy looked up at Wind Ryder.

Wind Ryder didn't answer. In one move, he picked the youth up in his arms and started back toward his own tipi with him, leaving the women to follow.

Wind Ryder had gone only a short distance when Bear Claw confronted him. Fury was etched in the other warrior's face.

"The captive is mine. Put him down," Bear Claw snarled.

Wind Ryder faced him without fear. "I will buy him from you. Name your price."

"The boy is not for sale," he said coldly. He was glad to be having this confrontation. He had made it a point to bring the boy back just so he could taunt Wind Ryder with him. It pleased Bear Claw to see his brother so angry.

Wind Ryder had known Bear Claw would challenge him, and he was prepared to fight him. He turned and set the boy on his feet near Shining Spirit and Crazy One.

"What are you doing?" Marissa asked, unable to understand what was being said.

"Do not worry," Wind Ryder answered in English. He turned back to Bear Claw.

"If you will not sell or trade him to me, then I will take him from you," Wind Ryder said simply.

Bear Claw had not wanted to fight Wind Ryder, at least not face to face. He'd lost to him in fair fights too many times already. If he fought Wind Ryder again, he wanted to have an advantage over him—like surprising him in an ambush. But all eyes were upon him now. He was trapped. He could not back down from Wind Ryder's challenge.

"You can try," he sneered.

Wind Ryder looked over at the women. He was proud of their courage in coming to the boy's aid. "Take him to our lodge."

Marissa and Crazy One led the injured boy away. Marissa kept an arm around him, for he was staggering and barely able to stay on his feet.

"What's going to happen to me?" the boy asked weakly.

"Wind Ryder has claimed you," Marissa told him.

"Is he a white man?"

"Yes." Marissa nodded. "And he wants to keep you safe."

She could feel how weak and unsteady he was,

and she was glad when they reached the tipi. After casting one nervous look back toward the men, she led the way inside. The boy and Crazy Woman followed her in.

Wind Ryder remained calm as he faced Bear Claw.

"The boy is mine now," he stated confidently.

Wind Ryder's arrogance infuriated Bear Claw. He was ready to erupt in fury when the crowd that had gathered around them suddenly parted and Laughing Woman appeared before them.

"Come," Laughing Woman said, rushing to Bear Claw and taking his arm. "There is no time for this. Your father—he has awakened and wants to see you."

Bear Claw looked at Wind Ryder. "It is not over between us," he threatened. "We will settle this later."

Wind Ryder only stared at him. There was no need to say anything more. For now, the boy was safe.

"He wants to see you, too," Laughing Woman told Wind Ryder, though it angered her to do so.

They started toward the lodge.

"Stay here," Crazy One told Shining Spirit. "Tend to the boy. I will go see what is happening."

Crazy One hurried back to watch Wind Ryder.

Marissa stood over the boy, who was trying to put on a brave face in spite of all he'd suffered.

"Don't worry," Marissa said. "Wind Ryder is the best warrior in the tribe. You will not be returned to Bear Claw."

At her words, he began to tremble. "I want to go home. I want my ma and pa."

"I know," she said sadly. "I know."

Kneeling down beside him, she took him in her arms and held him to her, offering what solace she could.

"What's your name?" Marissa asked gently. "My name is Marissa."

"I'm Joe. Joe Carter." Tears welled up in his eyes as he leaned back a bit to gaze up at her. "Thanks for helping me."

"You're welcome. Let's see what we can do to get you cleaned up a bit."

Marissa tried to distract herself by tending to the boy, but all the while she was straining to hear what was going on outside. She prayed fervently that if there was fighting, Wind Ryder would prevail.

As she bathed the youth's wounds, she began to understand how Crazy One had felt all those years ago when she'd tried to help Wind Ryder. There was no way she could let Joe return to Bear Claw's keeping.

Wind Ryder reached the chief's tipi first and went in. Bear Claw and his mother followed.

Chief Ten Crow lay unmoving on the blankets.

His eyes were closed and his breathing was shallow and labored. His coloring was gray and lifeless.

Wind Ryder stared down at the man he had called father for so many years. He wondered what would happen if Ten Crow didn't recover. The question haunted him.

"Father—" he said quietly as he went to his side.

At the sound of his voice, Ten Crow opened his eyes. He stared up at Wind Ryder as if seeing him for the first time. There was a distant look in his eyes for a moment before he focused.

"No—I need to see my son—I need to see Bear Claw." Ten Crow struggled to speak in a weak voice.

At Ten Crow's words, Wind Ryder stepped away. Pain stabbed him at being denied by the chief.

Bear Claw smiled confidently and went to his father's side.

"Yes, Father, I am here," he said triumphantly.

Laughing Woman, too, felt a moment of exhilaration. Her son was Ten Crow's favorite. The chief wanted Bear Claw by his side, not Wind Ryder.

Ten Crow gathered what little strength he had left to speak. He grabbed his son's arm for emphasis.

"Bear Claw—you must bring peace to the tribe. You and Wind Ryder."

Ten Crow turned his head and looked over at Wind Ryder. The effort cost him. Their gazes met for only an instant, and then his eyes closed.

The chief's hand fell away from Bear Claw's arm as his spirit left his body.

His fight was over.

"My husband!" Laughing Woman cried out in agony and threw herself across his chest.

Wind Ryder and Bear Claw remained silent as they realized their father was dead.

Wind Ryder knew in that moment what he had to do. There would never be peace in the tribe as long as he was there, and without Ten Crow, there was no reason for him to remain.

"I will leave the village. Now. Today," Wind Ryder said, breaking the silence.

Laughing Woman looked up at him. Her face was distorted and tear-stained in her grief. She was shocked by her husband's death, but a surge of perverse delight filled her at Wind Ryder's words. She was glad that she would never have to see him again.

"It was a bad thing that you were ever brought here," she spat out angrily. Now that Ten Crow was dead, she could finally give vent to her true feelings about this interloper.

Wind Ryder was more than ready to ride away and never look back, but he wanted to make his point before he left. He looked at Laughing Woman, his expression cold.

"You forget, woman, that I never asked to be brought here. I came to this village as a captive."

Then he looked at Bear Claw. "Shining Spirit, Crazy One, and the boy will go with me when I leave. I will not be back."

"Good," Laughing Woman said. "Go now. Leave us. You are no son of mine!"

Wind Ryder looked at them both and realized she was right—very right.

He left the tipi and walked away.

Bear Claw was furious.

"He cannot take my captive!" he raged as he started to go after Wind Ryder.

"Let them go!"

"The boy is mine!"

"Your father is dead, my son," she admonished. "Do you care more about some white captive? Let him go with Wind Ryder. Be glad they are gone."

Bear Claw longed to go after Wind Ryder, to somehow get the better of him.

"Remember, son, Wind Ryder is leaving, never to return. That is good—very good."

Bear Claw's anger knew no bounds, but he stayed with his mother as she mourned Ten Crow's passing.

Later there would be time to seek his revenge.

Chapter Eighteen

Wind Ryder returned to his own tipi to find the boy there with Shining Spirit.

Marissa looked up and was relieved to see Wind Ryder unharmed.

"You're all right," she breathed, quickly going to him. "Did you fight Bear Claw?"

"No. Laughing Woman came for us. Ten Crow is dead."

Marissa was shocked. "I did not know he had been hurt."

Wind Ryder explained what had happened.

She wasn't sure how to react to the news. She knew Wind Ryder had cared about Ten Crow, but somehow he seemed almost unaffected by the chief's death. "I'm sorry."

"Where is Crazy One?" he asked, not mentioning Ten Crow again. He wondered if he ever would.

"I don't know. She left us to find out what was happening with you and Bear Claw. She was afraid for you."

"We must find her."

"Why?"

Wind Ryder looked down at her and saw her questioning look. "We are leaving the village. We will take Crazy One and the boy with us."

Marissa was stunned by his announcement.

"We're leaving?" she repeated in a whisper. Her hopes were soaring, but she still wasn't sure she'd heard him right.

"There is no reason to stay here in the village any longer."

She wanted to throw herself in his arms. She had prayed for this moment but feared it would never come—and now it was here. She was going back to her own world.

"Is the boy strong enough to travel?" Wind Ryder asked.

Though he was weak, Joe jumped to his feet at this question. Excitement was coursing through him at the prospect of returning home. "I'm strong enough!"

"Strong enough to ride alone?" Wind Ryder asked.

"Yes."

Wind Ryder gave the youth an approving look.

It was good that he was strong and willing to fight. A child of lesser strength might not have been able to survive the trek they were about to make.

"Good." He glanced at Shining Spirit. "Find Crazy One and bring her here. I will get the horses."

"Wait for us here," Marissa told Joe.

Marissa hurried from the lodge, ready to search for the older woman. Wind Ryder followed her. She stopped and turned back to look at him.

"Thank you," she said softly.

He stood, staring at her for a long moment, then nodded once. He remained where he was, watching as she rushed off. When she'd gone from view, he let his gaze sweep over the village, committing to memory all the sights and sounds that had been so much a part of him for so long.

But this part of his life was over now.

Ten Crow, the man who had been like a father to him, was dead. There was nothing left to bind him there, nothing to hold him.

He was going to leave, and he would never come back.

Wind Ryder did not know what he would find in the white world. But even if he himself never fit in there, he knew he was doing the right thing. What mattered was returning the boy and Shining Spirit to their own people.

Wind Ryder realized that once they left the village, everything between him and Shining Spirit would change. He had taken her as his wife, but she did not know it, and in the white world he could make no claim on her. That realization saddened him, and he tried to prepare his heart for the loss.

"I cannot go!" Crazy One cried, backing away from Shining Spirit. "Leave me alone! Leave me alone!"

"Crazy One," Marissa said quietly, gently. "There is no reason to be afraid. This is Wind Ryder—the boy you cared about. He wants to take you with him. He wants you to return to your own people."

"No! No!"

"I will be with you, and so will the boy. Wind Ryder will take us to my uncle's ranch. We'll be safe there, I promise you."

Crazy One had been in the Comanche village for more years than she could count. Any dream she'd had of going home had been destroyed long ago. The thought that she might actually be able to leave the tribe was as frightening to her as it was thrilling.

Home—Could she really go back?

"You will be with me?" Crazy One asked, calming a bit.

"And the boy. He needs your help, too."

It seemed so simple, yet the older woman's terror held her frozen as she fought all her demons.

"Come with me, Crazy One."

"But who would want me now? No one. No

one." She shook her head in abject sorrow. She knew how the white world reacted to captives who were returned. They were made outcasts and subjected to all kinds of humiliation.

"Wind Ryder wants you. He asked for you. He said to find you and bring you to him."

"Wind Ryder said that?" She looked up, shock showing on her face.

"Yes. He wants you to go with him, and he is waiting for us with the horses at the lodge right now."

"He is?" Crazy One still sounded frightened.

"Yes. There is no reason for you to be afraid, but we must go now."

Finally, the old woman calmed. She was amazed by what Shining Spirit had told her.

Wind Ryder wanted to take her along. Wind Ryder wanted her with him.

"Yes. Yes, I will go with you. I will leave this place. We will go together." Crazy One smiled.

Marissa was startled, for she had never seen the other woman smile before. It transformed her, and for just an instant Marissa had an image of what Crazy One had looked like when she was young.

Crazy One moved to Shining Spirit's side, and together they walked toward Wind Ryder's lodge.

The nightmare that had been their captivity was about to end.

Wind Ryder had returned with four horses and was waiting for them. It took them only a short time to gather their belongings. They mounted up and started to ride out.

The mourning for the dead chief had begun. The wails of those who had loved and respected him echoed through the village.

Joe was frightened by the sounds. "Are they gonna come after us?"

"No," Wind Ryder reassured the boy. "No one will bother us."

In his heart, Wind Ryder, too, was mourning Ten Crow's passing. He looked back only once, then put his heels to his mount and rode away from the village for the last time.

Louise stood on the porch of the ranch house, staring out across the night-shrouded land. Her mood was as dark as the night. In the weeks since the search party's return, there had been no word about Marissa.

It was truly as if she'd vanished.

It was almost as if she'd never existed at all.

But Louise knew that wasn't true. Marissa was very much alive in her heart. If only they could find her!

A single tear traced a forlorn path down her cheek, and she brushed it angrily away. What good did it do to cry? Crying wouldn't bring Marissa back. It seemed that nothing would bring her back.

Louise sighed and turned around.

"Oh," she gasped when she found George standing just outside the front door, watching her.

"Are you all right?" he asked, crossing the distance between them.

He'd noticed that she had been very quiet at dinner and had excused herself to come outside as soon as they'd finished eating. He'd stayed indoors to give her some privacy, but then he'd started to worry when she hadn't come back in.

Louise drew a ragged breath at his question. She answered honestly, "I don't know, George. I don't know if I'll ever be all right again." She turned away from him to look back out into the night. "There are times when I think I should leave. I've gotten my strength back. Maybe I should go back to New Orleans. But then I realize I'd have to board a stagecoach again, and the thought terrifies me. I know I can't stay here forever, living on the hope that Marissa is going to return. At some point . . ."

Louise stopped, emotion overwhelming her as she was about to voice the horrible truth that was threatening to destroy her. George went to her and put a gentle hand on her shoulder, urging her to turn back to him. She resisted for a moment, not wanting him to see her this way, but then faced him. George gazed down at her, seeing her tears in the pale light that shone from the house.

"Don't cry, Louise," he said in a husky voice.

She lifted her gaze to his. "But I feel so helpless—I want to do something. I want to find Marissa and bring her home, but I have to accept that we may never see her again. She truly may be lost to us—especially after all this time. Oh, it's been so long, George, and with each day that passes . . ."

George gathered her tenderly in his arms. "We've done everything we can. If there was anything else that could be done, I would do it in a heartbeat, but there isn't. I know Marissa. If she's alive out there and there's any way she can come home to us, she'll do it. She's a strong, intelligent young woman. She's a survivor. I can't believe she's dead. I won't allow myself even to consider it."

"But what should I do? I don't belong here. I was her companion. I was supposed to keep her safe."

George had long suspected that Louise was feeling guilty that she had survived while her charge's fate was unknown. It hurt him deeply that she was so sad. He wanted to make things better for her. He wanted to help her and support her in any way he could. He wanted to make her smile, but he knew that only one thing could do that—seeing Marissa again.

"You almost died in the attack," he told her fiercely. "Don't ever feel that you failed Marissa in any way. You were trying to save her when you were wounded. I'm just thankful you're alive."

"You are?" Her breath caught in her throat at his unexpected declaration.

"Yes." George's answer was almost a groan.

In that moment, the careful control he'd been keeping over his own turbulent emotions was destroyed. He sought her lips in a hungry kiss.

Louise was stunned by the power of his embrace. He had kept himself so distant from her that she'd had no idea he harbored tender feelings toward her. When he broke off the kiss and stepped away from her, she found she was a bit lost.

"I'm sorry, Louise. That should never have happened," George told her.

"Are you really sorry?" she asked a bit breathlessly as she stared up at him.

He looked down at her in the moonlight and found himself smiling gently at her. "No. No, I'm not sorry. I've wanted to do that for some time now, but . . ."

"I know," Louise said a bit sadly. "It's hard to allow ourselves any bit of happiness while we're worrying about Marissa."

"But we both know that at some point we have to go on with our lives."

They fell silent, standing together there at the porch railing surrounded by the West Texas night.

"Tell me about yourself," Louise finally said. "Here I am, living in your home, taking advantage of your wonderful hospitality, and I know so little about you—only what Marissa told me." She smiled up at him as she remembered. "Marissa said you were—and I quote—wonderful and perfect and the best uncle in the whole world."

He returned her smile as he imagined his niece saying that. "She's one special girl. But considering that I'm her only uncle, there wasn't a lot of competition." He paused, then went on, "There's not much to tell about me. I was married many years ago, but my wife, Julie, died in childbirth. The baby, too."

"I'm sorry."

"It was a rough time for me, but it's been almost twenty years now." It surprised George to realize that he didn't think of Julie very often anymore. He supposed it was true that time was a great healer. "Since then I've just concentrated on building up the Crown."

"Well, you've done a magnificent job. It's a wonderful ranch."

"I'm proud of it."

"Marissa told me West Texas would grow on me, and she was right." As she thought of Marissa again, her smile faltered.

"What about you, Louise?" George asked, wanting to distract her. "I know so little about you. Were you ever married?"

"No—although I was engaged once, but then I found out that he was only marrying me for my money, so I broke off the engagement. My parents left me a substantial inheritance. Now I spend most of my time working for social causes and helping the poor."

"You're a very special woman, Louise."

At his gentle words, she looked up at him again and was mesmerized by the look in his eyes. "Thank you."

George really wanted to kiss her again, but knew he should wait. With an effort, he forced himself to be a gentleman.

"Well, it's getting late. I guess we should call it a night," he said.

Louise had been hoping that he might kiss her again, and she had to fight to hide her disappointment. "You go on in. I'm going to stay out here a little while longer."

"All right. If you need anything, just let me know."

She wanted to tell him that she needed him to kiss her, but the thought so surprised her that she only nodded in response. When George had gone inside, Louise stood there alone, wondering what had come over her.

She had always been prim and proper. She was a lady. Why was she thinking about George this way?

Louise frowned into the darkness, even as she remembered his embrace, and she smiled a bit. His kiss had certainly been wonderful. And he was so strong and so supportive, not to mention handsome.

For the first time in all the weeks she'd been there, her heart lightened a bit.

* * *

George lay in his bed angry with himself for having been so forward with Louise. He did not want to take advantage of her in any way, but at the time kissing her had seemed so right. And it had certainly felt right.

He rolled over and sought sleep, but the memory of how wonderful she'd felt in his arms was burned into his consciousness. Louise had been with him on the ranch for weeks now, and he'd discovered that he liked having her there. She was a calming presence, a gentle woman. She was pretty, too, there was no denying that. George thanked God that she had made a full recovery from her wound.

He thought of Marissa then. He missed his niece, longed to have her there with him, too. She had suffered so much losing her father, and then to have witnessed the horror of the raid and been taken by Comanche . . .

Happy memories of Marissa played in his mind, and he smiled in the darkness. She had been a beautiful little girl, and she'd grown into an even more beautiful woman. He prayed Marissa would come back to him. He vowed that if she did, he would protect her and make sure she was never in any danger again.

Sleep was long in coming for George that night.

Chapter Nineteen

Laughing Woman was devastated by the loss of her husband. She mourned him deeply. The only good she could find in all that had happened was that Wind Ryder was gone. It did not matter that he had taken the other whites with him. They meant nothing. Wind Ryder had been the one to cause all the trouble for Bear Claw, and now they were rid of him.

"Laughing Woman!"

She heard another woman call her name from outside her lodge, and she got up to see who wanted her.

"What is it?" she asked as she found Soaring Dove waiting there for her.

"It is Bear Claw—"

"What about my son?" Laughing Woman

frowned. Was something wrong? She knew the young woman cared for Bear Claw.

"He is getting ready to leave the village."

"Why?"

Soaring Dove looked nervous as she spoke, but she had to tell Laughing Woman. "Bear Claw is still angry with Wind Ryder. He says he wants to get his captive back."

Laughing Woman was instantly furious with her son. Wind Ryder was gone! Bear Claw should have been jubilant, not angry over a stolen captive. She was going to find him and tell him so.

"Where is he now?"

"By the horses," Soaring Dove told her.

Without another word, Laughing Woman hurried off to confront her son. She reached him just as he was about to leave.

"Bear Claw! I must speak to you!"

When Bear Claw looked at her, Laughing Woman could see the rage within him.

"What do you want, Mother?" He was irritated by her interference.

"Where are you going?"

"It is none of your concern where I am going, woman. I am no youth to be watched over and coddled," Bear Claw snapped, wishing she would go away and leave him to his plan.

Laughing Woman was hurt and infuriated by his dismissal of her. "You are my son. We have just buried your father. He has been dead only two days, and now *you* want to leave me, too?"

"There is something I must do," he told her seriously.

"Are you going after Wind Ryder?"

"Yes. There is much I have to settle with him."

"You are wrong! There is nothing for you to settle with him. He is gone! That was always our hope—that he would leave, and he finally has. Why do you chase after him? Your father's vision was right! There can be peace in the village now that Wind Ryder is no longer here."

"There can be no peace for me," Bear Claw said angrily. "He has stolen that which is mine! I will have the captive back!"

"Let them go! The whites have caused nothing but trouble for us here in the village. We are well rid of them. You are a fine and mighty warrior. There is no need for you to go after Wind Ryder!"

"There is every need, Mother," he said tersely. The humiliation he had suffered at Wind Ryder's hands through the years had only intensified after Wind Ryder had taken the boy from him in front of the entire village. He had waited a day to mourn his father's death, but now he would find his enemy and seek his revenge.

"You have nothing to prove!" Laughing Woman insisted, her desperation growing. She feared that if he left her, he might never come back.

"I have everything to prove," he said, swinging up on his horse's back.

"Bear Claw—my son—you should stay here and celebrate your newfound peace. There is no need for you to go after him."

"Out of my way, woman," Bear Claw ordered coldly.

He felt no tender emotion for his mother as he wheeled his mount around and galloped away. He needed no nagging woman trying to keep him from his destiny.

Wind Ryder had stolen his captive. Everyone in the tribe had seen it.

Too many times he had suffered embarrassment at Wind Ryder's hands. He was going to hunt Wind Ryder down. And he was going to kill him. And the boy. And Crazy One.

And Shining Spirit, too—but only after he'd had his way with her.

Bear Claw was smiling as he raced off, following Wind Ryder's trail.

"The ranch is west of Dry Springs," Marissa told Wind Ryder. "About an hour's ride out of town. Have you been there before? Do you know the area?"

Wind Ryder nodded. "The tribe has traveled that way. It will be a long trip."

"That doesn't matter," she said, smiling at him. "What matters is that we're going."

Wind Ryder stared at her, seeing the delight in her smile. He had always thought her lovely, but she had never seemed more beautiful to him than she did now. She truly was a shining spirit. His father had been very wise in naming her.

At that moment, Wind Ryder had a great desire to rein in and pull Shining Spirit from her horse. He longed to make love to her right there in broad daylight in the middle of the countryside. He fought down the impulse. It would be a little difficult to do with Crazy One and Joe looking on.

Wind Ryder started to smile at the thought, but stopped. It was then he realized that they might never make love again.

Everything was different now that they had left the village. He had protected Shining Spirit by claiming her as his wife, but soon she would no longer need his protection. He was taking her home—back to her own people. They would never be alone again.

He scowled, wondering what he would do after he had seen her safely home.

Marissa had been watching him, and she saw the change in his expression.

"Are you sorry we left the village?" she asked. She feared he was regretting his decision.

"No. All is as it should be," he answered without emotion. He did not want to betray the turmoil and pain that had arisen within him at the thought of never knowing her love again.

Wind Ryder did not want to talk anymore. He kneed his horse and rode ahead, leaving the rest of them to follow. In the mood he was in, he did not want to be too close to Shining Spirit. He needed to keep some distance between them.

Joe was unaware of Wind Ryder's mood. He had come to admire Wind Ryder greatly, and he wanted to stay by his side all the time. He hurried to catch up with him.

"Wind Ryder—" Joe looked up at him as he reached Wind Ryder's horse's side.

Wind Ryder glanced at the youth.

"Thanks for helping me get away," Joe said.

He hadn't had time to talk with Wind Ryder much or to get to know him. He was still feeling the pain of his injuries, but just being away from the Comanche village had lifted his spirits, so he could ignore the physical discomfort.

"It is good that we are gone from the village," Wind Ryder said. "There will be peace now."

"How long did you have to stay there? It musta been awful for you," the boy said, unable to imagine spending years with the Comanche. Just the short time he'd spent with them had been hell. He couldn't imagine how Wind Ryder and Crazy One had managed to survive.

"I was brought to the village when I was six," he answered.

"Were you scared like me?"

"Yes. It was not an easy time."

"Did you want to go home?" Joe shuddered at

the thought of being forced to spend the rest of his life with the Comanche.

"I tried to run away, but each time they found me and brought me back."

"Well, they aren't gonna find you and take you back this time," Joe said with confidence. "You don't ever have to go there anymore. Now you can go home, just like me."

Wind Ryder was almost certain he knew what the boy was going to find when they returned, but he said nothing. At least Joe was still alive. If he'd remained Bear Claw's captive much longer, there was no telling what torture the other warrior would have inflicted on the boy.

"How come your name's Wind Ryder?" Joe asked with a child's curiosity.

"Chief Ten Crow called me that because I could ride like the wind," he answered simply.

"Really?" Joe's eyes rounded in awe. "I want to be a good rider like you some day."

"You will be," Wind Ryder said with confidence.

The boy beamed up at him as they continued on.

Bear Claw rode hard as he followed the tracks of his quarry. It was good that Wind Ryder was not trying to hide his trail. It made what he planned to do very simple. True, he was a full day behind Wind Ryder, but with any luck, he would catch up to him soon.

The warrior's smile was feral as he thought of the pleasure he would get out of killing Wind Ryder. He had hated him from the moment his father had taken him into their family all those years ago. Bear Claw had been the oldest, and yet his father had always favored Wind Ryder.

The rage Bear Claw had harbored for all these years was now full-blown. Soon Wind Ryder would cower in submission before him. Soon Wind Ryder would die by his hand.

Just thinking about having that much power over Wind Ryder gave Bear Claw a rush of intense satisfaction, and the thought that Shining Spirit would be watching all the while made him feel even more powerful.

Soon he would find them.

Very soon.

Wind Ryder was still awake long after everyone else had fallen asleep. He lay unmoving, staring up at the star-studded night sky.

His thoughts were troubled, for it would not be long until they reached the white world, and it was then that he would have to begin thinking of himself as Zach again. It would not be easy.

Disturbed, Wind Ryder faced the truth: He was alone. His family had been murdered. And now Ten Crow was dead, too.

Wind Ryder had been forced to become self-sufficient. He had not allowed himself to care for anyone until now—until Shining Spirit. And he did care about her deeply, but he knew they could have no future together. She was excited about returning to the white world, but he had heard how the whites treated returning captives. He would do her more harm than good if he stayed with her. Though his skin might be white, they would always look upon him as a Comanche warrior.

More than anything, Wind Ryder wanted Shining Spirit to be safe and happy again. She had made it clear she wanted to return to the life she was accustomed to. He had nothing to offer her, and he had no idea what his future held. She would be better off without him.

Wind Ryder shifted to his side, and he immediately regretted his action, for there, directly in his line of vision, was Shining Spirit. She was sleeping just across the campfire from him. She was close—so very close.

Biting back a growl of frustration, Wind Ryder rolled back over. He was glad the others were sound sleepers or he would have awakened them by now with all his tossing and turning. He glanced back at Shining Spirit once more and could see that she slept peacefully next to Crazy One, completely unaware of his tormented thoughts.

Frustrated, Wind Ryder got up and moved silently out of the glow of the campfire. It was going to be a long night. He would regret the lack of sleep the next day, but he could not force slumber to come. He sat down some distance away with his back to the campsite; there was no reason to continue to torture himself by watching her sleep.

Marissa did not know what had disturbed her rest, but she awoke sensing that something wasn't right. She immediately noticed that Wind Ryder was gone. Worried, she got up to look for him.

She moved quietly, not wanting to wake the others. It didn't take her long to find him.

Wind Ryder sensed someone behind him and turned to find Shining Spirit making her way toward him. His expression was intense as he watched her. Cast in a golden glow by the low-burning campfire, she was a vision of loveliness.

"Is something wrong?" she asked softly.

"No. Nothing's wrong. Go back to sleep," he answered tersely as he stood up.

"You look worried." Marissa went to him.

Before he could move away from her, she put her arms around him and started to kiss him. At the touch of her lips, Wind Ryder tensed. He took her by the upper arms and held her away from him.

Marissa was stunned by his move. He had never treated her this way before. The change in him troubled her. He seemed so distant to her—so cold.

Before she could say anything more, the sound of Joe's worried call rent the night. "Wind Ryder?"

"We'd better go back," Wind Ryder told her, grateful for the boy's interruption.

He turned away from her and went back to where the boy was bedded down.

"Are you all right?" he asked Joe as he knelt down beside him.

Joe nodded sleepily. "Now that you're here, I am. I was worried about you 'cause you were gone. I was scared."

"I'm here."

Joe yawned and, secure once more, let his eyes drift shut.

Wind Ryder glanced at Shining Spirit; she had already lain down on her own blankets next to Crazy One, her back to him.

Wind Ryder did not try to sleep. There was no point. He returned to sit in the darkness alone. Peace was not his that night.

Marissa lay awake, trying to understand what had been troubling Wind Ryder. He had acted so strangely, putting her from him. She glanced toward where he should have been bedded down, but he was not there. He had gone off into the night again. For a moment, she considered going after him again, but she didn't. He obviously needed some time by himself.

Closing her eyes, she sought sleep. Her last thought as she drifted off was of the pleasure she always found in Wind Ryder's arms.

Chapter Twenty

"Wind Ryder is in a strange mood today," Marissa remarked to Crazy One as they watched him and Joe riding ahead of them the following day. He had had little to say to either one of them that morning.

"Yes, his mood is strange," Crazy One agreed. "Perhaps he is afraid."

"Wind Ryder? Afraid?" Marissa was shocked by the very idea. He was fearless and brave. She couldn't imagine that anything could trouble him, but then she remembered how she'd found him awake and sitting alone in the middle of the night. She realized Crazy One might be right.

"I am frightened. Aren't you?"

"No. I'm excited. I can't wait to get to my uncle's ranch. Don't be afraid. I'll be with you to help you."

"But all the whites will hate us now."

"No, they won't."

"Yes, they will. We are squaw women. They will think we are lower than dogs," Crazy One warned her.

Marissa had been thinking only of the joy of being reunited with her uncle, but now she faced an ugly truth she hadn't considered.

The whites would think her a ruined woman.

"I don't think it will be that terrible," Marissa said hesitantly.

"There will be some who will want us dead."

"It doesn't matter what they want, and we don't care what they think," Marissa said, realizing she truly didn't care what anybody thought of her. "The only thing that matters is that we are free again."

"Yes, we are," Crazy One agreed, an almost dreamy look coming into her eyes. She had never thought she would live to see the day.

Marissa admired her strength. "I don't know how you managed it—being all by yourself in the village for so many years."

"It was not easy, but once they thought I was crazy, they left me alone."

"Well, I just thank heaven that Wind Ryder is taking us back. Even if the whites do consider me an outcast, I'd rather be an outcast in the white world than a slave in a Comanche tribe."

"Slave?" Crazy One looked at her, a bit confused. "You were not Wind Ryder's slave. You are his wife."

"What?" Complete shock stunned Marissa to silence.

Crazy One saw the younger woman's look of surprise. "He did not tell you?"

"Tell me what?"

"After your fight with Moon Cloud, he claimed you as his wife to keep you safe. No one would dare harm the wife of one of the tribe's fiercest warriors. It was a fine thing for Wind Ryder to do—protecting you that way."

The whole time Crazy One was talking, Marissa's mind was racing. Wind Ryder had claimed her as his wife?

"It does not matter that he did not tell you. What matters is that he kept you safe."

Marissa looked at Wind Ryder as he rode so proudly and confidently ahead of them. He was a tall and powerful warrior. And, according to Crazy One, he was her husband.

"You have come to love him, haven't you?" Crazy One asked.

Love him? Marissa asked herself. Did she love him?

Why else would she have given herself to him with such abandon? Why else would his kiss and caress leave her weak with wanting him?

"Many women wanted to be Wind Ryder's wife," Crazy One went on, "but you were the one he chose." She smiled at her, thinking Shining Spirit would be happy about the news.

"I—I have to talk to Wind Ryder."

Marissa's thoughts and emotions were in turmoil as she put her heels to her horse's sides and rode to catch up with him. It seemed so clear to her now. She loved him—he had protected her—he had saved her—and now he was taking her home. She was ready to tell him of her love for him, but first she wanted to know why he hadn't told her of their marriage.

"Joe, I need to speak with Wind Ryder alone for a moment."

The boy was surprised, but reined in and fell back to ride with Crazy One. Crazy One made sure they stayed a good distance back.

Wind Ryder looked at Shining Spirit. He could see that she appeared upset about something, and he wondered what could be wrong.

"Crazy One just told me that we're married. Is that true?"

In her heart, she was hoping he would declare his love for her. She waited almost breathlessly for his answer.

Wind Ryder had never intended for her to learn that he had taken her as his wife in the tribe. He was glad that she was angry, for he needed to put distance between them. It was going to hurt him to face her, but he was doing it for her own good.

"I claimed you as my wife to keep you safe while

we were in the village, but you are not bound to me in any way. A Comanche marriage means nothing in your world."

Marissa had expected declarations of love and devotion. She stared at him, her expression frozen. She couldn't believe their loving had meant so little to him.

"Did you really take me as your wife to protect me—or just so no other warrior could have me?" she challenged angrily.

"I did not force you. You came to me willingly."

His statements were cold, and her heartbreak and misery were complete. What they'd shared had only been sex to him. She could never let him know that it had meant much more to her.

"I had no choice," she said. "I did what had I to do to survive—to stay alive."

Wind Ryder's mood turned black as he recognized his own words—his own desperation from his early days as a captive. She had submitted to him because she had had no other choice. She had surrendered to him out of fear. She thought of him just as he knew all the others would once they reached the white world.

To Shining Spirit, he would always be a Comanche warrior.

"I will see you to your uncle, and then I will take care of Crazy One and Joe."

Wind Ryder did not know what he would do

once he'd made sure the captives were safe and settled.

He didn't belong in either world—Comanche or white.

He would truly be alone.

Marissa said nothing more, but slowed her horse's pace. She almost wished that Crazy One wasn't there, for she didn't want to speak with anyone. But she took her place by the old woman's side, while Joe returned to ride with Wind Ryder.

"All is well with Wind Ryder?" Crazy One asked.

"Yes," was all she answered.

Crazy One was curious about their conversation and glanced at Shining Spirit. The younger woman's dark expression surprised her. As a warrior's wife—especially Wind Ryder's—she should have been proud. Crazy One wondered what had transpired between them, but she did not ask.

Bear Claw's rage drove him relentlessly. He was glad Wind Ryder had the women and the boy with him. It slowed his pace and made him more vulnerable. He could tell their tracks were fresher, that he was closing in. If all went as he hoped, he would catch up with them that very night. The anticipation excited him.

The day passed quickly for Wind Ryder. There wasn't a lot of conversation, but Marissa did speak of how her uncle had worked to establish his ranch and make it a success.

Joe told them about his family and their spread near Sidewinder.

Wind Ryder and the women shared a pained look, thinking about what the boy was going to face when they found out the truth, hoping someone in his family had survived.

Crazy One remained quiet. The years of living in fear and misery with the Comanche had taken their toll on her. Fear was eating at her, and she still had trouble believing they were going back. It would be a difficult transition for her. She just hoped that once they were among the whites, she would find some measure of peace.

Wind Ryder glanced over at the older woman and saw her troubled, haggard expression. He had always known that life was hard for her in the village, but for the first time now, he realized how strong a woman she was to have survived her captivity. He had never forgotten the savage beating she'd gotten for trying to take care of him as a child.

"Everything will be all right," he said to her.

Crazy One glanced at him.

Their gazes met, and the fear in her eyes faded.

"You would not lie to me." It was a statement of fact. She trusted him.

"No."

For the first time in many years, she smiled at him.

The smile touched his heart, and he smiled back. He was going to do everything he could to make life better for her.

Wind Ryder glanced at Shining Spirit. She had said little directly to him, and he doubted that she ever would again. He had wanted to distance himself from her. He knew it was best to let her go. But he wondered if he could bear the pain.

They made camp near a small stream that night. They had covered a good distance, and they all were tired. They fell asleep quickly, even Wind Ryder. His lack of rest the night before had taken its toll on him.

Bear Claw knew he was closing on Wind Ryder. He was about to bed down for the night when he caught sight of the glow of a campfire ahead in the distance. Leaving his horse behind, he moved forward on foot. He did not want to risk making any sound that would alert Wind Ryder to his presence.

He was certain Wind Ryder had no idea he was being followed. The thought left him smiling. He wanted that element of surprise.

Bear Claw went close enough to see the four people bedded down around the fire.

An immense feeling of power overcame him. He would kill Wind Ryder first, then worry about the others.

* * *

Crazy One did not know what had awakened her from her sound sleep. There were many nights when she woke up and lay for hours, unable to rest. She didn't bother to stir or get up. There was nowhere to go. It would be dangerous to wander around in the wilderness this late at night. She glanced at the fire, but it was still burning, so there was no need for her to tend to it. She tried to relax. She closed her eyes again.

And then she heard it—

The sound of a small rock dislodged in the distance.

Crazy One held her breath. She knew it might be nothing more than an animal hunting in the night, but the chill that shivered up her spine warned her otherwise. She waited, wishing she had a weapon close at hand. Ever so cautiously, she turned her head to look out into the darkness in the direction the sound had come from.

The light of the campfire glinted off a gun barrel, aimed in their direction.

"Wind Ryder!" The scream erupted from her just as the first shot was fired.

He reacted instantly. He threw himself sideways and, by a miracle, avoided being shot dead as he slept. The rifle bullet slammed into his blankets. Wind Ryder grabbed up his gun and dove into the darkness for cover.

Marissa and Joe were both shocked from their

sleep by Crazy One's warning shout and the gunshot. Joe scrambled away into the night, all the horrors of the Comanche raid on his home fueling his mindless panic.

"Run!" Crazy One was shouting as she herself started to flee.

Bear Claw was furious at the old woman's interference. In that moment, he had never hated anyone as much as he hated her. He knew what he was going to do. He took careful aim.

Crazy One was turning, ready to follow Joe, as the second shot rang out. The bullet tore through her. She cried out in a bloodcurdling scream that rent the night. She looked once toward Marissa as she collapsed to the ground.

Marissa was horrified by what she'd just witnessed.

First Louise—

Now Crazy One—

Time seemed to pass in slow motion as she turned toward the older woman, wanting to help her.

She heard the sound of someone running toward her and thought it was Wind Ryder.

He would come to save her.

He would help her.

And then she looked up.

Horror unlike anything she'd ever felt before filled her at the sight of Bear Claw charging toward her.

Chapter Twenty-one

"No!"

Bear Claw was there before she could grab her knife. In a violent, punishing move, he jerked Shining Spirit to her feet. He pinned her savagely against his chest and held his knife to her throat as he backed away to stand before some rocks. He didn't want to give Wind Ryder the chance to sneak up on him from behind.

It would have been a simple thing to shoot her down like Crazy One, but he wanted Wind Ryder to suffer.

Marissa tried to fight him.

He jerked her even more tightly against him and pressed the sharp blade harder against her throat. A line of blood appeared on her fair skin.

She went still.

Bear Claw chuckled evilly in her ear. He lifted his gaze to stare out into the night. Wind Ryder was out there somewhere watching, and Bear Claw planned to give him quite a show.

"Well, *brother,* where are you? Can you not show your face? Or are you too afraid of me now?"

"I fear no coward." Wind Ryder's voice echoed through the night.

Bear Claw glanced around but couldn't determine where the voice had come from. "Show yourself or watch your woman die!"

Silence reigned as Bear Claw waited and listened. He felt no fear of Wind Ryder. He had Shining Spirit. There was no way Wind Ryder could take a shot at him and not hit her. He was safe.

Wind Ryder would have to come out—

And when he did—

Bear Claw pressed the knife harder against her throat, wanting to encourage Wind Ryder to take action. He smiled at Shining Spirit's whimper. The power he had over her made him feel invincible.

"Wind Ryder! You hide in the darkness. Shall I go ahead and slit Shining Spirit's throat as I did your dog's?" he called out. "Your dog did not fight much. Do you think your woman will?"

Wind Ryder's blood ran cold at Bear Claw's words. Hidden in the darkness with Joe huddled by his side, he watched and waited for a chance to make his move against the man he'd once considered a brother. He knew Bear Claw's threats were real, and he knew he had to take action. He could not let Shining Spirit suffer at this man's hands. His grip tightened on his rifle.

Joe looked up at Wind Ryder, his expression questioning as he waited for his hero to save Shining Spirit. Wind Ryder picked up a stone and handed it to the boy, motioning for him to throw it to the far side of the campsite on his signal. The boy nodded in understanding, ready to do whatever he could to help.

Marissa could feel the blood seeping from the mark Bear Claw had made on her neck, and she was desperate for some way to help Wind Ryder. He was out there watching. She knew he was trying to save her.

Her only hope was her knife. Bear Claw didn't know she had it. The way Bear Claw was holding her with one arm across her chest, pinning her against him, her lower arms and hands were free. If she could pretend to sag weakly just a bit and somehow manage to get a hand on her weapon, she might be able to stab him. Then she could get away, and Wind Ryder would be able to get a clear shot at him.

The pain of the knife on her throat convinced her to take the chance.

Marissa readied herself.

"Wind Ryder! Are you too afraid to show yourself?" Bear Claw called out. "Are you mourning Crazy One? I enjoyed watching Father beat her whenever she was kind to you. There were times when I would chase her down and hit her myself. She is dead now."

Marissa did not understand what Bear Claw was saying in the Comanche tongue, but she could restrain herself no longer from trying to get away. She let herself go limp for an instant and snatched the knife from her waistband.

Bear Claw shifted his hold on her, trying to tighten his grip, as Wind Ryder ordered Joe to throw the rock.

At the sound of the rock tumbling in the distance, Bear Claw turned in that direction, expecting to see Wind Ryder.

Marissa knew the time was right, and she attacked. With all the force she could muster, she swung her lower arm back, stabbing at any part of his body she could reach. She heard him grunt in pain as she buried the knife in his thigh. For an instant, his hold on her loosened. She jerked free and threw herself to the ground.

In that moment, Wind Ryder's shot rang out in the night.

Bear Claw stood motionless for an instant, his expression one of disbelief as he stared in the direction the shot had come from. His knife dropped from his hand. Blood poured from the knife wound on his thigh and from the bullet wound in his chest.

Wind Ryder stood and showed himself.

Across the distance in the pale light of the campfire, their gazes met and locked.

"Wind Ryder—" The name was a curse on his lips as Bear Claw crumpled to the ground.

Dead.

Wind Ryder ran forward, rifle in hand. He could think of nothing except getting to Bear Claw and making sure he was dead. He knelt beside him and turned him over. He stared down into the face of the man he had come to hate. He did not understand how a man like Bear Claw could be born of a father like Ten Crow. It saddened him to know that he had taken his life, but Bear Claw had left him no choice. It had been kill or be killed.

Certain at last that Bear Claw would never harm anyone again, Wind Ryder stood up and went to Shining Spirit.

"Are you all right?" Wind Ryder asked, his voice gruff. He wanted to hold her, to tell her of his feelings, but he held himself back.

"Yes," she answered tightly, the injury to her neck very slight. She wanted to go into his arms and stay there for eternity, but she knew it wasn't to be. Instead, she looked worriedly for the boy. "Where's Joe?"

Joe came out of hiding when he heard them talking.

"She's dead," Joe said, staring down at Crazy One, who lay unmoving.

Marissa and Wind Ryder hurried to console him.

"Are you all right?" Marissa asked Joe, worried about him. He was so young to have witnessed so much death.

"Yes—I think so," Joe said hoarsely. "Crazy One saved us." He looked up at them. "She saved all of us."

"Yes, she did," Wind Ryder answered.

He knelt beside the old woman and took her lifeless hand in his. He was tormented by the promise he'd made to her that very afternoon. He had told her everything was going to be all right. He had believed they would be safe on the trip to the ranch. He had never suspected that Bear Claw would come after them. He had never thought he was putting her in any danger.

Guilt and anger assailed Wind Ryder.

He had promised Crazy One a better life, and now she was dead.

Marissa was as torn by the older woman's death as he was. She did not understand why fate had spared her again. The only thing that kept her from breaking down was her firm belief that there was a better life after this one—that Crazy One would find peace in heaven—far more peace than she'd ever known on Earth. There, she would at last be reunited with her family.

"Oh, Crazy One, I'm so sorry."

Marissa gave vent to her tears.

Wind Ryder almost took her in his arms, but he stopped himself.

"What are we gonna do?" Joe asked. He was trying to be brave, but he was visibly shaking. He looked around nervously. "Are there any more Comanche coming after us?"

Marissa went to hug the boy.

Wind Ryder shook his head. "Bear Claw came alone. He is dead. There will be no more bloodshed."

Joe looked relieved.

"You did a fine job," Wind Ryder praised him. "Without your help, I might not have been able to get off that shot."

The boy brightened a bit at the praise. "Can we go home now?"

His question was so pitiful, it tore at Wind Ryder.

"Yes, Joe. We're going home."

Wind Ryder hoped, for the boy's sake, that when they got back they would discover he had a home to go to.

They did not sleep the rest of the night.

Marissa tended to Joe, trying to calm and reassure him, while Wind Ryder buried Crazy One and Bear Claw.

At first light, Wind Ryder rode out to look for Bear Claw's horse. It was a fine animal. When he found it, he was tempted for a moment to take the mount for Joe, but then changed his mind and turned it loose. He wanted no reminders of the man who'd tried to kill them while they slept.

He returned to the campsite, and they said their final good-byes to Crazy One. They stood over her grave, and Marissa offered up a prayer.

Joe looked up at her when they'd finished praying.

"We never knew her real name," he said sadly, tears welling up in his eyes.

"I know it," Wind Ryder said softly.

They both looked at him expectantly.

"When I first came to the village, I remember she told me her name was Elizabeth."

"Elizabeth," Marissa whispered as she gave Joe a loving hug.

They stood over her grave a little longer, then Wind Ryder quietly went to get their horses.

His mood was dark. Any connection he'd had to the tribe had died with Crazy One and Bear Claw. He was leaving that part of his life behind forever.

He led the horses back to where the others were waiting for him, eager to leave this place of heartache.

"Let's go home, Wind Ryder," Marissa said wearily.

"From now on, my name is Zach, Marissa," he told her.

She was startled, but as their gazes met, she understood. "Let's go home, Zach."

They mounted up and rode for the Crown Ranch.

The terror of the night had taken its toll on Marissa. She had honestly believed that things were going to be all right for all of them—that they were all going to find happiness once they returned to the white world. But now Crazy One—Elizabeth—was dead. Marissa wondered what else the future held for them.

Zach looked back toward the graves one last time. Sorrow filled him. He had wanted to protect Crazy One, and yet she had been the one to protect him—just as she had when he'd first come to the village.

He turned away and stared out across the wide expanse of land. His future lay somewhere out there before him. He kneed his horse to a quicker pace. He was done with the past.

The days and miles passed slowly.

At first, Marissa couldn't stop looking back, fearful someone else might be following them. but with each passing mile she grew calmer, and her spirits lightened as they shortened the distance to her uncle's ranch. At the ranch, she would find peace.

Marissa was proud of how well Joe was handling himself. She prayed that they would find a way to put his life back together. He had already suffered enough.

Marissa often found herself watching Joe and thinking that Zach must have been much like him as a boy. She was glad that they had gotten Joe away from the village so quickly. Life had been hard on him, but not as hard as it had been on Zach.

The days and nights were difficult for Marissa. As angry as she'd been with Zach, she could not forget the intimacy they'd shared. Nor could she forget that he had taken her as his wife to protect her and now he had given up everything—his whole life—to see her home.

They had been traveling for two weeks when one night, as they were getting ready to bed down, Zach came to her.

"We passed near the way station where you were taken captive today," he told her.

"We're that close to Dry Springs?" Marissa asked excitedly.

"Yes. We should be at your uncle's ranch very soon."

"That's wonderful," she said as a torrent of emotion tore through her.

"It will be good to see you returned to your family."

He stood there staring at her. The last thing he wanted to do was give her over to her family. What he really wanted was to take her in his arms and kiss her and know the beauty of her love again.

But since the day of their confrontation, everything had changed between them. He had never dreamed it would be so difficult to be with her, and watch her, and want her, and yet have to stay away from her.

"If only—" she began, then stopped, knowing there was no point in speaking of Louise again. She couldn't change what had happened. She could only pick up the pieces of her life and try to go on. But at least she was going on—in the white world, and it was all thanks to Zach. She looked up at him, a myriad of emotions showing in her eyes. "Thank you."

He managed to nod in response, then turned away to busy himself with Joe.

Marissa lay down. She was exhausted from the long days of riding, but this night, sleep would not come. As much as she tried to fight them and keep them at bay, memories of the raid tormented her. The turmoil kept her tossing and turning long into the night. It wasn't until the early morning that she finally drifted off. Her sleep was filled with disturbing visions of violence and death.

Chapter Twenty-two

"You're sure you want to do this?" George asked Louise as they rode away from the ranch.

"I'm sure," she answered with conviction.

George nodded and said nothing more for the time being. He'd learned what a fighter she was. Her recovery had been amazing. He'd been even more impressed when she'd asked him the week before to teach her how to ride astride. Louise had been a quick study and had already mastered the technique on the quiet mare he'd given her. But her request this morning had still shocked him.

Louise was aware of George's silence and wondered if it meant disapproval. "I have to do this, George. I have to make sure I can take care of myself. I don't ever want to be afraid again."

George wanted to tell her that he would take

care of her, but he knew she wasn't ready to hear that yet.

"All right, we'll start with a handgun, and once you've mastered that, we'll practice with a rifle."

She nodded her approval. "Good. And, George—"

He looked over at her.

"Thanks for taking me seriously."

"Most of the women who live out here know how to use a gun, so it's good that you're interested in learning," he said.

They rode on companionably to a place down by the creek where he figured it was safe enough for her to start practicing. They reined in there and dismounted, tying up their horses.

George took out the handgun he'd brought along in his saddlebag and the tin cans she'd use for targets. He checked to make sure the gun was loaded.

"Let me set up these cans, and we'll see what you can do," he said.

They walked to a fallen tree and he lined the tin cans up along the trunk. Moving back a ways, he handed the sidearm to her.

"Be careful, it's loaded."

"It's heavy." Louise was surprised by the weight of the weapon.

"You can use two hands if you need to."

"No, I'm going to learn to do this right. There wouldn't have been time during the raid to worry about aiming with both hands. I've got to get good at this."

"All right, let's see what you can do."

George went to stand behind her. He lifted her arm to help her take aim.

"Just remember to squeeze the trigger slowly," he advised, trying to ignore the scent of her perfume as it drifted around him.

A shiver trembled through Louise at his touch. She told herself it was because she was nervous. But it did feel wonderful to have George standing so close to her. She thought fleetingly of the kiss they'd shared, then remembered the purpose of their excursion. This was no time to think about kissing. She needed to learn how to use a gun—and not just for target practice.

Louise took her time as she aimed at a can. She got off her first shot. It went wide, not even coming close to the can.

"Oh, no. I'm horrible at this! I missed all of them by a mile!" she cried in embarrassment.

"It wasn't quite that bad."

"No wonder you brought me out here so far away from everything. If we'd tried this near the house, I might have shot somebody." She had to laugh.

"Let's try it again," George said, smiling. She was only partly right about why he'd brought her away from the house. The truth was, he'd wanted some time alone with her, and this seemed the perfect place. "It's not easy. It takes a lot of practice and a lot of patience to get it right."

"I'm ready. I've waited too long as it is." Louise turned back to look at the cans. Her expression grew serious. There was an almost deadly glint in her eyes.

George understood her mood. Once more he went to stand behind her. This time he leaned in even closer to help improve her aim. Again he forced himself to ignore her sweet perfume and the soft press of her body against him. It wasn't easy.

"What do you think?" Louise asked.

"You're fine. Go ahead and shoot," he told her, but he wondered what she would have thought if she'd known exactly what he was thinking just then.

Louise fired and came much closer this time.

"Is the third time the charm?" she asked over her shoulder, not quite as embarrassed as the last time, but still not satisfied with her performance.

"Let's find out," George said encouragingly, stepping back. "Why don't you try it on your own?"

He didn't want to tempt himself too much. She was a lady, and it was broad daylight.

Louise was fiercely determined. With utmost care she took aim at the tin can and pulled the trigger.

The can went flying.

"I did it!" Louise cried out in complete and utter surprise.

She wheeled around and threw her arms about George, taking care to keep the gun pointed away from both of them.

He was a bit taken aback by her display of excitement, but enjoyed every moment of it. This was the first time he had seen her truly happy.

As he gazed down at her, the mood between them suddenly changed.

"Yes," he said solemnly, "you did do it."

George had never expected to fall in love again. After the death of his wife and child, he'd deliberately kept himself so busy with building up the ranch that he'd never thought about getting seriously involved with another woman.

And now Louise had come into his life.

Every day George gave thanks that she'd survived the Comanche raid. He still remembered how she'd looked when he'd seen her at the doctor's office that first day. She had looked so beautiful, so fragile, so delicate, but he had learned what a strong woman she was. Now that she was back in good health, he found himself fearing that she might start making plans to return to New Orleans. He decided it was time to let her know the truth of what he was feeling for her—that he'd fallen in love with her.

Ever so slowly, George lowered his head and kissed her.

* * *

"Are we there yet?" Joe asked. The seemingly endless days on the trail were wearing on him.

"Not yet, but we're getting close," Zach told him.

"How much farther do we have to go?" Joe asked.

"We should be there very soon, maybe even today," Marissa said, even more eager than he was to reach the ranch.

"Today? Really?" He looked over at her, his eyes wide with excitement.

"Really," she answered, smiling at him.

Marissa could only imagine how wonderful it was going to feel to see her uncle again. Overnight, she had managed to deal with all the horrible memories of the raid and Louise's death.

Marissa missed Louise terribly. If there were some way to turn back time and change everything that had happened that day, she would have done it, but there wasn't. She couldn't change the past. With an effort, she fought back the sorrow that threatened to overwhelm her.

This was to be a happy time.

She was almost home.

It was then they heard gunshots echoing in the distance.

"What's happening?" Marissa reined in and looked at Zach worriedly.

"I don't know," he answered, studying the horizon. He wasn't sure what they might be riding into. "Stay here. I'll go see."

"Be careful," she said nervously. She knew how any white in the area would react to seeing him.

"Who do you think it is, Marissa?" Joe asked.

"It's probably just some folks out hunting. Zach will check for us."

"White people?" The boy's expression grew hopeful.

"Yes. Why?"

Before she could say more, Joe turned his horse and urged it to a run, galloping after Zach, needing desperately to see white people again.

Louise had been mesmerized by the wondrous feeling of being in George's arms. As his lips met hers, her eyes drifted shut, and she gave herself over to the myriad of delightful feelings that were coursing through her.

Louise had not forgotten the kiss he'd given her on the porch. But when he had made no further romantic advance, she'd come to believe that he'd thought it was a mistake. The way he was kissing her now, though, she knew it hadn't been a mistake.

She started to draw him nearer when the weight of the gun in her hand reminded her of where they were and what they'd been doing.

"Oh—the gun." It startled Louise that she'd completely forgotten she was holding it.

George gave her a lopsided grin as he let her go. "It wouldn't be too good if it went off when we weren't expecting it."

He took the revolver from her and laid it carefully aside.

"Now—where were we?"

"I think we were celebrating," Louise said, blushing at her own brazenness. She told herself she was a mature woman, but there was something about George that made her feel young again—young and happy.

"I like celebrating with you," George said in a husky voice as he took her back in his arms.

They came together a bit timidly at first, for they were finally fully acknowledging their attraction to each other. But the moment their lips met, all awkwardness was forgotten. His mouth moved over hers in a possessive brand, evoking feelings within her she'd never known before.

"Louise—"

She opened her eyes to look up at him when he broke off the kiss.

"I think we'd better head back now," he told her regretfully.

"Don't I need more practice?" she asked with a teasing smile, not wanting to be out of his arms.

"I would love to stay here and practice with you, but I'm not sure it's safe."

"Safe?" She frowned.

He smiled even more. "I wasn't talking about the gun. I was talking about keeping you safe from me."

"Are you dangerous?"

"Right now I feel like I am," he said tightly. Then deciding to be honest, he went on, "I've been taking care to keep my distance from you since that night I kissed you on the porch, but it hasn't been easy. I didn't want to take advantage of you, but then I didn't believe I could ever feel this way again."

She was afraid to let herself hope what he was going to say. "Feel what way again?"

"Louise, I love you," he declared earnestly. "I want you to marry me and stay here with me. I don't ever want you to leave me."

"Oh, George." His name was a heartfelt whisper on her lips. "I love you, too. You've been my strength. I don't know how I would have gotten through all this without you."

She found herself back in his arms.

"I don't even want to think about it," George said. "All that matters is that we're together."

He kissed her once more, deeply, passionately.

"Louise—will you marry me?" he repeated, wanting to hear her say it.

She had never believed this moment would come in her life. She had resigned herself to her spinsterhood, but now George had changed all that. She wanted him as she had never wanted another man. She loved him.

"Yes, George, I'll marry you." Louise lifted her lips to his, ready to seal her answer with a kiss.

As she did, she happened to glance over his shoulder, and she went still.

There on the hilltop across the way, silhouetted against the sky, was a Comanche warrior.

And he was staring down at them.

"Oh, my God!" Louise gasped as she froze in George's arms.

"What?"

He had been ready to kiss her when he felt the sudden change in her. He released her and turned to see what had frightened her.

"Get on your horse and ride out of here, now!" he ordered as he grabbed up the gun she'd been using for practice. "Don't look back!"

"No! I will not leave you here!" She stood her ground. "Give me that gun!"

She all but snatched the revolver out of his hand. They looked at each other for an instant. It seemed almost an eternity before he nodded.

"Get down behind the tree trunk," he ordered.

"Where are you going?"

"To get my rifle."

George ran for their horses and got his rifle and saddlebags before racing back to join her where she was taking cover behind the fallen tree.

"Why hasn't he attacked?" Louise asked. She was frightened, terrified actually, but she wasn't helpless—not this time. Her grip tightened on the gun as she waited.

"I don't know—I—"

As George spoke, a rider came charging past the warrior, galloping down the hill in their direction. George feared it was an attack. He lifted his rifle and took careful aim—

But he stopped before pulling the trigger.

He dropped the gun and stood up.

"What is it? Why didn't you shoot?" Louise demanded.

"Look," was all George could mutter as he watched the young white boy racing toward them with the warrior following.

Louise went still as she realized the rider was only a child. "Why, it's a boy—a white boy." She looked at George, incredulous. "But why is he with that warrior?"

As soon as Joe rode past him, Zach gave chase. He was afraid someone might take a shot at the boy and wanted to warn him to go slowly so he wouldn't threaten the white people.

"Joe—wait. Be careful, they don't know who you are!" Zach called out to him.

But Joe was in no mood to listen to Zach. He had no intention of slowing down. There were white people here!

He was almost home!

Louise and George were watching their approach cautiously.

"What should we do? That warrior is right behind him," Louise said, still holding her gun in a death grip.

George had his rifle in hand, too. "We wait. Neither one of them has a weapon that I can see."

And then they heard the boy's frantic calls.

"Don't shoot! Don't shoot!" Joe was gasping for breath as he rode at full speed toward their hiding place.

George stood up, showing himself to the boy.

"George! What are you doing?" Louise grabbed his arm, wanting to pull him back down to safety.

He stood his ground and hoped his instincts were right.

Joe saw the white man stand up, and his heart leaped for joy. He rode straight toward the man, tears streaming down his face.

Zach slowed his pace and stayed a short distance behind. He did not want the whites to feel threatened, but he wanted to make sure Joe was not harmed. He reined in as the boy stopped and all but threw himself from the horse's back to run to the white man who'd come forward to meet him. Zach was still worried. The white man had a gun.

Joe stopped right in front of the stranger and looked up at him. He knew he was dirty and battered and bruised, but he also knew he was almost back home.

"We're coming home—Zach brought us back," he blurted out.

George had no idea what the boy was talking

about, but he could see that the child had been through a rough time. "Easy, son."

"We been riding for weeks now. I didn't think we'd ever get here." Joe was gasping in his excitement.

"What happened to you?" George asked.

"I was taken captive in a raid, but Zach's bringing me home."

"Zach?" George could not make much sense out of what the boy was saying. He looked up at the warrior who had stopped a distance away, wondering whom the boy was talking about.

"Yes, he knew the way. He brought us." He was babbling.

Before George could respond, he heard Louise cry out in shock.

"George! Look!"

He turned toward Louise, expecting more trouble. He didn't know what had frightened her, but he would defend her with his life. He would shoot to kill if need be.

Louise had come to her feet and was staring off toward the crest of the hill again, her expression one of complete amazement.

George turned back to look, expecting to see an entire raiding party there, expecting to face death.

Instead he saw only a solitary mounted figure—

A woman—

And the sun was glistening off her golden hair—

Chapter Twenty-three

"Oh, my God," George muttered as he began to tremble with the force of the emotions that besieged him.

He feared he was dreaming. He feared if he blinked she would be gone.

But she was still there.

"Mister—are you all right?" Joe asked, a little frightened by the way the man looked—almost as if he'd seen a ghost.

George was too numb to answer.

His rifle dropped from his hand, and he started running past the warrior and up the hillside.

Louise still couldn't believe her eyes.

There was the boy—

And the Comanche warrior—

But on the hilltop—

Was it really Marissa? Had she returned to them?

Suddenly she didn't care about her gun or the warrior.

Suddenly all that mattered to Louise was getting to Marissa—touching her and holding her—and reassuring herself that she was truly alive.

Louise laid the gun down and started to run after George.

Marissa had reined her horse in at the top of the hill to see what was happening below.

The sight that greeted her touched her to the depths of her soul. There below, standing with Joe, was her uncle. When Uncle George looked her way, she knew he recognized her almost immediately, for he started running toward her.

"Marissa!"

She heard him call her name, and a thrill unlike anything she'd ever known filled her heart.

"Uncle George!" She put her heels to her horse's sides and raced down the hill.

Joe looked at Zach, who had ridden down to his side and dismounted to stand with him.

"He's her uncle?" Joe asked, confused by all that was happening.

"I think so, Joe."

They waited and watched as Marissa quickly

dismounted and threw herself into the white man's arms.

"You're alive!" George said over and over as he held her to his heart. "You're alive!"

He leaned back a bit to stare down at her, his expression both joyous and wondrous. He didn't know how this had come to pass, and it didn't really matter. All that mattered was that Marissa was there. She was alive and had come home to him.

"Uncle George—it really is you! It is! I never thought I'd see you again!" Marissa was crying as she clung to him frantically, unable to believe that she had really found him.

"Oh, yes, sweetheart, it's me—and you're home. At last you're home and you're safe! We searched for you for weeks! We thought we'd never see you again. We were so afraid you were dead."

"We?" Marissa asked.

"Yes, we," he replied. Gently he took her by the shoulders and turned her a little so she could see Louise.

Marissa's breath caught in her throat at the sight of her friend—alive and well and rushing toward her at that very moment.

"Louise," she whispered in a strangled voice. "Dear God—" Marissa looked up at her uncle, awed, stunned, almost speechless. "She's alive? You saved her?"

"Yes, darling, Louise is very much alive."

At that moment, Louise reached them.

She stopped a few steps away to stare at Marissa. She remembered the last time she'd seen her as the Comanche had grabbed her up. Pain stabbed her at the bloody, vivid memory, and her tears fell silently.

"Marissa—I thought I'd never see you again," Louise said in a voice just about a whisper.

"I thought you were dead," Marissa returned before rushing to hold her.

They came together in an embrace of love and desperation, of pure loving reunion. The two women stood wrapped in each other's arms, crying in joy over the gift of life they'd been given.

George went to them and put his arms around them both. It was a long moment before they even thought about moving apart, so great was their need to reassure themselves that this was reality and not a dream.

"Come, you have to meet Joe and Zach," Marissa said when they finally stopped crying and were calm enough to talk. She looked over to where the two stood watching them.

They followed her to meet the strangers.

"Uncle George—Louise—this is Joe Carter, and this is Zach Ryder. Zach brought us back."

"Zach?" George was stunned when he realized the warrior was a white man. He looked at him critically, fighting to control his initial feelings of hatred and violence toward this man who, to all outward appearances, was a Comanche warrior. Finally he stepped forward and offered him his hand.

"Thank you, Zach, for saving my niece," George said earnestly. He clasped Zach's hand in a firm handshake. "Thank you for bringing her back to me."

"You are welcome," Zach returned.

The two men looked each other in the eye, and each recognized the other as a worthy opponent and an honorable man.

"And, Zach, this is Louise," Marissa said, her eyes welling up with tears again as she accepted the wonderful truth that her friend was alive.

"Louise?" Zach said in surprise as he faced her for the first time. "You survived the raid—"

Louise was staring at him, frightened yet trying to fight her fear. "You're not an Indian—"

"He was a captive—like me, Louise," Marissa quickly explained.

"Oh—" Louise suppressed a shiver at standing so close to him. She tempered her terror by telling herself he really was a white man—not a warrior. "Yes, I survived the raid. I was the only one. It wasn't easy, but I had George to help me."

George understood her fears and kept a supportive arm around her to give her the strength she needed to accept all that was happening.

"This is Joe," Marissa continued, going to the

boy. "He was brought into the village right before Zach decided it was time for us to leave. Zach got us all away from the tribe and brought us safely here." Marissa thought about telling them of Crazy One and her tragic death, but decided against it. She would talk of her friend later, when things had settled down.

George faced Zach. He wasn't sure of the right way to phrase his question, so he decided to come out and ask forthrightly. "Are you staying here with us or returning to your tribe?"

"Zach is staying," Marissa answered before Zach had a chance. "He's not going back."

George was a bit surprised by the answer, for he knew how difficult it would be for Zach to fit in, but that didn't matter. Zach had saved his niece, and in doing that he had earned George's eternal friendship. He would help him in any and every way he could.

"Well, let's get on back to the ranch. I think it's time for a celebration."

Zach went to Joe. "Are you ready?"

"Oh, yes. Soon I'll be home!"

George went to get their horses. He stopped only long enough to pick up the weapons and then returned to where everyone was waiting. They mounted up and rode for the ranch.

Marissa rode between George and Louise. She kept looking from one to the other, wanting to reassure herself that she was truly home.

"When we get near the house, I'll ride in first," George told them, catching Zach's eye. "We don't need any trouble today."

When the house came in sight, George galloped ahead to tell everybody the news.

"Marissa's back?" Sarah repeated, staring at George as he tied his horse to the hitching rail.

"She's coming right now," he told her, pointing to where the four riders were approaching. "A man named Zach, who was raised by the tribe, is the one who led her here. He brought a young boy who'd been a captive, too."

"This is so wonderful. Our prayers have been answered," Sarah said tearfully.

"Yes, they have," George agreed gruffly. Then, thinking how his men were going to react to Zach, he added, "We'll have to find them some clothes."

"I'll take care of that as soon as I've seen Marissa. How is Louise?"

He smiled. "Louise is beside herself. Who would have thought they'd just come riding in this way?"

"I'll go get Claude and Mark."

She rushed off to find the men and give them the exciting news.

George knew Mark would be thrilled. He remembered how hard it had been on him when they'd had to give up the search.

Sarah, Claude, Mark, and all the other men who were working in the stable came up to the house to join George in welcoming Marissa back.

"Marissa!" Sarah cried out excitedly when she saw her riding up.

Though Sarah had cautioned the men that the travelers were in Comanche dress, there was still some tension among them at the sight of the warrior riding in with the women and boy.

"Easy, boys," George said in a low voice. He knew a few of the hands had short tempers and no love for the Comanche. He didn't want any trouble.

The men relaxed at his order. They prepared to welcome Marissa home.

Sarah rushed forward and hugged Marissa the minute she dismounted.

"Damn—I ain't never seen no white warrior before," one of the men said in a low voice to Claude.

"It'll be fine. He's the one who got Marissa and the boy out of there alive."

The men heard the comment, and their opinion of the stranger went up, but white or not, they wouldn't be comfortable around him as long as he looked like an Indian.

Mark was standing back, watching everything. His gaze went over Marissa as she hugged Sarah. It surprised him that he was both disgusted and aroused by the sight of her wearing the buckskin Indian dress. It reminded him far too clearly of where she'd been and of what had, no doubt, happened to her there. Still, he was glad she had returned. It looked like his fortunes had changed. His prospects were bright again—as long as he could manage to hide his reaction to seeing her this way.

"It is so good to see you!" Sarah was crying. "You have to tell me everything that happened. We were so worried about you. And when we thought you were lost . . . well, George and Louise have been inconsolable. We all have."

Marissa was warmed by Sarah's affection. "I'm glad to be here, believe me."

"And who is this?" Sarah asked as she looked past Marissa to the boy and man standing by their horses.

Marissa quickly made the introductions.

"I'm gonna be going home soon," Joe piped up as Sarah took him under her wing. "Zach promised."

Marissa and Zach glanced at each other but said nothing.

As Sarah took charge of Joe, Louise and Marissa started inside. It was then that Mark stepped forward.

"Marissa—" Mark's voice was deep and his expression earnest as he went to her.

"Mark—" She stopped and gazed at him, delighted to see him. She'd been so busy with Joe and Sarah, she hadn't noticed him standing back with the ranch hands.

"I'm glad you're back," he said.

She smiled at him. "I am, too."

She had no time to say more as Louise drew her on toward the house.

"Let's all go inside and celebrate!" Louise urged.

"That will be wonderful, but I really have to have a bath first," Marissa told her.

"That's fine. You can all get cleaned up first, and then we'll have our celebration."

They went inside.

Zach had been standing off by himself watching Marissa's reunion. He'd expected the whites to be suspicious of him, and they had been. Nothing had troubled him, though, until one man had stepped forward and stopped Marissa to talk to her. Something about the way he'd looked at her—and she had looked at him—bothered Zach.

It startled him when he recognized his reaction as jealousy. He scowled to himself. He had no reason to be jealous. He had no claim on Marissa.

Now that she was safely back with her family, he could be moving on as soon as he took care of Joe. But seeing how the woman named Sarah had taken over tending to the boy, he was tempted to cut his ties and ride out right away. He wasn't needed or wanted at the ranch.

"Why don't you give us about an hour and then come on up to the house?" George said to his men after the women and the boy had gone inside. "We're going to have us one fine party."

"We'll do that, boss," Claude said. "Come on, boys, let's take care of their horses and go back to work for a while."

Claude stopped before Zach and stuck out his

hand. "Thanks for bringing our Marissa home."

Zach nodded.

None of the others came over to speak to him.

"Coming, Zach?" George called from the bottom of the porch steps where he was waiting for him.

Zach followed him inside.

Chapter Twenty-four

"Let's see what we can find for you to wear," Louise said as she started to go through the closet in the bedroom she was using. "All of our possessions were destroyed during the raid. George was kind enough to buy me some new clothes. I know they'll be a little bit big on you, but we can go into town tomorrow, if you want, and buy everything you need."

"I don't care how big everything is. I just want to be out of this buckskin."

"Here." Louise laid out one of her prettiest day-gowns along with shoes and the necessary undergarments. "While you start getting undressed, I'll go help Sarah bring up the water for your bath."

"You don't know how delicious having a bath sounds."

"What did you do in the village?"

"There was a stream nearby, and everyone washed up there."

"I promise you will enjoy this bath much more."

"I have no doubt about it," Marissa said, actually laughing a bit.

"I'll be right back."

Left alone in the bedroom, Marissa sank down on the edge of the bed. She stared at Louise's bathtub, thinking of how, very shortly, she would be soaking luxuriously in a tub of hot water and using real soap. As her thoughts drifted, memories of her "bath" after the fight with Moon Cloud returned. She remembered the icy water, her fury with Wind—Zach—and the way it had felt when he'd held her in his arms in the middle of the stream.

That had been their wedding night.

The thought took her by surprise.

She'd had no idea that he'd claimed her for his wife that day. And then—when he'd taken her back to the tipi—

Marissa got up and went to the window to look out. She had to distract herself. She had to banish those memories once and for all.

As she waited for Louise's return, she let her gaze sweep over the panoramic view of the countryside, and then she glanced toward the stable. She could see Mark working with one of the unbroken horses in the corral. Claude was holding the horse's bridle as Mark mounted and prepared to ride it. She couldn't hear what they were saying, but she grew excited as she waited for Claude to release the mount.

He did.

The horse spun crazily and bucked once.

Mark went flying off and landed heavily in the dirt.

Marissa knew that Zach would never have been thrown. He would have broken the horse in no time.

When she realized the direction of her thoughts, she turned away from the window. It was time to put Zach and her time in the village in the past.

Louise and Sarah returned shortly, and after filling the tub and making sure she had the linens she needed, they started from the room. Louise stopped at the door and went back to Marissa to take her in her arms.

"You have no idea how thrilled I am that you're here—safe and healthy and—"

Marissa hugged her back. "Oh, yes, I do." She smiled at her. "Because I feel the same way about you. When I saw you coming toward us, it was a dream come true. I was so sure you were dead—It was so terrible—"

"I know. I still don't know how I managed to hang on long enough for them to find me. But once they brought me into town, George found out who I was, and he took care of everything from then on. He even hired the best tracker in the area to help him try to find you, but a bad storm came through and washed out your trail. They didn't want to come back without you, but there was no way for them to keep going."

"Uncle George is a very special man."

"Yes," Louise agreed. "He is."

Something in her friend's tone of voice made Marissa look at her questioningly.

"I have to tell you—" Louise said quickly, unable to keep the secret any longer.

"Tell me what?"

"The good news. Your uncle—George and I—well, he's proposed to me, and I've accepted."

With that, Marissa threw her arms around Louise again in absolute joy. "That's wonderful! Now you truly will be family!"

"I know." Louise could think of nothing better. "You hurry and take your bath now, so we can really celebrate."

"I'll be down as soon as I can."

"We'll be waiting."

Louise left her to her privacy, and Marissa took off the buckskin dress for the last time. She stepped into the steaming water and sank down into its welcoming heat. The soap Louise had given her was scented, and Marissa felt as if she were in heaven. She gloried in the silky lather, and once she'd finished bathing, she washed her hair, too. The towels were soft against her skin, and she was eager to put on real clothes again—to feel like a lady.

* * *

"I think I can find some clothes to fit you," George told Zach as he took him to his own bedroom at the back of the sprawling ranch house.

Zach had known the time would come when he would have to dress as a white man again, and it seemed that time had arrived. He wasn't certain he was going to like it.

"I will find a way to repay you as soon as I can," Zach told George.

"Don't worry about it. After what you did for Marissa, this is the least I can do to help you," he answered.

George went through his dresser and took out the things he thought would work for Zach.

"Here—these should fit you," George said, handing him the clothing he needed along with a pair of boots.

"Thanks."

"And you can have this room over here." He directed Zach to a bedroom across the hall from his own. "You'll be needing a bath, too. There's a bathhouse out back that the men use. I can show you where it is now, if you want."

"All right."

Zach knew that things would be more comfortable around the ranch once he was dressed as a white man. The way the whites felt about the Comanche, he was surprised that none of the hands had tried to start a fight with him. From the looks they'd given him, he was certain a few of them had thought about it.

"So, how did you come to be living with the Comanche?" George asked as they walked out to the bathhouse. He was curious about this strong young man who'd been brave enough to help Marissa and Joe.

"I was taken captive when I was young. I was about the same age as Joe. Then I was adopted into the tribe."

"So you've lived most of your life with them."

"Yes, I did."

"Do you remember anything about your own family? Where your home was?"

"Somewhere near San Antonio, I recall, but I doubt there's anything left of it—not after all this time."

"We can check for you, if you want," George offered.

"No. There's no need. My family was killed in the raid."

"Are you sure?" he asked.

For an instant, Zach looked haunted; then he hid his emotion. "Yes, I'm sure. I do want to check on Joe's family. Is there any way to find out if he has any relatives?"

"We can go into Dry Springs and wire the town nearest his family's ranch. The law there might know something."

"Good. If there's any chance he's got family left, I want to find them for him."

"That's kind of you."

"He's a good boy."

"And what about you? What do you intend to do once you've taken care of Joe?" George asked.

"I'm not sure. I was mostly worried about bringing Marissa back. Now that she's here with you, I can move on."

"There's no reason for you to go. You're welcome to stay here at the Crown for as long as you want. And if you want a job, I can always use an extra hand."

"Thanks."

George left him at the bathhouse.

Zach went in and quickly bathed. When he'd finished, he dried himself off and began to dress, donning the clothing George had given him. Everything felt foreign to him—the underwear—the denim pants—the shirt that buttoned—the socks and boots. He felt awkward and unable to move quickly, but he knew he would have to adjust. He cut a narrow piece of leather from his loincloth and used it to tie back his hair. He started to gather up his few things before leaving the bathhouse, then stopped and stuck the knife in the waistband of his pants. He did not want to be completely unarmed. Zach drew a deep breath as he opened the door and stepped outside.

In that moment, he left his time with the Comanche behind.

He was once again Zach Ryder.

As soon as George returned to the house he sought out Louise.

Sarah was tending to Joe, so Louise had taken over in the kitchen. She was just starting to prepare dinner when she heard someone behind her and turned to see George. She didn't say a word but went straight into his arms and laid her head upon his chest.

"She came back to us," Louise said in a tear-choked voice.

"Yes, thank God, she's back."

They stood that way for a long moment, offering up thanks for Marissa's safety.

"Is she all right? Really all right?" George asked quietly when they finally moved apart.

His expression was dark and concerned as he looked down at Louise. He had put on a good face for everyone until now, but deep inside, his worries about Marissa were eating at him. It was no secret how the Comanche treated their captives, and it sickened him to think she had been tortured and abused.

Louise understood what he was thinking as she lifted her gaze to his. "She seems fine, George. We haven't talked about any of what actually happened, but she was acting as if she was all right."

He swallowed tightly. "I want to help her. I want to do everything I can for her."

"You are," Louise told him, kissing him softly. "You're loving her, and that's all she needs right now—your love and the safety of being here with you."

He nodded, feeling a little better. He was a man who liked to fix things, to make things better when he could. But in a situation like Marissa's, he was helpless to change what had happened.

"Well, she certainly has my love," he said gruffly. "She's suffered so much lately—"

"She has, but she's a strong young woman. Marissa will do just fine, you'll see."

George gathered Louise near again and kissed her warmly. She watched him as he left the room, then turned back to her work. In her heart, she was hoping and praying that she was right—that everything would be all right—with Marissa.

Only time would tell.

George saw Zach coming up to the house and went out to meet him. The change the clothes made in him was amazing.

"Everything fit all right?" George asked as Zach drew near the porch.

"Fine, thanks."

"You want to take your other things to your room? We're just sitting in the parlor."

"I'll be right back," Zach said.

George watched him as he walked inside and down the hall. He seemed a bit uncomfortable in the clothes, but that would pass. Smiling, George returned to the parlor to join the others.

Zach entered his bedroom and stopped dead as he looked up. Directly across from the door was a dresser and its mirror, and he found himself staring at his reflection.

His mirror image startled him.

So this was what Zach Ryder looked like.

The shirt he wore was a bit tight across the shoulders and the pants fit more loosely. The change was dramatic. He looked like the other white men he'd seen today.

Feeling as ready to begin his new life as he ever would, Zach left his old clothes in the room and turned back to join the celebration.

"Here he is!" George called out when he saw Zach standing in the doorway of the crowded room. "Come on in, Zach."

Zach went to his side, and George pressed a glass of whiskey into his hand.

"Here, relax a little," he said in a low voice.

Zach nodded and took a quick drink. He had had whiskey before in the village and knew its powers. He would have to be careful not to drink too much, for he had seen how it made some of the warriors crazy.

Joe ran over to talk with him.

Mark was there with the other hands, enjoying

a drink and waiting for Marissa to appear. It had been a good day—a very good day. His plans were going to work out after all. There was no way of telling what had happened to Marissa while she was a captive of the Comanche, and none of the men had dared to bring up the subject. They were too loyal to George to question her reputation. And Mark would play that game, too. He would do whatever it took to make his own dreams come true. He smiled to himself and glanced toward the hall, wondering when Marissa was finally going to join them.

Marissa sat at the dressing table and worked at pinning her hair up. It felt good to look like a lady again. It had been so long that she'd forgotten how much she enjoyed dressing up. After the months she'd spent living the life of a Comanche woman in buckskin and moccasins, it was definitely a change to be wearing petticoats and shoes.

When she had finished with her hair, she paused to stare at her reflection. Except for the fact that she was tan now instead of pale, she looked no different from the young woman she used to see in the mirror at her home in New Orleans. But she knew better. Inwardly, everything had changed.

Marissa found herself wondering how Zach was doing. She was certain Uncle George was helping him, but she knew this was going to be a difficult time for him. She wanted to do all she could for him, but she didn't know if he even wanted her help.

After one last glance in the mirror, Marissa left the bedroom. She was eager to spend time with her uncle and Louise. She wanted to relax and to laugh again.

Instinctively, Zach knew Marissa was near. He had been standing with his back to the doorway and turned when he felt her presence. He stood there, drink in hand, staring at her.

Zach had always thought Marissa was lovely—beautiful, in fact—but seeing her this way, dressed as a lady, he was amazed. Her hair was done up on top of her head, revealing the slender arch of her neck. Heat centered low in his body at the thought of pressing kisses along the sweet line of her throat. He took a drink of whiskey as his gaze dropped lower. The gown she wore was simple and modest. It was a little big on her and so it only hinted at the sweet curves he knew lay beneath it. She looked a perfect lady, a far cry from the Comanche maiden he'd ridden in with—a far cry from the fierce, fighting woman he'd taken as his wife.

"Here she is!" George said happily as he went to embrace her.

Sarah and Louise bustled in from the kitchen where they'd been busy putting together a big meal while George had been serving up the drinks. At his announcement, all eyes turned to Marissa.

"Thank heaven, you're back!" the men were saying as they all came forward to talk with her.

Marissa made small talk with them, but found herself looking around for Zach. She didn't see him at first and thought maybe he hadn't joined them yet.

And then Marissa caught sight of him. Standing across the room was a tall, handsome white man. Her eyes widened in shocked recognition as he looked up at her and their gazes met.

Zach Ryder was there.

Chapter Twenty-five

Mark had been getting himself a drink when Marissa came into the room. He went straight to speak with her, glad to see that she was back to looking like herself. There was no telling what had happened to her while she'd been gone, but he wasn't going to worry about that. He had his eyes set on a bigger prize than any woman's virginity. Money and power were what mattered in life, and that was what he was after. He would get both by marrying her.

"Evening, Marissa," Mark said, coming to her side.

"Hello, Mark." She smiled at him a bit distractedly.

She had been watching Zach, trying to reconcile the man standing across the room from her with the warrior she'd known and loved. Zach looked so different—so wonderful—this way. She was hard put not to just walk away from Mark and go to Zach. It took an effort, but she managed to give the other man her full attention.

She'd always thought Mark nice-looking. He was tall and lean and blond. It surprised her to find that the attraction she'd felt for him during her last visit to the ranch had faded. She didn't let her reaction show as they talked, though. She pretended to listen to his every word, while in truth she was longing to be with Zach.

From across the room, Zach was keeping watch over Marissa. She appeared happy, and he was glad. Deep within him, though, an ache had grown, for he knew they would soon be parting. It saddened Zach to think he would never see her again, but he knew it was for the best. He was an outcast among these people. When Mark had approached Marissa, Zach had been hard put to stay where he was and keep his distance. There was something about the man that troubled him, but Mark wasn't his concern. Marissa was home. She was no longer his to protect.

"Zach!"

Joe's call distracted him, and he was glad to be drawn away to join the boy and Sarah outside on the porch.

"Miss Sarah says we can go into town tomorrow

and send a telegram to my family," Joe told him excitedly.

"We'll do that," Zach agreed. "With any luck, we'll hear back from them right away."

"We will," the boy said with certainty.

"Well, while you're here with us, let's have some fun. What do you say?" Sarah said with a smile.

"Yeah." Joe's eyes lit up, and he sounded like an eager, innocent child once again.

Sarah and Zach smiled. Zach seemed a little uncomfortable, and she wanted to make him feel welcome.

"Would you two like to walk down to the stable and take a look at the horses?" she asked.

"Sure," Joe answered quickly.

The three of them got up to go.

Zach cast one quick glance back inside to see that Marissa was still talking with Mark before following Sarah and Joe. His gaze lingered on Joe, and he found himself wondering what his own life would have been like if he had been rescued from the Comanche early on as Joe had been. Zach put the thought from him. There was no point in thinking about it. He couldn't change the past.

Marissa had watched Zach disappear outside. She wanted to excuse herself from Mark to follow him, and she was just about to do that when Claude and several other hands came over to talk with her, and the opportunity was lost.

Some time later, after walking through the stable

and seeing the Crown's fine horses, Sarah and Joe decided to return to the house. Zach wanted to remain outside awhile longer.

"Are you sure you don't want to come with us?" Sarah asked.

"I want to see Marissa," Joe said happily. "Don't you, Zach?"

"I'll be in later," Zach said.

He wanted to see Marissa, too. He wanted to be with her, but he knew it was best if he stayed away—especially while Mark was hovering over her. He didn't like the way he felt when he saw the other man with her.

"Well, the food will be ready soon. Don't miss out."

She led Joe up to the house, leaving Zach alone with his thoughts down by the corral.

Zach appreciated all the work George had done to carve his empire out of the West Texas wilderness. He was sure it hadn't been easy fighting nature and the Comanche, but George had done it and survived. The Crown Ranch was a beautiful spread.

As he thought of the Comanche, Ten Crow slipped into Zach's thoughts. He realized Ten Crow's vision had been real. He was certain there was peace in the tribe now that both he and Bear Claw were gone.

He found he did not miss anything about the village. His only regret was Crazy One's death. She had suffered so much in her life, and he had hoped to somehow make it up to her. All he could do now was to make sure things turned out better for Joe. He wanted him returned to his family, just as Marissa had been returned to hers.

Thinking of the boy, Zach headed back toward the house to be with him.

The rest of the day passed quickly and pleasantly for Marissa. George and Louise made their happy announcement, and everyone was thrilled by the news of their upcoming marriage. The company was wonderful, the food was delicious, and just being back with Uncle George and Louise made everything seem perfect.

Joe stayed with her, needing the security she offered, and she enjoyed having him near. He only left her when Zach came back inside.

When it grew late and everyone was ready to call it a night, the men went to the bunkhouse and Sarah and Claude retired to the small outbuilding where they lived.

"Are you sure you're up to going into town tomorrow?" George asked Marissa.

"Oh, yes," she answered. "I think it's important we send the wire about Joe as quickly as we can."

"All right, then, we'll leave first thing in the morning."

"I'll be ready. Good night, Uncle George," Marissa said, kissing him on the cheek.

"Good night, sweetheart," he said, all the love he felt for her shining in his eyes.

"And I am truly thrilled about you and Louise," she said as she looked from one to the other. "I think it's wonderful."

"So do I." George gave Louise a grin.

Louise kissed him good night, and went with Marissa to her room for a chat.

"Did you enjoy yourself?" Louise asked as she helped Marissa out of her dress.

"Oh, yes. I'm still finding it hard to believe I'm actually here with you."

"I feel the same way. Joe seems to be doing quite well, considering all he's been through."

"I only hope that when we send that wire tomorrow, we get some good news back."

"What will you do if . . . you don't?"

"I haven't talked to Zach about it, but I would want Joe to stay here on the Crown with me. I don't think Uncle George would mind."

"Oh, no. Of course not. Your Zach . . ." Louise paused for effect. "He's quite an interesting man. He looked like a different person dressed in George's clothes, don't you think?"

"I didn't even recognize him for a moment," Marissa admitted.

"Well, he's quite handsome."

"Yes." She was reluctant to say anything more, fearful of revealing the truth of her feelings. Louise had a way of reading her mind sometimes, and this was one time when she didn't want her friend to know what was in her heart.

"Marissa—when you were in the village—what was it like? What happened?" Louise asked, sitting down on the side of the bed.

Marissa sat beside her. She had known they were going to have to talk about it eventually, and this was as good a time as any. "After the raid, we rode for days on end."

"Was Zach part of the raiding party?"

"No."

"Oh, good." Louise was visibly relieved. As much as she'd appreciated his bringing Marissa back to them, the thought that he might have been in the raiding party that had killed so many people had disturbed her.

"I wasn't given to Zach until we reached the village."

"You were 'given' to Zach?" Louise was shocked.

"Yes, I was his captive. He was very good to me," she added quickly when she saw Louise's horrified expression.

"What happened next? Were you hurt in any way?"

"No. Zach protected me. One of the other warriors tried to hurt me, but Zach saved me."

"So you really are all right?" Louise desperately wanted to believe that nothing bad had happened to Marissa, that she hadn't been raped or abused.

"I'm fine. I really am. Nothing happened to me," she answered, her heart breaking as she said it.

She was lying. Something had happened. She had fallen in love with Zach.

"I'm just so glad that you're back with us, safe and sound." Louise gave her a loving kiss and a warm hug. "Good night, darling. Sleep well."

"I will," Marissa murmured as Louise left her alone.

She had honestly thought she would sleep well that night. She was exhausted, and she was back at the ranch, resting in a comfortable bed. But sleep eluded Marissa, and she lay awake long into the night.

George looked over at Zach and Joe. "How are you two doing?"

"We're fine," Zach answered. "Thank you for everything you've done."

"No, Zach, it's like I told you before—thank *you*."

"Good night."

Zach and Joe went together to the room George had given them. A cot had been brought in for Joe to sleep on, and it didn't take the boy long to undress and seek its comfort.

"Zach—I'm sleeping in a real bed again," Joe said, grinning as he pulled the covers up to his chin. "G'night, Zach."

"Good night, Joe."

Zach blew out the lamp, then got ready for bed himself. Still feeling a bit uncomfortable and uneasy, he decided to sleep with his pants on just in case there was any kind of trouble. He sat down on the edge of the bed and marveled at its softness. He tried to remember the last time he'd slept in a real bed. A vague and distant memory of his mother tucking him in and saying a prayer came to Zach as he settled back on the pillows and pulled the blanket up.

Closing his eyes, Zach sought rest. It had been a long and adventuresome day. He was glad that everything had turned out so well and that Marissa was home safely. He wanted only her happiness.

As he lay there in the dark thinking of Marissa, pain filled his heart. He would soon have to leave her. He didn't want to, but there was no future for them together. He had seen her with Mark and knew the cowboy was the kind of man she deserved—not someone like him, a man raised in the wild by the Comanche—a man without a future or a home.

He'd felt awkward and unsure of himself at the celebration, so he'd remained quiet, keeping to himself. There was no point in making friends at the ranch. He would be leaving soon, and he wouldn't be back.

He would be leaving Marissa.

Hot, exciting memories of their nights together in his lodge assailed him. Her kiss, her caress, the claiming of her innocence. The pure pleasure of making her his own.

Zach bit back a miserable groan as he fought down his desire for her.

She was his wife—

But not with her consent, he argued with himself. And only in the Comanche world.

Louise went to look for George and found him outside, sitting on a bench on the porch.

"Enjoying the peace?"

"Yes. Join me?"

"I'd love to." Louise went to sit beside him.

"You were right about Marissa. She seems fine."

"I think so. It's been a difficult time for her, but she's a strong young woman. We're so blessed to have her back."

George looked over at her in the moonlight, then leaned down and kissed her softly. "Just yesterday, I would never have believed we'd be sharing this moment—but we are."

She smiled up at him. "It's a dream come true for both of us."

"Will you help make the rest of my dreams come true?"

"I'd love to."

"How soon do you want to get married? Let's set a date."

"Tonight?" Louise asked, her voice a soft purr.

George chuckled. "Don't tempt me, woman."

"Why don't we speak with the reverend when we go into town tomorrow?"

"I guess I can wait that long."

They kissed one last time before going inside for the night.

Zach lay in the darkness, unable to sleep. His surroundings were too strange; his thoughts were too troubled.

In frustration, he finally got up.

It was well past midnight. After checking to make sure Joe was sleeping soundly, he took his own blanket and left the room. He silently went out of the house. He bedded down some distance away and lay there, staring up at the stars. The night sky and the hard ground were familiar to him, and he relaxed a little.

Many thoughts plagued him. As a boy, he had longed to escape from the village. He had prayed to be rescued. He had waited and hoped, but he had finally been forced to give up his dream of going home. He had accepted his fate and done what he'd had to do to survive. Yet even after he'd become a fearless warrior, he acknowledged that in the deepest recesses of his heart, a secret part of him had always longed to go home again.

And now he was free.

He was back among the whites.

But he felt no joy.

He only felt alone.

In irritation, he got up. He didn't like the direction of his thoughts. He was not a man who felt sorry for himself. He was a man who took action. Restless as he was, he knew there would be no sleep for him that night. He had just resigned himself to that when he heard Marissa say his name.

"Zach—"

The sound of Marissa's voice so close behind him sent a thrill through Zach. He turned, surprised to find her there within arm's reach. He had been caught up so deeply in his own troubled thoughts that he hadn't been aware of her approach.

"Marissa—what are you doing out here?" he asked softly, knowing the sound of their voices would carry in the night.

"I was awake and looked out my window, and I saw you here. I was worried about you. I thought something might be wrong. I wanted to make sure you were all right."

He longed to tell her that he was all right—now that she was with him—but he didn't. "I'm fine. I'm just not used to sleeping indoors yet."

She nodded thoughtfully, understanding. "It is quite a change after all we've been through. I was sorry we didn't get any time to talk tonight—"

"You were busy." He deliberately sounded as if it were of no importance to him.

His tone of voice was so cold and indifferent that it put Marissa off a bit.

"I know. I wanted to spend as much time with my uncle and Louise as I could."

He held his tongue, but he wanted to mention all the time she'd spent with Mark.

"Zach—" Marissa took a step closer to him. She sensed that he was angry with her about something. "I really never got the chance to thank you properly for bringing me home. I never really allowed myself to believe that it was going to happen until today."

She boldly went to Zach and lifted her arms to encircle his neck.

"Thank you." Her words were a hushed whisper upon her lips.

Ever so gently, she drew him down to her, seeking his lips in a cherishing, loving exchange.

The sweetness of her embrace sent a shaft of almost painful desire jolting through Zach.

He wanted her—

How he wanted her—

Zach responded instantly, any restraint he'd had upon himself destroyed by the touch of her lips on his. He crushed her to his chest, deepening the kiss to a hungry, devouring exchange. He needed this. He needed her.

He didn't know how he was going to stay away from her, but he had to. Because he cared so much about her, because he loved her.

The cold emptiness of the despair that besieged

him gave Zach the strength he needed to end the kiss. He put her physically from him.

"Go back inside now, Marissa. It's where you belong."

She belonged in a soft bed in a safe, comfortable ranch house, not out here, sleeping under the stars with him.

She didn't need to be worrying about where the next meal was coming from or what danger the next day might bring.

Marissa was startled and confused. She had felt the flame of their passion for an instant while in his arms, but, just as quickly, the passion had vanished and now he was sending her away.

She stared up at Zach in the starlight. In that moment, he was her warrior again—strong, powerful, and determined. But no trace of emotion played on his handsome features. He looked cold and distant. And he had sent her away from him.

Heartbroken, Marissa turned away from him without another word and made her way back to the ranch house. She took care not to make any noise as she entered her room and lay down for the night.

Zach remained standing, watching her until she was out of sight. Only then did he lie back down.

In the distance, down by the stable, Mark had been watching all that transpired. Fury and disgust had filled him at the sight of Marissa kissing Zach. The woman was a slut.

He'd hoped that she hadn't changed too much while she'd been a captive, but now he knew the truth.

As annoyed as he was by what he'd witnessed, he would not change his plans. His feelings for her had certainly changed. It was hard to care for any white woman who would let herself be kissed by a Comanche. Mark didn't care if Zach was white or not. He'd been raised a Comanche. Nothing could change that. And Marissa had acted like some kind of whore, going to him in the middle of the night.

He wondered if he could live with the knowledge of what she'd done. He decided he could. The prize that awaited him made it all worthwhile.

Chapter Twenty-six

In the past, Marissa had never thought much of Dry Springs, but today it appeared a booming metropolis to her as they rode down Main Street toward the mercantile. She had made the trip in the buckboard with Louise and Joe, while Uncle George and Zach accompanied them on horseback.

Sheriff Spiller happened to be making his rounds when he saw George coming up the street. He didn't pay any attention to who was in the buckboard. He'd heard back from the Rangers and wanted to let George know that they had no new information on his niece.

"George!" the sheriff called out as he flagged him down.

"Morning, Sheriff," George said, grinning as he reined in before him.

Sheriff Spiller was surprised by how happy the rancher looked. Ever since Marissa had disappeared, George had been a very somber man.

"I got some news from the Rangers," he began.

"Well, I got some news for you, too," George said as the buckboard pulled to a stop next to them.

"You do?" The Sheriff couldn't imagine what he might have heard.

"Our prayers were answered, Sheriff. Marissa's come home to us."

"What?" The lawman was shocked. He looked over at the buckboard and realized who was riding in it. Marissa was seated next to Louise and a young boy, and she looked in fine health. He stared at her in complete disbelief.

"Hello, Sheriff," Marissa said with a smile.

"Well, I'll be damned—er, uh, excuse me, ladies," he said awkwardly, blushing a little at having forgotten himself. "How did you manage to get away?" He was amazed and delighted by the good news.

George motioned for Zach to come forward and introduced the two men. He told the lawman how Zach had gotten both Marissa and Joe out of the village.

"It's a pleasure to meet you, Mr. Ryder," Sheriff Spiller told him, shalling his hand. "Welcome to Dry Springs."

"Thank you, Sheriff."

"We're thrilled to be here," Marissa told him happily.

"We're thrilled to have you here," he answered, tipping his hat to her. It wasn't often that anyone got good news where the Comanche were concerned. "Enjoy your stay in town."

"We will."

They moved on and reined in before the mercantile.

"We may be a while," Louise warned George.

George just smiled, glad to have the problem of having to wait for them while they were shopping.

"We'll take care of sending the telegram. Then I imagine Zach and Joe will want to stop off at the barbershop. We'll plan on meeting you back here after we've finished our business."

Marissa and Louise went inside as the men started off toward the telegraph office.

"We need to send a wire," George told the man at the desk.

"Yes, sir. You're in the right place. Where to?"

"Sidewinder," he answered firmly.

"Who you wanting to send it to?"

"Just to the sheriff there. We're trying to contact the Carter family." He quickly explained the boy's situation.

"I'll take care of it," the telegraph operator told them, giving the boy an encouraging look. "How long will you be in town?"

"Just for the day. Otherwise, you can notify us out at the Crown."

"The minute I hear anything, I'll get word out to you right away."

"My ma and pa will be here soon, won't they, Zach?" Joe asked, looking up at him, his eyes round with excitement as they left the telegraph office.

"I hope so, Joe."

"You two ready to see the barber?" George asked, wanting to distract the boy. There was no telling how long it would be before the reunion would take—if it took place at all.

"Let's go," Zach said, ready to shed the last visible reminder of his Comanche life.

"What about you, Joe? You ready to have your ears lowered?" George teased.

The boy immediately covered his ears with his hands and looked a bit scared. "He ain't going to cut my ears off, is he?"

Zach and George both laughed.

"I was just teasing you, son," George told him, putting a calming hand on his shoulder.

Joe was openly relieved as they entered the barbershop.

"Afternoon, George. How you been doing?" Pete, the town barber, asked.

"Life is good, Pete. My niece is back, safe and sound, thanks to this gentleman here. Say hello to

Zach Ryder. Zach, this is Pete Wilkins, a good friend of mine."

They shook hands.

Pete got a look at Zach's hair and frowned a bit.

"Kinda long, isn't it?" he asked cautiously.

"Yes," was all Zach answered.

"The boy needing a trim, too?"

"If you got the time," George said.

"I sure do. Who wants to go first?"

Joe quickly volunteered. He hopped eagerly into the chair. Zach and George settled in to watch. As the barber went to work on Joe, George told him about Marissa's miraculous return and how Zach had saved Joe, too.

"You're a brave man, Zach," Pete told him.

"I was glad I was able to bring them back," he answered as the barber finished the boy's hair, and he and Joe switched seats.

Pete set to work on Zach.

"You had a lot of hair," Joe said, looking down at the strands that lay on the floor when the barber finished.

"It's been a few years since I had my last haircut," Zach said.

He got out of the chair. He rubbed the back of his neck and glanced over his shoulder to catch a glimpse of himself in the mirror on the wall. He had known the change in his appearance would be dramatic, and it was. He didn't stare at himself for long, but he knew the truth: he was a white man now.

George paid the barber, and they left the shop.

"There's one other person I want you to meet before we go back to the mercantile, Zach," George said, telling him about Hawk. "Let's take a walk down to the stable."

He led the way. They reached the stable and went in.

"Hawk?" George called out to his friend.

Hawk appeared out of the back, leading a haltered horse behind him.

"George—what brings you to town? Did you get news about your niece?" Hawk asked as he came forward.

"I've got two friends here I want you to meet," George said. "Hawk Morgan, this is Zach Ryder and Joe Carter. Zach brought Marissa and Joe back, Hawk. He got them out of the Comanche village."

Hawk was astounded at the news. Such escapes were rare, almost unheard of. He looked at the stranger with even more respect as he held out his hand to him.

"I don't know how you did it, but I'm sure glad you did. We tracked that raiding party for weeks, but after the storm, we could never find the trail again. How did you get them out? Did you have enough men with you to attack the village, or did you sneak in and steal the captives away?"

"Neither," Zach answered, instinctively liking Hawk right away. "I was already in the village. I'd been raised there as a Comanche, but I knew the time had come for me to leave and take the captives with me."

Hawk nodded in understanding as he looked at Zach with even more respect. This man had sacrificed a lot to bring Marissa and the boy back to their families. He was a good man. "If you need anything while you're here in Dry Springs, just let me know, but I got a feeling George will take good care of you." He looked over at George. "And Marissa is all right?"

"She's fine—thanks to Zach."

Hawk nodded and smiled. "It's nice to hear good news every once in a while."

"That it is," George agreed.

They talked awhile longer, then left Hawk so he could get back to work.

"Now all we have to do is get you two some new clothes," George said as they made their way through town to the mercantile.

"I won't need much," Zach told him.

"Let me take care of this."

"I'll pay you back."

"Consider it a gift—a small way for me to thank you."

"Do you think that man at the telegraph office heard back from my pa yet?" Joe piped up eagerly, interrupting them.

George answered in a calming tone, "It's a little soon yet, Joe. Sometimes it takes a while for messages to get through, but I know he'll find us right away when he does hear."

Joe nodded, but his excitement didn't lessen. He was positive that he would be going home any day now, and he could hardly wait to see his ma and pa again.

Zach saw the mercantile ahead and found himself looking for Marissa.

As they drew near the store, two women came out. The women hurried past, barely taking notice of their presence as they talked to each other in hushed voices.

"Can you believe they even let her in the store?" one woman was saying in outrage.

"I shudder to think she actually was touching some of the merchandise. Why, she even tried some of the dresses on," the other woman remarked hatefully. "I don't know if I will ever shop in there again. Who would want to buy something she'd touched?"

Zach knew immediately whom they were talking about. It was what he had long feared might happen to Marissa when they returned. Crazy One had warned them how the whites might react, and he had just witnessed some of it firsthand. He glanced over at George and saw his pained expression. He had heard the women, too.

They went inside.

"That looks like it fits you perfectly," Louise was saying as Marissa stood before her in a sedate day-gown. She noticed George and smiled at him. "We're just about done, I think."

Marissa turned to greet them, and her gaze fell upon Zach. Once again, he was dramatically changed, and she could only stare at him as her heartbeat quickened. Long ago in the village, she had imagined how he would look this way. He was every bit as devastatingly handsome as she'd thought he would be.

"Don't Zach and Joe look handsome?" Louise asked happily.

"Yes, they do," Marissa answered.

"We'll be over here," George said, indicating the men's side of the store. "They need some clothes, too."

"We only have a few more things to get and we'll be ready to go," Louise assured him.

"Well, Tom, how's my credit with you? Think I can afford to keep these two women?" he joked with the owner.

"I don't know, George, they're doing a pretty good job of running up your bill," Tom warned facetiously.

"Good," he answered. "Let them have whatever they want. Same for my two friends here. They need to be outfitted, too. Think you can help them out?"

"Let's see what we can do," Tom said, hurrying

to wait on them. He liked it when the rancher was in a spending mood. The man had money, and he liked to spread it around. It wasn't often the store had so many good customers at once.

An hour later they had finished their shopping.

"Louise and I have one last stop to make before we return home," George announced, giving her a knowing look. He glanced at Zach. "You want to see about packing up everything while we pay a visit to the reverend?"

"We'll take care of it," Marissa promised, delighted, for she knew they were going to the preacher to set a date for their wedding.

It didn't take George and Louise very long. Zach had just finished stowing the last of their purchases when the couple returned, and they were smiling in delight.

"Well?" Marissa asked excitedly.

"It's all set," Louise told them.

"We're going to be married next month," George said.

"Congratulations!" Marissa hugged them both.

Zach offered his good wishes, too.

There was going to be a wedding.

Zach thought of the day he'd claimed Marissa as his wife in the village, then told himself it meant nothing. It had been a Comanche marriage. He did not look her way.

Marissa did not look at Zach either. She kept her thoughts focused only on Louise's happiness.

"Let's go home," George said. He helped the women up into the buckboard while Joe climbed in the back on his own.

"Thank you for your business," Tom said, following them outside to see them off.

"We appreciate all your help," Louise said.

"Well, don't forget the big dance next Saturday night," Tom reminded them.

"We won't," Louise said.

They set out for the Crown.

Zach turned his thoughts to the weeks to come as they made the trip back. He was uncomfortable with the amount of money George had spent on him at the store. Though George had told him the clothes were a gift for helping Marissa, Zach was determined to find a way to repay him. He'd already made up his mind to do all the work he could around the ranch until Joe was taken care of.

After they'd ridden out of sight, Beatrice, Tom's wife, appeared at his side. She had not come out the entire time Louise and Marissa had been in the store. She had stayed in the back in their living quarters. Tom had been bothered by her absence. He could have used her help.

"Thank God, they're gone!" Beatrice spat out hatefully.

Tom looked at her in disbelief. "What are you talking about, woman?"

She shuddered visibly for effect as she faced him.

"That—that woman! I can't believe you actually let her into the store."

"Which woman?"

"Why, Marissa Williams, that's who! Tom, she's been living with the Comanche."

"Yes, and she's home now. She's safe again."

"Well, I don't want the likes of her in my store ever again. You hear me?"

Tom grew furious with her close-minded attitude. "Shut your mouth, Beatrice! That poor young woman was a victim. She didn't ask to be taken captive. I just thank God that she's back with George."

"We're going to lose business if you wait on her!"

He gave her a smug look. "No, we won't."

"Of course we will! None of the self-respecting women in town will want to go anywhere she's been."

"Yes, they will, dear wife. They'll have no choice, since we're the only mercantile in town."

She hated his logic. "It still doesn't make it right to let her in our store."

"Marissa Williams is George Williams's niece, and she is a valued customer." He showed her the bills George had just rung up—bills that he knew would be paid in a timely manner, unlike those of some other regular customers.

"Oh, my! They spent that much today?" She was shocked.

"That's right. I don't think we have to worry

about offending our other customers. They'll come around, and if they don't, that's too damned bad. George and his family will always be welcome in my place of business."

With that, Tom turned his back on his small-minded wife and went back to work.

Chapter Twenty-seven

Once they returned to the Crown, Zach made sure he kept busy. As each day passed with no news about Joe's family, the boy became more unhappy and more worried. Zach worked with George to find small chores to keep the boy active. He watched over Joe and grew even more fond of him as the days passed. He knew he would miss him greatly if the time ever came for him to be reunited with his relatives.

The day of the dance in town arrived almost too quickly.

George went to find Zach in the stables where he'd been working with the horses.

"Zach—I need to talk with you," George said.

"Is something wrong?" he asked, wondering why the rancher sounded so serious.

"No, nothing's wrong. I just wanted you to know that we'll be riding out a little after noon today. So be ready to go."

"Go? Where?"

"We're going to town for the dance tonight."

"There's no reason for me to go along," Zach said. He didn't know how to dance, and he had no interest in returning to Dry Springs.

"I don't want to hear any arguments. As hard as you've been working around here, you deserve a night off. You're going with us, and here—" George handed him an envelope with money in it. "I don't want to hear a word out of you," he said gruffly. "You're supposed to be a guest here on the Crown, not hired help. But if you insist on acting like hired help, I'm going to pay you."

"I owe you too much already," Zach argued, trying to give the envelope back.

George wouldn't hear of it. "Go get cleaned up. I'll be expecting you to be ready to ride out when we are. I thought we'd take Joe along, too. Mark and a few of the other men are also going."

"I can stay here and watch over things for you."

"No need. Sarah and Claude will be staying behind to keep an eye on things."

Zach knew he was defeated, so he offered no further protest. He was not looking forward to going to the dance, though. It was difficult enough seeing Marissa around the ranch every day, but going into town and watching her dance with other men was going to be hard on him. He told himself he could do it—mainly because he had no choice.

"Plan on spending the night in town, too," George went on. "I always rent some rooms at the hotel so we don't have to worry about riding back to the ranch late at night. We'll attend church services in the morning before we start home."

Zach agreed and went on to finish what he was doing. When he was done, he got ready for the trip. He was resigned to the fact that he would have to be around Marissa. There could be no avoiding her company on the trip to and from town, but he hoped he could find some way to stay away from her at the dance. It wasn't going to be easy, but he would do it.

Marissa couldn't believe the week had passed so quickly. Now here they were back in Dry Springs at the hotel, getting dressed for the dance.

"I'm just about ready to go downstairs," Louise announced from where she was sitting at the dressing table, putting the finishing touches on her hair.

"So am I. If you'll just fasten the last few buttons on my dress, I'll be ready, too," Marissa said as she came to stand before her and presented her back.

Louise made short work of buttoning the gown. "Now turn around so I can see you."

Marissa did as she was told.

"It's even lovelier on you than I thought it would

be," Louise said, very pleased with the way the gown had turned out.

She and Marissa had picked out the dress pattern and material at the mercantile, and Louise had worked hard all week to have the gown ready for the weekend.

"You are so talented, Louisc. I have no sewing ability whatsoever," Marissa said as she looked in the mirror. "Oh, my. It does look pretty, doesn't it?"

The turquoise gown fit her perfectly. The modestly cut neckline revealed nothing untoward, but did flatter her figure, as did the fitted waistline.

Louise stood up, ready to meet George.

"You look pretty, too," Marissa said.

"I hope so. I want to look nice for your uncle," Louise replied as she smoothed her skirts.

"Uncle George will be pleased, I'm sure. Tonight should be fun," she said, remembering the dance they'd attended the last time she'd visited the ranch. For an instant, she thought about how much had changed in her life in the last year—her father's death—the raid—Zach—Then she pushed the thoughts aside. Tonight she wanted to be happy.

They left the room and made their way downstairs to find George cleaned up and waiting for them in the small lobby. He looked very handsome in his dress clothes, and Louise told him so.

It was dark outside, and as they left the hotel,

they could hear music playing in the distance.

"I'm the luckiest man in Dry Springs," George said with a grin. "I've got a beautiful woman on each arm."

Marissa and Louise both laughed, delighted by his compliment.

When they reached the dance, the festivities were already in full swing. Couples were dancing on a raised platform surrounded by colorful hanging lanterns as the band played a lively melody.

They had just come to stand at the side of the dance floor when Mark appeared.

"May I have this dance, Marissa?" he asked, sounding quite the gentleman.

"Why, yes, thank you, Mark," she replied courteously, but she had really been looking for Zach in the crowd.

Mark squired her out among the other couples as George took Louise in his arms and followed.

Marissa enjoyed dancing with Mark. He was a good dancer, and twirling to the music reminded her of her last visit with her father. She had not missed one dance that night. She had been very popular with all the young men in town.

As she followed Mark's lead, Marissa wondered where Zach and Joe were. They had an ridden into town together that morning, but she had not seen either of them since earlier that afternoon.

It had been a sad day for Joe. They'd checked with the telegraph office as soon as they arrived, only to discover that there was still no response to their wire to Sidewinder. Joe's disappointment had been obvious. She thought that perhaps Zach had taken the boy off to keep him entertained so he wouldn't have time to think about what they'd learned.

When the dance ended, Mark escorted her back to join her uncle and Louise. They were standing with a group of neighboring ranchers.

"Thank you, Marissa," Mark said in a courtly manner.

"It was my pleasure," she assured him.

He excused himself from her side.

The music started up again. There were many single young men around. George noticed that several glanced in Marissa's direction every now and then, but not a one of them came over to ask her to dance. George wasn't about to let Marissa feel lonely.

"This dance is mine," George stated possessively. "Louise, if you'll excuse us?"

"Of course. You two have fun," she told them with a smile.

Marissa enjoyed every minute of their dance, but she knew why Uncle George had invited her. Crazy One had warned her that the whites would consider her a ruined woman when she returned, and apparently she'd been right. Except for Mark and her uncle, no other man had come near her.

Though for a moment the realization was painful, Marissa quickly dismissed her hurt feelings.

She had told herself when they left the village that being an outcast in the white world was infinitely better than being a slave to the Comanche. And she had meant it. Not being the belle of the ball was not going to bother her.

She was free and she was safe.

That was all that mattered.

Mark came to claim Marissa for the next dance.

"Are you having a good time tonight?" he asked.

"Oh, yes."

Mark had been watching her from across the way, and he knew no other man had danced with her except her uncle. That pleased him. He didn't want any competition for her affections. He wanted her all to himself.

It annoyed Mark a bit to think Marissa was truly ruined socially, but in the long run, it was only her inheritance that mattered to him—not her.

Money meant a lot to Mark, and Marissa had money.

Mark had resigned himself to suffering the taunts of men who would say he was taking some Comanche warrior's leftovers. He couldn't argue with them, since it was probably true. After all, he had seen her kiss Zach that night out at the ranch.

The memory of their kiss still angered him. He knew he couldn't waste any time before proposing to her. He would have to make his move soon.

He would woo her and court her tonight. In a few weeks, he'd propose.

Feeling quite confident, Mark drew Marissa a little closer as they danced. He enjoyed the feel of her body pressed against him. It wouldn't be long before he'd be able to take her any time he wanted her. The prospect pleased him.

When the music ended, Mark escorted her back to her uncle's side.

"Would you like me to get you a drink?" he asked.

"Yes, Mark. Thank you."

Marissa had an ulterior motive in accepting his offer. She wanted to get away from him for a while, and if he went to the crowded refreshment table, she'd have a moment without him.

Something about Mark was bothering Marissa. The way he'd held her so close during that last dance troubled her. Zach's touch had always excited her and sent shivers through her. Mark's touch sent a different kind of trembling through her. He made her nervous and wary and uncomfortable.

Thinking of Zach, Marissa glanced around but saw no sign of him. She told herself it was ridiculous to think he would ask her to dance. This past week, he'd stayed as far away from her as he could without leaving the ranch completely, and she admitted to herself that she missed him.

The music started again. It was a slow melody

this time. Marissa stayed where she was, expecting Mark to return with her drink. She would use the beverage as an excuse to avoid a slow dance with him.

"May I have this dance?"

Marissa went still at the sound of Zach's voice. She turned to find him coming up behind her.

Zach had been watching Marissa from afar all night long. He had seen how she'd been treated by most of the townsfolk, and he'd watched her dancing with Mark.

He had had enough of seeing her in Mark's arms. Mark had held her too close. The jealousy he'd been fighting and trying to deny could not be ignored any longer.

A thrill went through Marissa, and she answered quickly, "Yes. I'd love to dance with you."

The sight of Zach dressed in dark pants and a white shirt made her acutely conscious of what an attractive man he was. Her heartbeat quickened as she took a step toward him, more than ready to go into his arms.

Zach had been observing the other couples on the dance floor, too, and though he knew he wasn't practiced in the art, he thought he had learned enough by watching to make it through one dance with Marissa. Actually, he didn't care if they danced at all. He just wanted to take her in his arms and hold her close.

They moved out among the other couples, unmindful of anyone watching them.

Zach kept the steps simple. He concentrated only on the pleasure of having Marissa in his arms as they moved to the slow, sensuous rhythm.

He looked down at Marissa, and their gazes met.

They were lost in a haze of sensuality as they both remembered other times when their rhythm together had been at a much quicker pace. The memories sent heat through him. He swallowed tightly as he fought for control.

He wanted to hold Marissa closer. He wanted to kiss her and strip away the clothing that was a barrier between them. He wanted to be one with her, to know the beauty of loving her again.

He looked away from her and forced himself to settle for a dance.

Marissa closed her eyes and became a creature of sensation as she moved with Zach to the tempo of the music. It was heavenly being in his arms. The touch of his hands sent delight coursing through her.

She never wanted to be away from him. She wanted to hold him close and never let him go. Marissa made up her mind right then and there. She was going to tell Zach that she loved him.

She certainly had nothing to lose. The worst that could happen had already happened. At least, if she told him, she would know that she had been honest with him about her feelings. What he did after that would be his decision.

Marissa was ready. She girded herself and prepared to tell Zach the truth of her love.

And then she heard Mark say, "Excuse me." His tone was terse. "I'm cutting in."

Her eyes flew open. Mark was standing next to them, a belligerent look on his face.

Zach was surprised by the other man's intrusion. When he felt Mark's hand on his shoulder to stop their dance, he was almost ready to fight him. But he stopped. He did not want to make trouble for Marissa. Zach dropped his hands away from her as Mark boldly stepped in front of him and took over.

Marissa stiffened as Mark's hand settled possessively at her waist to guide her through the rest of the dance. She was upset, very upset, but she fought not to let it show. She managed to smile up at him.

Zach walked to the edge of the dance floor and looked back. He saw Marissa smiling at Mark as if she hadn't a care in the world.

He stalked off into the night.

He had the money George had given him and he had seen a saloon on his way to the dance earlier that evening. He was glad Joe was with Louise and George, so he could get away for a while.

Zach strode angrily toward the saloon.

Chapter Twenty-eight

Hawk never attended the town dances. He knew he wasn't wanted. He stood at the bar in the Palace Saloon, enjoying a whiskey and minding his own business. The place was emptier than usual on this Saturday night because of the dance, and Hawk was glad.

He heard someone come into the bar behind him, but he didn't turn to look as the man settled at the end of the bar. He kept on drinking, minding his own business.

"Whiskey," the new customer ordered.

The voice sounded familiar, and Hawk looked up in the mirror behind the bar to see the other man's reflection. It surprised him to find it was Zach Ryder. Picking up his glass, he moved down to speak with him.

"Evening, Zach," Hawk said. "Good to see you in town."

"Hawk," Zach answered, nodding to him as he paid the bartender for his drink. He hadn't really wanted to talk to anyone when he'd come into the bar, but he hadn't thought he'd run into Hawk. He was the exception.

"Come on, you want to sit at a table?"

"Sure." Zach took his tumbler of whiskey and followed Hawk to the back of the saloon.

"How are you doing out at the Crown?" Hawk asked once they'd settled in.

"George is a good man. Marissa will be well taken care of. We're still waiting to hear about the boy's family. We sent the telegram to Sidewinder a week ago, but there's been no word at all," he said as he took a deep swallow.

"What's going to happen if his family's all dead?"

"I don't know. Joe's a good boy. He's suffered a lot, and I don't like to think of him being alone." Zach knew those words described himself, as well, but at least he was a man. He could make his own way in the world, unlike Joe.

"Let's hope it turns out all right."

"I know. It was hard enough on him in the village, but if he finds out his whole family is dead . . ."

"Is that what happened to you?" Hawk asked perceptively.

"That was a long time ago." Zach looked up at

him. "From what I can remember, there was no way any of my family could have survived the raid on our ranch. I'm hoping things will be different for Joe."

"I'm sorry about your family."

"So am I."

They both fell silent for a moment. Each took a drink.

"How did you end up in Dry Springs?" Zach asked, changing the subject. "Do you have family here?"

"No. I don't have any family. I settled here on my own a few years back."

"And I'm real glad he did," purred the bar girl known only as Red because of her flaming hair color. She came to stand beside the table. "Evening, Hawk." She smiled seductively down at him, then looked at Zach "You're new in town, aren't you?"

"Yes."

"This is Zach Ryder, Red," Hawk told her. "He's the man who brought Marissa Williams, back from the Comanche."

"I heard you were raised by the Comanche," Red said, eyeing Zach thoughtfully.

"That's right," Zach answered, expecting condemnation from her.

"Well, welcome back to civilization—if you can call Dry Springs civilized," she said with a wicked grin, not the least bit put off by his background.

"Hey, Stan! These boys need another round—and make it on the house!"

She sashayed to the bar to get them two more drinks, then served them at their table.

"You enjoy yourselves tonight, and if you need anything—anything at all—you just let me know. All right, Hawk?" Her tone left no doubt as to her meaning.

"We will, Red," Hawk promised.

She winked at him and went off to wait on another customer.

Zach and Hawk had been there for quite a while when a group of men came in and went to the bar to order drinks. They were loud and raucous and intent on having a good time.

"The dance must be over," Hawk remarked as the place started to fill up.

Zach noticed that Mark was among the group at the bar. Zach wasn't at all glad to see him, but he was quietly pleased that, at least, the cowboy wasn't with Marissa. Zach shifted his chair so his back was to the bar. He wanted to ignore the other man's presence. He'd seen enough of Mark already that night.

Mark was more than satisfied with the events of the evening. Marissa had seemed quite receptive to him, and he believed it would only be a matter of a few weeks or maybe a month before he could propose. The only annoyance he'd had all night had been when Zach danced with her. He didn't know what was going on between the two of them, but it was going to stop. He was going to have several stiff drinks to celebrate his success.

Red worked the crowd. She enjoyed flirting with the cowboys, and she wasn't averse to taking one of them upstairs to make a little extra money on the side. She lingered at the bar, laughing with the men, trying to decide which one to set her sights on.

"Hey, Mark!" one of the men called out in a slurred voice. "Why don't you take Red upstairs and have some fun?"

Mark could have used some female companionship that night, but it wasn't the saloon girl he wanted. He wanted Marissa.

"Not tonight," he answered.

The drunk wasn't about to be ignored. "But, Mark—at least Red is honest about her trade. She ain't no damned Comanche squaw like that Marissa Williams you was dancing with all night. How many of them bucks you think the Williams girl did while she was a captive? You know she was probably bedding half the tribe."

Mark laughed at the man's insults. The drunk hadn't said anything that he hadn't already thought himself. He was only speaking the truth.

Mark downed the rest of his drink and signaled the bartender to refill his glass as he responded, "Yeah, she probably did. But so what? It don't matter that she's a slut. It only matters that she's got money. I can forgive just about anything when there's money involved."

Zach had been listening to Mark and growing angrier by the minute. It had been hard enough watching him with Marissa at the dance. But to learn now that he was just using her broke his self-control.

He pushed his chair back, ready to fight.

"Zach—" Hawk saw the fury in his face and knew what he planned to do.

Zach didn't answer. He just got to his feet and walked straight up to the bar.

"Looks like you got company," one of the men said to Mark.

Mark turned to see who was coming.

Zach hit him full-force and sent him sprawling to the ground. Chaos erupted around them as everyone scrambled to get out of the way.

Though he had been caught off guard, Mark was ready to fight. He launched himself at Zach. The two men grappled in a violent confrontation. Each man landed powerful, bruising blows.

Zach's fury was intense. This man had danced with Marissa and acted like he cared about her. But it had all been a lie.

The hatred Zach felt for Mark fueled his anger. He gave a roar of rage as he threw himself bodily at his opponent and knocked him down. With savage intensity, he beat the other man into submission. His last, most powerful blow caught Mark squarely on the chin, leaving him unconscious.

When Zach realized Mark was out, he stood up in complete disgust. He looked around at the others in the saloon, ready for more trouble. When he had no takers, he relaxed a bit, spitting blood as he turned away from Mark's prone body.

Hawk was there.

"Let's get out of here," Hawk told him. He looked over at the bar girl. "See you later, Red."

Red just nodded as she watched them go. She'd seen many fights in her time, but never any as intense as this one had been. She realized the others in the bar were staring at Zach and Hawk as they walked out.

"Hey, what are you looking at?" she asked. "I guess Zach didn't like what Mark was saying about the Williams girl. The excitement's over. Let's all have another drink."

Red looked one last time in Zach and Hawk's direction. They were two tall, fine men, the likes of which weren't seen very often. She didn't show it, but deep within her she felt a bit sad. No man had ever defended her honor that way.

Hawk and Zach hadn't gotten far down the street when Zach stopped at a watering trough to wash up. He could feel his cheek swelling, and he was tasting blood.

"And I thought it was going to be a quiet night," Hawk joked.

"It was, for you," Zach countered. He tried to grin as he straightened up, but his cheek hurt too much.

"Do you love her?" he asked.

"Yes." Zach knew there was no point in lying to Hawk.

"What are you going to do about it?"

"Nothing. She's better off without me. I have nothing to offer her."

Hawk knew how pride could get a man in trouble. "Sounds like she's got all the money she needs."

"A man should be able to take care of his family."

"So get a job," Hawk said simply.

Zach growled something unintelligible at him.

"Think about what I said," Hawk told him. "You need me for anything, my house is the one out behind the stable."

Hawk walked off, hoping things would get better for Zach. He understood the difficulties the other man was having in adapting to the white world. He hoped Zach would be able to sort out what it was he really wanted before it was too late and he missed his best chance at happiness.

As Zach made his way back to the hotel, he was glad it was late so he wouldn't run into anyone on the streets. The lobby was deserted as he crossed it and went upstairs to his room. George had gotten him his own hotel room that night so he didn't have to worry about Joe, and he was relieved. He didn't want the boy to see him this way. It was going to be awkward enough the next morning when he came face to face with Mark again.

Marissa and Louise were up bright and early the next morning. They were sharing a room, and enjoyed having the time together. They were looking forward to attending church services.

"I wonder what happened to Zach last night?" Marissa said.

Her tone was nonchalant enough, but she was worried. She had only seen him for that one dance, and then Mark had cut in and ruined everything. She'd kept hoping that Zach would return and ask her to dance again, but he hadn't. There had been no sign of him, either, when they'd returned to the hotel.

"I don't know," Louise said. "I didn't see very much of him last night, but I'm sure he'll be joining us for church this morning."

They left their room and met George and Joe in the lobby.

"Did you see Zach on your way down?" George asked.

"No. I guess he's still in his room," Louise said.

"I'll go get him and be right back."

George went upstairs and knocked on Zach's door.

"Yeah?" came Zach's muffled response to the knock.

"We're ready to go to church. Should we wait for you?"

"No, go on. I'll meet you there." Zach answered through the door.

George returned to escort the ladies and Joe to the church.

"Zach will be along," he told them, trying not to smile. Judging from the sound of his voice, he had a good idea where Zach had disappeared to last night.

Zach stifled a groan and sat up on the side of his bed. He stood and went to the washstand, ready to get cleaned up. It was then that he made the mistake of looking in the mirror. He looked just like he felt—as if he'd been in a bad fight. He would have preferred to just ride on out to the ranch without seeing anyone that morning, but since George had stopped by to get him, he knew he had to show up at church. They would be expecting him.

Zach wondered if George had seen or spoken to Mark yet. He figured he hadn't. If he had, George would certainly have had more to say to him when he'd come by the room.

As quickly as he could, Zach finished washing and then donned his best clothes for church. He was going to be late as it was.

Chapter Twenty-nine

Marissa was sitting with Joe, trying to listen attentively to the minister's sermon. She wanted to concentrate on the good news he was sharing, but her heart was distracting her. She kept wondering where Zach was. Uncle George had said he'd promised to meet them at church, but so far he hadn't shown up.

Marissa scolded herself for caring so much about Zach, but she couldn't forget how it had felt to be in his arms the night before. They had danced only once, but it had been wonderful. She was certain Zach had to feel something for her. How else could they have moved so perfectly together? They had seemed so attuned to one another—and then Mark had cut in.

"God bless you all," Reverend Gibson said, ending his sermon.

Marissa had been so caught up in her thoughts about Zach that she was surprised to find he was finished. She stood up with Joe to follow Louise and George as they left the pew. Glancing around the crowded church, she hoped to catch sight of Zach. Her heart stirred within her when she saw him. There was no mistaking his tall, broad-shouldered form as he walked out the main doorway ahead of them into the sunshine.

Marissa was glad to know he'd kept his word, even if he hadn't come to sit with them. She realized he'd probably arrived late and had sat in a back pew. A part of her wanted to rush down the crowded aisle and seek him out, but she couldn't. She was trapped there, and she realized it was for the best. There was no point in throwing herself at him. Zach had made it clear he didn't want anything to do with her. Bringing her wayward emotions under control, Marissa offered up one last prayer as she departed the church.

She asked God to help her find a way to win Zach's love.

"It won't be long," Louise said to George in a quiet voice as they moved down the center aisle. She gave him secret smile.

They both realized that in a few short weeks they would be getting married in that very church.

"I can hardly wait," he said, taking her hand in his.

"Me, either."

They followed Marissa and Joe from the church.

"There's Zach," George said, pointing him out.

Zach was standing off to the side, facing slightly away from them.

George thought nothing of the way Zach was standing as they drew near to speak with him.

"I'm glad Zach made it in time to hear at least a part of the service," Louise said. "Will we be going back to the ranch now?"

"Yes. It's that time. Most of the men have already started back. Not all of them stay around for services."

"I wondered where Mark was this morning."

As they drew near and got a look at Zach's face, everyone stopped dead.

"What happened to you?" George demanded. Evidently, Zach had been in a fight, a serious one judging by the look of him.

"Whoa!" Joe said, shocked as he stared up at Zach. "Who hit you?"

"Zach," Marissa gasped. "Are you all right?" She wanted to go to him, but controlled the desire with an effort. "Your face—"

"The other man looks worse," Zach told her, remembering her fight with Moon Cloud and the answers she'd given him when he'd confronted her about it.

Marissa's gaze caught and held his.

Zach stared down at her, entranced by her innocence and beauty. It was all he could do not to take her in his arms and hold her to his heart. He remembered how angry he'd gotten listening to Mark in the saloon last night. This woman deserved only the best in life. She did not deserve the fate she'd been dealt.

"But are you all right?" she repeated.

"I'm fine," he answered.

"You sure? Where did this happen?" George asked.

Zach wanted to answer George honestly, but he wanted to do it when Marissa wasn't around. What he had to say to him needed to be said in private.

"I'll tell you later," Zach answered George, glancing at the women. "Now's not the time."

George scowled, but respected his wishes. "Are you feeling well enough to make the trip to the ranch?"

"I can ride. We need to get back."

"Why don't you come with me to the stable?"

"Fine."

They left Joe with the women and arranged to meet them at the hotel. Then they went to get the buckboard and the horses.

Louise and Marissa wondered what was going on, but said nothing in front of Joe. They were sure they would find out later.

* * *

Once they'd gotten away from Louise and Marissa, George turned to Zach.

"All right. We're away from the women. What happened? Did you get drunk and end up in a fight with somebody?"

"I was at the Palace with Hawk last night when some men came in," Zach began.

"And?"

"Mark was one of them. I didn't like was he was saying, and I let him know it."

"Mark?" George was surprised. "You fought with Mark?"

Zach nodded.

"What about?" George thought for a moment, then remembered Mark cutting in when Zach and Marissa were dancing. "Did you fight over Marissa? I know Mark cares deeply about her."

It pained Zach to speak up, but he knew George deserved the truth.

"Mark cares about Marissa's money," he stated flatly.

"What?" George was shocked.

"When he was at the Palace last night, some comments were made." Zach told him all that had been said in the saloon.

George was shaking with barely controlled fury when Zach finished. "That lowlife son of a bitch!"

Zach couldn't have agreed more.

"You say he looks worse than you?" The older man's mood lightened at the thought.

"That's right."

"Good."

George was glad Mark was no longer in town. He wasn't sure he would have been able to control himself if he ran into him. He knew exactly what he was going to do once they got back to the ranch.

Hawk was working at the stable when they arrived. He helped George hitch up the buckboard while Zach went to saddle the horses.

"You were there at the bar, too, last night, weren't you?" George asked Hawk.

"I was there. You'd have been proud of Zach. He's a good man."

George nodded. "I'm just sorry I missed it. I would have enjoyed helping Zach make his point to Mark, but I'm going to have my chance to deal with Mark very shortly."

Hawk was glad George wasn't mad at him. He knew what a determined man George Williams could be. It didn't pay to be on the wrong side of him.

Zach and George returned to the hotel to pick up Joe and the women.

They rode for the Crown.

George was outwardly calm as they made the trip, but with every passing mile, his anger grew. He was looking forward to facing Mark down.

"Did you have a good trip?" Sarah asked as the party reined in before the house.

"Oh, yes," Louise answered. "The dance was very nice, and we got some more shopping done."

Claude saw the packages stowed in the back. "Let me help you with those."

"Have you seen Mark around?" George asked.

"Not so far this morning," he answered.

"I'll be back."

George wheeled his horse around and rode down to the bunkhouse. He wanted to talk to Mark, and he wanted to talk to him now.

"Where's Mark?" he bellowed as he stuck his head in the bunkhouse.

"Down at the stable last I seen him, but that's been a while."

"Well, get off your ass and go find him!" George bellowed. "Tell him I want to see him up at the house."

"Yes, boss," the hand replied, moving quickly at his order.

It wasn't often that George got in one of these moods, but all the men knew better than to mess with him when he was angry. Most of them knew better than to make him angry in the first place.

George returned to the house to await Mark. The women were still busy unloading the last of their purchases from the buckboard. He went to help and had just started up the front steps when he saw Mark coming.

"Here, Joe. Take these inside," George ordered

gruffly. "You might want to stay in there for a few minutes, too."

Joe looked from George to Mark and nodded in response as he hurried indoors. Everyone was about to go back outside for another load.

"You shouldn't go out there right now," Joe warned them.

"Why not?" Louise asked.

"George just told me I had to stay inside," he answered.

Louise thought that was odd. Zach and Claude took a look out the window and saw Mark talking with George in front of the house. They hurried toward the front door. Louise, Marissa, and Sarah exchanged puzzled looks. They glanced outside and saw Mark—his face battered and one eye swollen almost shut.

"Did Zach fight Mark last night?" Louise asked Marissa.

"I don't know."

The women hurried after Zach and Claude to see what was going on.

Joe wasn't about to be left out. He was curious, too.

"What the hell do you mean, I'm fired?" Mark was shouting.

"Get your things and get off my property—*now*!" George was glad Mark looked much worse than Zach did. He hoped the man was suffering greatly.

"You can't fire me!"

"I just did."

"I've worked my ass off for you on this ranch!"

"I paid you. You could have quit at any time."

"When we were on the trail trying to track down Marissa, I was the one who didn't want to give up."

"And we all know why now, don't we?" George's tone was deadly. Hate filled him. He wanted Mark gone right now, and he never wanted to see him again.

"Hell, after she'd been with the Comanche, nobody else in town would want her!"

At his words, Louise stepped to Marissa's side and slipped a supportive arm around her.

Mark went on. "At least I planned to make an honest woman out of her! I was going to marry her!"

Joe was confused by all that was going on. He was frowning as he stepped to the edge of the porch. "I don't understand," he began. "You can't marry Marissa. She's already married. She's married to Zach."

"What?" George looked back at Zach and Marissa, shocked.

"Isn't that right, Zach?" Joe went on. "Crazy One told me so."

Zach glanced at Marissa. Neither spoke.

The truth Zach had denied to protect her had been revealed. He hadn't meant for her to be hurt. He loved her. He had married her in the Comanche world to protect her. But what had protected her there would ruin her in the white world.

Mark laughed, a harsh, cruel laugh. His plan of marrying for money was ruined, so he decided to be as vicious as he could. "So Marissa really is a squaw! She was Zach's squaw! Wait till I tell the boys in town!"

Until that moment, Zach had held himself back, but he could no longer stand by and let this man say such things about the woman he loved. He started forward, ready to fight him again.

But George held out an arm to block Zach's way. "There's no need for violence."

Zach didn't want to stop. He wanted to teach Mark a lesson once and for all. He stood there, his jaw locked, his hands clenched into fists at his sides.

Mark looked at them, feeling cocky. George might have fired him, but he'd had the last word.

George had listened to Mark's comments in disbelief. He had trusted this man. He had thought a lot of him, but now he knew the truth.

George had stopped Zach from hitting him because this was his fight. And he intended to fight it.

He swung out at the now unsuspecting Mark. His one fierce, violent blow knocked the younger man to the ground. Mark lay flat on his back, sprawled in the dirt, stunned and bleeding.

"Get off my ranch," George ordered, glaring down at him. "And don't ever come back."

Chapter Thirty

George ordered Claude to make sure Mark packed up and got off the Crown. Once Claude had escorted Mark away, George turned to Zach.

"I think we need to talk," George said.

Zach respected George, but there was one thing he had to do before he spoke with him. "I understand, but first I need to talk to Marissa."

George didn't argue the point.

Zach turned back toward the house, where Marissa stood on the porch with Louise, Sarah, and Joe.

"Is something wrong?" Joe asked, feeling the tension in the air and not understanding it.

Mark was gone. Everybody should have been happy.

Zach walked slowly to the porch. It seemed the

longest distance he'd ever crossed in his life.

He had tried to let Marissa go.

He had wanted what he'd thought would be a better life for her—a life without him. But now he knew the truth. He loved her and he could not let her go.

He had told her the Comanche marriage meant nothing. He'd been wrong.

And if she would have him, he would spend the rest of his life proving it to her. It wouldn't be easy. He had no real place in the white world, but he would do what he had to do to keep her by his side.

Marissa watched Zach coming toward her, and she thought he had never looked more wonderful than he did in that moment—bruises and all. He had fought to defend her and her honor.

If Zach didn't care about her, why had he fought for her?

Hope soared within her, but she remained unmoving, more than a little frightened by the power of the emotions sweeping through her. When Zach stopped at the bottom of the porch steps, she wanted to run to him, but she feared being rejected.

And then Zach held out his hand to her.

Marissa took a step forward and put her hand in his.

Zach drew her down the steps and away from the house. He took her to the place where he'd slept out under the stars their first night at the ranch, down to the place where he would tell her he loved her and didn't want to live without her.

"Louise—what's wrong?" Joe asked, seeing the tears in her eyes.

"Nothing, Joe, dear. Nothing at all." Shc hugged him impulsively as George came to stand with them.

"Let's go inside," George said.

He gave Louise a soft, quick kiss, then held the door for her and Sarah and Joe to enter ahead of him.

Zach stood gazing down at Marissa.

It was time for the truth between them.

"I thought you would have a better life without me. I thought Mark was the better man for you," he began slowly. "I thought I could let you go—but I can't. I love you, Marissa. Though a Comanche marriage may not be recognized in the white world, in my heart you are my wife."

Marissa gazed up at him, her love for him shining in her eyes. "Zach—without you, I have no life. You're the most wonderful, bravest man I've ever known. I want to be with you—to spend the rest of my life with you."

"But I have nothing to offer you," Zach said, deeply troubled. "I don't even really know who I am."

"I know who you are. You are the man I love, Zach Ryder, and your love is all I'll ever need," she said simply.

Marissa reached up and looped her arms around his neck, drawing him down to her.

"I love you," she whispered as her lips met his.

Zach crushed her to him, deepening the exchange. In that moment, they both knew there was no greater joy in the world than true love.

They would find a way to be together.

They would find a way to happiness.

With love, all things were possible.

The church was filled with well-wishers as Reverend Gibson intoned, "I now pronounce you man and wife. George, you may kiss your bride."

George drew Louise near and kissed her sweetly. He had never been this happy before, and he knew the future was only going to get better.

The reverend then turned to the other couple standing before him.

"I now pronounce *you* man and wife," he repeated with a smile. "Zach, you may kiss your bride."

Zach needed no further urging.

He gazed down at Marissa, his wife now in all ways—Comanche and white.

With utmost care, he kissed her.

* * *

"Now they're really married," Joe told his grandpa.

They were sitting together in the first pew, watching as Zach and Marissa and George and Louise started back up the aisle, the ceremony over.

"That they are, Joe," Al Carter said as he returned his grandson's smile.

"And now we can go home to Pa, right, Grandpa?" Joe asked.

"That's right. He's waiting to see you."

Al Carter had been overjoyed when he'd received the telegram in Sidewinder telling him that Joe was alive and well in Dry Springs. The only survivor of the raid on Joe's ranch had been Joe's father, Steve. Al had taken Steve in and had been nursing him back to health since the Comanche attack. When the news had come about Joe, they had been thrilled.

Al knew their homecoming would be a sorrowful, bittersweet one, but at least they had each other, and they would be together again. Joe was alive—that was all that mattered.

Al had thanked Zach a thousand times, it seemed, for saving Joe. He would be eternally grateful for the man's help.

Al smiled up at Zach and Marissa as they passed by the pew on their way out of the church. In his heart, he wished them happiness forever.

* * *

Marissa was in heaven as Zach escorted her from the church.

She had never known she could be this happy.

Zach loved her, and she loved him.

Tonight was their wedding night, and this time she would *know* that it was her wedding night.

Tonight they would make love for the first time in a real bed.

The thought made Marissa's smile even brighter.

Zach was looking down at her and saw her expression. There was a definite twinkle in her eyes. "What are you thinking about?"

"You'll see," Marissa answered, and she pulled him down for another kiss.

When the kiss ended and they moved apart, Zach thought of the chain and cross from his childhood that he carried in his pocket, and he was filled with an overwhelming sense of peace. The past had been difficult for him, but as they stepped out into the sunshine, he knew their future would be as bright as this day was—and just as full of love.